Coldsmith

Also by Ron Schwab

Coldsmith

Ron Schwab

Uplands Press

OMAHA, NEBRASKA

Uplands Press
1401 S 64th Avenue
Omaha, NE 68106
www.uplandspress.com

Publisher's Note: This is a work of fiction. Names, characters, places, and incidents are a product of the author's imagination. Locales and public names are sometimes used for atmospheric purposes. Any resemblance to actual people, living or dead, or to businesses, companies, events, institutions, or locales is completely coincidental.

Ordering Information:
Quantity sales. Special discounts are available on quantity purchases by corporations, associations, and others. For details, contact the "Special Sales Department" at the address above.

Uplands Press / Ron Schwab -- 1st ed.

ISBN 978-1-943421-54-1

Chapter 1

September 1877

Custer County, Nebraska

RANCE COLDSMITH HAD paid no attention to the echo of gunshots drifting in with a westerly breeze from the Baker farm a half hour earlier. Baker was likely shooting at some jackrabbits or scaring off an unwelcome coyote. But the smell of smoke wafting eastward was not something a man ignored with the sea of drying grass that surrounded his sod house on the southeast fringes of the Nebraska Sandhills. He stepped out of the barn, where he had been trying to mend harnesses before the setting sun turned off his light.

His eyes searched the western horizon where only a sliver of near-red sun peeked above the hills. Then he saw the smoke plumes, so black they contrasted sharply with the graying sky. A few moments later, angry flames shot through the billowing smoke. It was the Baker place, not more than a mile down the rutted trail some folks called a road. Rance wheeled and returned to the barn to saddle Rusty, his big sorrel gelding.

When his mount was ready, Rance led it out of the barn, stopping by the house to buckle on his gun belt and pick up his Winchester. Slipping the rifle into its scabbard, he swung into the saddle, his lanky frame settling easily into place. The rider sat tall in the saddle, his standing height being four or five inches over six feet, his wide-brimmed Plainsman hat adding some inches to those numbers. The hat, pulled down on his forehead, nearly hid his steel-gray eyes and covered most of his short-cropped, sandy hair.

As he headed toward the Baker farm, he had no idea what to expect or whether he would be welcome. Carl Baker, a man in his early forties, Rance supposed, was not a friendly sort and had always seemed angry about his lot in life. He had been told that the man had homesteaded a quarter section almost ten years back, and it was obvious Baker barely made a go at it farming. But this was cattle country, fit only for a cowman like Rance. Three years earlier, Rance had bought out other flailing homesteaders to acquire his 640 acres—a full section. That was not near enough, and he had to admit he coveted Baker's quarter that adjoined his land at the western boundary and offered a perfect gateway into the lush, open grazing presently offered by the Sandhills. He hoped to buy Baker out when the farmer finally surrendered.

In the meantime, Rance had tried to be a good neighbor, paying the cost of barbed-wire fencing and cutting trees along Wildcat Creek and making the posts. Then he had hired his friend, Ben Rice, to help install it, so that his cow herd would not graze on Baker's land. Baker had neither lent a hand nor said "thanks," only scowled as he confirmed the fence was going up on the surveyed line.

Baker's wife, an auburn-haired woman whose long hair gleamed like copper in the sun, had brought cookies, cake or other snacks midafternoons with coffee and cool water from the well while the men fenced. She had seemed a bit subdued and quiet, but her gestures were friendly and appreciated. That had been two summers back, and he had seen her only from a distance when working that side of the small ranch or passing by since that time. He remembered her, though, a tall woman, just short of skinny, a freckled face that might have been pretty if it had not seemed so tired and haggard. The Bakers had two children, a boy and a girl, but they had been standoffish when they joined their mother on the walk to the fence line. He guessed Lisbeth Baker's age to be a year or two on either side of thirty, about five years younger than his thirty-five.

When he arrived at the Baker farmstead, he saw a stocky man sprawled out face down in the yard; Carl Baker, he assumed. The roof of the house, apparently at least partly grass-covered, was in flames, and smoke and fire belched from the windows. A naked woman stood in the open doorway, obviously dazed or confused, acting as if she were waiting for flames to consume her. He dismounted, dropping the horse's reins and raced for the house. He grabbed Lisbeth Baker's hand and pulled her from the doorway, leading her away from the burning house.

"Your children? Where are the children?" he asked, as he began unbuttoning his shirt.

"Children?"

She was clearly out of her head. "You have a son and a daughter." He pulled off his shirt and began slipping her arms into the sleeves. The shirttail fell over her rump and reached her upper thighs. That was the best he could do for the moment. It was only now, as he fastened a single button on the shirtfront, that he noticed her face was red and swollen and that blood was dripping down her face from a cut above one eye.

"Oh, yes. That would be Morgan and Marissa."

The roof collapsed and disappeared into the cavern formed by the soddy's thick walls. The children were dead if they were in the house, he thought.

As if reading his mind, Carl Baker's wife said, "I sent them out the back window to the root cellar behind the house when the men shot Carl. Thank God, I did. At least they did not see what those men did to me. Of course, they probably would have been killed."

She seemed to be regaining her senses some. She had obviously been beaten and raped, probably left to burn in the house. Rance said, "Take me to the root cellar. If they don't see their mother, they will be afraid."

She nodded. "Yes, follow me."

She was buttoning the shirt as they circled round the house, so she was becoming aware of her appearance now. Surrender of his shirt had left his torso still covered with the flour sack undershirt Tillie Rice had fashioned for him.

When they got to what appeared to be a large door lying flat on the ground with a steel handle protruding from the top, Baker's wife said, "You just slide the cover back. There is another handle on the inside that allowed Morgan to pull the cover over them."

She stepped to the root cellar and bent over the wood cover, obviously unaware she was exposing her bare backside. Rance made a token effort to turn his eyes away, but he knew he was unlikely to erase the picture from his memory.

"Morgan. Marissa," she called. "It's Mother. It is safe to come out now. The man with me is our neighbor, Mister Coldsmith."

Rance moved in next to the woman, grabbed the cover handle and slid the barrier away from the opening. He estimated that the pit was some four feet deep, and at first, he did not see the children crouched in the corner among gunny sacks that were probably filled with potatoes, carrots, and assorted garden vegetables. The boy stood up, his head rising above the top of the hole. "Help your sister get on top of one of the bags," Rance said, "and I'll pull her out."

The boy complied, and Rance reached out, grasping the little girl under her arms and easily hoisting her from the pit and passing her to her mother. The boy clambered out on his own. Rance positioned the cover back on the root cellar. "Wait here," he said, "I am going to check on your husband."

She said, "You cannot help him."

Rance thought she made the statement rather matter-of-factly and devoid of emotion, but it was not unusual for people who had recently endured a crisis to react to events in unexpected ways, sometimes even inappropriately. He returned to the front of the smoldering house, knelt beside the blood-smeared form and quickly confirmed Carl Baker's death. The man had taken two slugs in his chest and another above his ear, any one of which would have killed him quickly. Baker was a soft, paunchy man with a scruffy black beard, probably about his wife's height, five feet and nine or ten inches, Rance guessed. No gun belt at his waist and no sign of a rifle nearby. It appeared Baker had been unarmed. Of course, the killers could have taken his weapons.

The question was what to do with him? What to do with Missus Baker and the two youngsters?

"We could put him in the root cellar for tonight, so the coyotes and other scavengers don't get to him. I suppose he ought to be buried."

Rance turned at the sound of the woman's voice and got to his feet. She stood only five or six paces behind him, holding the little girl in her arms and the boy standing silently an arm's length away. He could not make out their faces in the darkness that now blanketed the scene, but he heard no sobbing and detected no other signs of grief. Carl Baker might have been a mere stranger from his family's reaction to his death.

"Do you have friends nearby?" Rance asked, realizing it was a foolish question the moment it escaped his lips. The only other neighbors within several miles were Ben and Matilda Rice and their eight children, located less than a mile east of Rance's house. Another mile beyond the Rice farmstead was Johnny Whitehorse, a Pawnee who had squatted in a soddy abandoned by a homesteader some years back.

The woman did not dignify his question with an answer. She simply turned away and headed toward the small plank-walled barn with the children.

Rance called after her, "Ma'am, what can I do to help you?"

"Wait there. I will leave the children in the barn. They can feed the milk cow and chickens while I come back and help you move Carl."

While he waited, Rance went back to the root cellar and rearranged the sacks of produce to form a pocket on the dirt floor where they might deposit a bloody corpse. By the time he returned, Lisbeth Baker was kneeling by the body rummaging through her late husband's trouser pockets.

When she looked up at him, the moonlight caught her face, and he saw the anger in her eyes. "The bastards even took his timepiece and the ten-dollar gold eagle I'm sure he had in his pocket. And they found my private stash in the old bean can I kept in the cupboard, all the money I had—over a hundred dollars—while they were tearing the house apart. I'd been saving that up a half dollar at a time ever since we got to this hellhole."

"Uh, I think I can drag your husband to the root cellar if you want to look after your children. Then we'll go to my place, and you can stay there until you figure things out. I will come back and get him buried proper in the morning. I'll see if my friend, Ben, can help look after things here."

"He's the colored man, isn't he?"

"Yes, he is. A good man and my best friend. Is that a problem?"

She gave a wry smile that might have turned her face pretty if it was not so beat up, he thought.

"No, not a problem for me. But Carl hated colored folks—that's not what he called them. Ironic, that he would be buried by a black man. I like that idea. Anyway, I will stick around and help you if you need it. Before we move him, though, I want his clodhoppers and britches.

I can make do with them until I find or make something better."

She knelt and took Baker's belt from the trousers and then untied his work shoes and pulled them, along with the socks, off his feet. That accomplished, she got up and bent over to grab the end of the trouser legs, revealing her perfect behind again when Rance's loaned shirt hiked up. She tugged on the denim trousers, lifting Baker's legs off the ground as the garment slid down his legs and over his feet. "Now," she said, "let's dump him in the root cellar. Too bad I don't have some hogs I could feed him to. That's what my papa used to do with snoopy Yankee carpetbaggers who got to be a problem at our place in East Texas. They just sort of disappeared in the hog pens. Carpetbaggers finally won, though."

Rance had thought he heard a hint of Texas in Lisbeth Baker's speech. She sure was not grieving over the late husband. They must have had a marriage made in hell.

Chapter 2

LISBETH WAS NOT keen on taking her children to a bachelor's house, but she could not come up with another option. All but the sod walls of her home had been reduced to coals and ashes. She had no money. She owned the buckboard that she was driving and Plato, the mule that was pulling it, and, of course, the quarter section they had proved up on in accordance with the Homestead Act. Any remnants of her family, consisting of a few cousins—if they were still alive—resided a world away in Texas. It was late September and, although the Sandhills that tapered into their prairie lands had been enjoying balmy breezes of an Indian summer, the ravages of winter blizzards were on the horizon. It might be a few months or a few days, but inevitably the freeze would arrive.

She wondered if Coldsmith might buy the quarter section. Probably. Ranchers never had enough land to suit them. She had so many decisions in front of her. Take a deep breath, she told herself. Think it out. Don't do something stupid. In a delusional moment she had essentially sold herself to Carl for the security she thought an older man would offer. Things had gone sour fast, and she had not had the courage to escape. And then Morgan came, then Marissa. She loved the two more than life, but they had tightened the noose that held her to Carl.

Coldsmith's Rising Sun Ranch was no more impressive than the Bakers' pitiful farm, she thought, when they pulled into the ranch yard, which was no different than a farmyard beyond its label. Coldsmith dismounted and walked over to the wagon. "I'm going to go in and light some lamps. Then you and the kids can make yourselves at home, such as it is, while I put up my horse and your mule in the barn."

When Lisbeth entered the house with her children and her deceased husband's shoes and britches, she was struck by the immense size of the interior in comparison to that of the burned-out hovel from which she had fled. It consisted of a single room with a curtained-off area at the west end, which she supposed concealed a bed and sleeping area. She estimated the interior space at almost thirty feet in length and fifteen feet wide. The walls were plastered smooth, probably with a mix of clay and ashes, and flat stones were pressed together and imbedded in the dirt to form a floor that could be swept. This was a sharp contrast to the dirt floor of the Baker soddy and the crumbling walls which consisted of the interior side of the sod brick.

The ceiling furnished by the underside of an A-framed, planked roof supported by sturdy posts showed no signs of water leakage, so it was likely covered by tar paper or some other water resistor. A floor without mud. She could hardly remember such luxury.

Cooking was apparently done in the large sod fireplace along the north wall. Three Dutch ovens of different sizes were stacked on the floor off to one side. A small, solidly crafted, oak table with two matching chairs sat near the area set off for kitchen workspace. In the northeast corner were shelves filled with pans, skillets and other cooking and eating utensils. There was also a tin sink set into a boxlike structure. Two rocking chairs sat in front of the fireplace, and a high-backed bench rested under one window. Clothes and extra blankets were stacked on pallets along the wall just outside the curtained area.

"Ma," ten-year-old Morgan asked, "are we going to live here?"

She wrapped an arm about each of her children. "No. Mister Coldsmith is allowing us to stay tonight so we can figure out what to do."

Six-year-old Marissa began to sob, "I'm scared, Mama, and I'm tired."

Lisbeth said, "Why don't you stretch out on the bench over there? Morg, you go stand by the door and watch for Mister Coldsmith and tell me if you see him coming toward the house. I'm going to slip behind the curtain and see if I can get your papa's britches on."

Morgan went to the door without protest. He was always her protector and exhibited newly raised welts on his back and behind to prove it. She led Marissa to the bench, taking a folded blanket from one of the pallets to place under her head and wrap about her shoulders. The chill that had started to settle in outside had not yet worked its cold fingers through the three-feet-thick sod walls, so it was comfortable enough that firewood or old buffalo chips and dry cow dung would not be wasted on a nighttime fire.

She slipped behind the curtain at the soddy's west end and found an unusually long double bed and a four-legged stool with an unlighted kerosene lamp on the seat, an improvised lamp table, she guessed. She was surprised to see that the bed was made up with tidy, military precision. She wondered if Coldsmith had been a soldier.

Of course, Carl had served in the Confederate Army, or at least had claimed so with some vagueness, but had not carried such habits away with him. The long bed was easily explained by the man's exceptional height.

She rolled Carl's trousers out on the bed. They would be a trifle short, for she was longer in the leg than her late spouse, but they should reach the ankle-high clodhoppers. The waist was another matter. Two of her would fit in the waist—well, that might be an overestimate. She picked up the denim britches and pulled them on, confirming that she swam in them. Underwear would have been welcome, but she would settle for being alive with her children unharmed. Anything else was luxury.

The belt would not help without additional holes punched. She sat down on the side of the bed and pulled on the oft-mended wool socks. Then the shoes. She tugged the laces to snug the shoes as tightly as possible. For once, her long narrow feet carried benefits. She stood up and tested the shoes. The clodhoppers were still loose, but with the heavy socks they were serviceable.

"Mom, Mister Coldsmith just left the barn," Morgan yelled.

She grabbed the belt and stepped out from behind the curtain, struggling to work it through the trouser loops. When Coldsmith came through the door with a rolled feather mattress wrapped in his arms, she was struggling to fold the pants' waist in order to pull the britches tight around her. However, it quickly became evident that if she got a new hole punched in the belt, the end was still going to reach out and sway like an angry snake. Coldsmith paused at the entryway and looked at her questioningly and then put the mattress down and went to the cupboard below the sink, opened the door and pulled out several strands of twine.

He walked over and handed her the twine. "Pick one. We can cut it down if need be. I can tie two together, but I'm guessing one will be enough."

She yanked the belt back through the loops and began stringing the twine. Coldsmith turned to Morgan. "What's your name, son?"

"Morgan, sir. Ma calls me Morg."

"Okay, Morg, would you help me lay out the mattress? Then, we'll get a few blankets from the stack, and you and your sister can sleep on it tonight. It should be cozy and soft enough, even on the stone floor."

Now, Lisbeth thought, we know where the kids are sleeping. If he had any thoughts of her sharing his bed, he was a dead man. Ever since she was eighteen-years old, she had slept with a man she hated, and tonight she had been ravaged and beaten by two others. More than enough men for a lifetime as far as she was concerned. She had finished tying the twine belt when she felt a rivulet of blood running down her cheek. She did not want to soak the borrowed shirt with blood and cast her eyes about for a rag.

She saw that the mattress and blankets were laid out and was surprised to see that Coldsmith had placed a sleeping Marissa on the makeshift bed and that Morgan was removing his sister's shoes and straightening the tattered dress she had outgrown a year earlier.

"I need something to wipe the blood off my face," she said.

"Use the shirt sleeve. That one's about due for the rag pile. Morg," Coldsmith said, "why don't you settle in. Your mother and I need to talk a spell."

Morgan looked at Lisbeth for approval. She nodded her consent.

She saw that Coldsmith was starting a small fire in the fireplace.

"I'll make some coffee," he said. "You just sit yourself down at the table and catch your breath."

She accepted his offer and pulled back one of the chairs and sat down. She watched him make the coffee and scrape some smoldering coals from the flames for the pot. He got two tin cups and placed them on the table with some worn leather coasters and a matching pot mat. She doubted many men would take such care, and she wondered again about his background.

He sat down across the table from her, saying nothing, waiting in silence for the coffee pot to heat. His mind was obviously elsewhere, and she was in no mood for social conversation as the reality of what had happened this night began to strike her. Up till now, it all had seemed a bad dream, a nightmare from which she would awaken.

Coldsmith got up, retrieved the coffee pot and poured two steaming cups of the brew, placing one on the coaster in front of her.

He asked, "Would you let me look at the wound above your eye?"

She had been dabbing at the cut with her shirtsleeve, trying to abate the renewed bleeding. "Uh, yes. That would be okay, I guess."

He stood and carried his chair around the table, placing it so near to her that their knees touched when he sat down.

"Lean your head forward," he said.

She obeyed and flinched when his fingers pressed against the tender flesh around the cut.

"They gave you a nasty beating," he said.

"The cut came from Carl. He struck me with the fire poker when I wouldn't tell him where I had hidden his

Colt." She decided to tell Coldsmith the truth. The man had to be curious about the lack of remorse she and her children had shown over her husband's killing.

"I see. What did the men take from your place? Besides the money?"

"Two horses. A bay gelding and a young black mare. She's a sweetheart. Gentle and relaxed disposition. I taught Morg to ride on her, and I started working with Marissa this summer. The two saddles and tack were missing from the barn. Oh, they took my gold wedding band. Obviously, I'm not sentimental about it, but it might bring a few dollars."

"You need stitches, or you will have an ugly scar and it will be a long time healing. I can do it quickly, but it won't be painless."

"Do it."

"A question," Rance said. "Morg is hurting. I can tell by the way he is moving, and he is sleeping on his stomach. Maybe that's normal for him but not for most."

She looked down at Morgan, who was already asleep on the mattress. She got up and knelt beside him and pulled his shirt up and slid his britches part way down his upper buttocks. It was worse than she had realized. Angry red welts, and bleeding slashes covered his back where the razor strap had struck. "He tried to protect me," she said.

"I have some liniment that will relieve the pain and speed the healing. It is in a jar that I keep in a leather bag under the bed." He nodded toward the boy's back. "Carl, I assume."

"Yes, Carl. And I had hidden the Colt and know how to use it. He would not have lived the night anyway."

Lisbeth reclaimed her chair, and Rance placed a small kettle of water on the hot coals in the fireplace. He walked to the end of the room and opened the curtain in front of the bed and retrieved a leather bag with a rawhide drawstring and returned to the table.

"This is the bag with the liniment. I'll just leave it on the table." He pulled the drawstring loose and plucked out a small box that contained several sewing needles and a spool of thread. When the water was boiling, he substituted the kettle for the coffee pot on the table and found a near-full whiskey bottle to place beside it. He dropped two clean dishtowel-sized cloths on the table and sat down facing Lisbeth again. He was grim-faced as he chose his needle and threaded it. The reality of the needle made her anxious, and her stomach was queasy.

"Do you want a drink?" Coldsmith asked.

"No, thank you."

He dipped one of the cloths in the hot water and washed about her wound before cleaning the rest of her face. He poured some whiskey on the cloth's other end, and she flinched when the liquid stung the flesh above her eye. She noted that he poured a bit of the whiskey on his fingers and rubbed it into the skin.

"Lean forward and hold still," Coldsmith admonished her.

She complied and closed her eyes, gritting her teeth as the needle pierced her skin. He worked with deft fingers, though, and it was over quickly.

"Three stitches. Use the liniment on the eye, too. New stuff. It's called Vaseline. More for people than critters, but I have used it on a few horses and cows with success. It will reduce scarring," he said.

"Thank you."

Coldsmith set his needle on the table. "I would leave the stitches in a week. I can take them out when I get back if you don't want to do it yourself."

"You are going somewhere?"

"I have an errand to take care of."

Chapter 3

"HERE'S THE PLAN I've worked out in my head, Missus Baker," Rance said. "You make yourself at home in the soddy while I'm gone. I shouldn't be more than three or four days but don't worry if it's a week. Ben Rice will come by in the morning with his oldest boy, Jake. They will take you back to your place and tend to burying your husband. You can search your farmstead and see if there are things you would like to bring here with you. Ben and Jake will help you move anything. I will see if Ben can bring Sue Ellen to stay with your kids at my place. She's sixteen, and Morg and Marissa would be better off here, I think. They'll get along fine with Sue Ellen. She and Jake—he's eighteen—are the two oldest of Ben's and Matilda's herd."

"You seem to have my life all worked out for me, Mister Coldsmith. What if I have something else in mind?"

"You're not a captive here, ma'am. You can do what you darn well please." Rance cut her some slack. After what she had been through, Lisbeth Baker had good reason to be testy about taking instructions from those of the male persuasion.

"I guess I don't have that much choice under the circumstances. I will be thinking about my dilemma while you are away and try to have plans made when you return."

"Stay as long as it suits you, Missus Baker. You and your kids will have a roof over your heads for as long as you need it. Not much, maybe, but it will keep the weather out. Now, I want you to do something for me."

She looked at him suspiciously. "If it's reasonable."

"Describe the men who, uh, attacked you and killed your husband."

She sighed and answered. "One was a tall man, not as tall as you, though. Rail thin, full blond beard and hair falling to his shoulders. Younger than the others but seemed to be the boss. Drooled tobacco on my face while he . . . Anyhow, he was a man without conscience, but I suppose the same could be said for the others, also. The other man who took me was average height, I guess, thick in the waist and chest but not what you would call fat. Black hair, no beard but it had been a spell since he had shaved. The third man was older. He didn't touch me but stood there and grinned while the others had their ways. He was shortest of the three. Had a droopy, white mustache."

"Names? Did you hear any names?"

"One of them—I think it was the older guy—called the young leader 'Tobe,' I am almost certain. Yes, that was it, 'Tobe.'" Her cocoa-brown eyes shot sparks of anger when she spoke her attacker's name.

"Were they wearing anything special that you noticed?" Rance asked. "Anything unusual, like riding a horse that might catch somebody's eye?"

"Tobe rode a black and white piebald gelding. Handsome animal. I noticed that when they first showed up in the yard. The other two were mounted on bays. Good horses, I guess, but they wouldn't stand out."

"Your husband went out to meet them unarmed?"

"Yes. But he could have taken the Winchester with him even though I had hidden the pistol. He wasn't much good with the Colt anyway. He acted like he knew the men, or at least the leader."

"Interesting."

"Last week, Carl was gone for three days. He said he went to North Platte to collect some information he was to be paid for. I wonder if it had anything to do with those men?"

Rance shrugged. "Likely we'll never know."

"I've got a milk cow. A Guernsey. I will need to milk her in the morning. Do you have a place for her here if I bring her back?"

Rance said, "There is a small, fenced pasture next to the barn. I have a few horses in it now, but it wasn't grazed much the past summer. You can run her into the barn to milk. No stanchions but there are empty stalls and halters and ropes hanging on the walls. You can find the grain hopper in the barn, too. I'm going to ask Tillie Rice to stop by tomorrow afternoon."

"That's Ben's wife?"

"Yeah, you should meet her, and she would be good to talk to if you need a woman's ear."

Lisbeth Baker looked dubious but said nothing.

Rance said, "The Winchester above the door is loaded. Do you know how to use it?"

"I do."

"There is a steel bar next to the door. Slip that through the slots when I leave. The door wouldn't give in to a battering ram. Ben and Jake will take care of critter chores about the place while I'm gone."

"I would be more comfortable if I knew what you were up to. I feel like you're going after those men."

"I'm going to see if I can pick up their trail. I am thinking they won't be looking for anyone to follow. If I get right on it tonight, odds are I can catch up with them."

"And then what?"

"I will try to recover your horses and money and anything else they took from the place."

"What about the men?"

"I hope they will surrender, in which case I will take them to the county sheriff's office in North Platte."

"And if they don't?"

"I will offer some encouragement."

"Are you going alone?"

"I intend to invite my friend Johnny Whitehorse. He lives up the trail along the river along Wildcat Creek. He's Pawnee, he can track and handle a gun if need be."

"You don't have to do this for me. I'm not sure I like the idea."

"I'm not doing it for you. I'm doing it for me. None of us can live in this country without law." He wheeled and disappeared through the doorway, swallowed quickly by the blackness of the night.

Chapter 4

AS HE APPROACHED the Rice farm, the Redbone Coonhounds started baying. Ben Rice had brought the original stock with him all the way from Georgia, and he bred and raised the dogs, finding a good market in the growing rail city of North Platte some forty miles distant and among the scattering of neighbors in the area. Lamplight flickered in the windows of the Rice sod house. It was a solid structure with a two-story bedroom wing, the only two-floor soddy Rance had ever seen.

It was nearly ten o'clock, but with October just a few days away, corn harvest kept Ben, Tillie and the eight kids ranging from five to eighteen years of age working dawn to well past dusk. Rance chided himself for not thinking of Ben's current farming commitments and wondered if he should back away from soliciting his help.

"Come on up, Rance," came a mellifluous voice from the east corner of the house. Y'all would be easy pickings in the moonlight out there."

"Didn't figure you'd be too quick to squeeze the trigger. Those hounds aren't going to let anybody take you by surprise."

He nudged the gelding toward the house as Ben Rice stepped out from hiding and walked out to meet him. He was a formidable figure emerging from the shadows, only a few inches shorter than the towering Rance and beefier in the shoulders and chest and thick-waisted.

Rance dismounted, and Ben, wearing bib overalls hitched over naked shoulders and a tattered straw hat, approached with extended hand and a warm smile. Rance finished hitching the horse to the rail in front of the house and took his friend's hand in a firm grip. "Sorry for the late visit," Rance said.

"I'm betting it ain't social."

"Nope. Afraid not."

"Y'all look kind of sour, like somebody died or something."

"As a matter of fact, somebody did. Carl Baker was shot and killed, and his house burned out."

"Smelt smoke when we was still in the cornfields. Jake claimed he saw a glow beyond your place but didn't see nothing when we come in. Baker, huh? Didn't like the sumbitch, but I don't wish harm to no man. His wife? Kids?"

"They're at my place. The killers beat and raped the wife, left her for dead and thought they'd burn her up with the house. She made it out, but barely."

Ben said, "Why don't you come up and sit in one of the porch rockers and I'll go in and get some coffee? Then, you can tell me the tale and explain what you're here for."

Ben turned and headed for the porch, which was just a twelve by twelve-foot, wood platform resting on stones in front of the house. He went into the house, and Rance claimed the smaller of the two rockers, usually occupied by Matilda, or "Tillie" as most called her. His long legs pushed his knees up level with his chest when he sat down. He figured the chair had been crafted for Tillie, a petite, pixie-like woman who might stand five-feet tall on her tiptoes.

When Ben returned with two big tin cups of coffee and handed one to Rance, the big farmer sat down in his own rocker and said, "Now, tell me what you're up to."

Rance gave his friend a quick summary of the evening's adventure.

"And you're aiming to go snake hunting, ain't you?"

Rance sipped at his coffee. "Good. You didn't make this. I've tasted your mud mix on the trail."

"Tillie won't let me near the coffee pot in the house. Y'all don't need to answer my question. You still ain't got the law out of your blood. I know what you're up to. Looking for company? I'll ride along."

"Ordinarily, I wouldn't turn you down, but it's harvest, and I might be gone for a spell. You could help, though, if you and Jake would take a buckboard by my place in the morning and accompany the lady to the Baker farmstead to bury her husband. Then help her collect what she wants to salvage to move over to my property until she decides where she's going. She's got a milk cow she wants to lead over. She's already got a mule and wagon in my barn that she can take along. I suppose she has a few items of farm equipment and such, but you can just the leave the big stuff there. No passerby is going to bother that."

"We can sure enough do that much for the poor thing."

"She needs help, but my sense is she is far from helpless. I didn't mention that she's not grieving for her husband. He did some of the damage to her face before the killers showed up."

"I'll just keep my mouth shut and let her tell us what she wants. Do you think Tillie should visit later? Does Missus Baker know we're colored folks?"

"I was hoping Tillie would visit. Remember, she brought us refreshments when we were fencing the Baker place? She's got Texas roots, I think she told us then, but that doesn't brand her one way or another. Her husband might have been a problem, but my impression was that she doesn't care about the color of a man's hide one way or the other. Her experience with white folks hasn't been all that pleasant. If she turns nasty, just walk away."

"Wouldn't do that till the job's done."

"One more thing. Do you think Sue Ellen would look after the kids at my house while you're at the Baker farmstead? I don't think they should go back there just yet."

"I'll tell her. She'll welcome a day off from picking corn."

Rance stood, "Ben, I can't tell you how much I appreciate your helping me out with this. I know it's a bad time to pull you out of the field. Save my place for last."

Ben lifted himself out of the chair. "Don't you worry yourself none. Matthew and Mark will keep the crew going. Luke and John's getting pretty fair at shucking corn themselves."

Matthew and Mark were fourteen-year-old twins. Luke had turned twelve recently and John was ten. Missy had arrived two years after John, and at age five, Louisa had given Tillie a three-year break. Rance suspected Tillie would not feel shorted if Louisa turned out to be the last of her brood.

"I'll leave the Baker woman to your care, then. I've got to be moving out."

"Y'all ain't taking off by your lonesome, are you?"

"Depends. If Johnny Whitehorse is home, I'll see if I can hire him on to go with me."

Chapter 5

JOHNNY WHITEHORSE HAD been waiting on a bench outside his log and mud-caulked shack when Rance arrived. He did not require a Redbone Coonhound to warn him that company was coming from along the path that threaded through the trees that fringed Wildcat Creek. Rance had offered the Pawnee five dollars per day to join him on the search for Baker's killers. As an additional carrot, he had promised a twenty-five-dollar bonus if the quest should be successful. Rance knew this would be a fortune to the Indian, who supported a young Sioux woman who shared his ramshackle abode.

Primrose was likely half Whitehorse's age, which Rance guessed to be a bit on the short side of sixty. She was a friendly woman, who spoke a smattering of English. She was pretty enough but probably outweighed her smaller, wiry husband by a solid fifty pounds, Rance figured. They had been a couple when Rance moved to the area over three years earlier. Whether they were married or not, Rance had no clue. Primrose had waved happily as Whitehorse rode off into the darkness with Rance and had seemed unconcerned about her husband embarking on a journey that might take him away for some days. She was likely accustomed to Whitehorse's absences, and Rance knew her to be proficient with a double-barreled shotgun she kept in the little single-room house.

They were at the Baker place now. The fire in the house had been reduced to smoldering, red-hot coals. A quick look through the soddy's doorway confirmed there would be nothing to salvage there. The soddy had turned into a giant oven. He walked with Whitehorse to the barn. The moon shot some light through the wide barn door, but it was still too dark to see much. A cow mooed from some-place and acknowledged their presence, and he heard a few chickens clucking.

"They owned a mule and two horses. The mule is at my place. The killers took the horses. One is a bay gelding. The other is a black mare."

"Ain't easy picking up the trail in the dark," White-horse said, "but where would they go but North Platte? Only place within two days' ride to sell the horses. Only place to get liquored up, too. You said they thought the

Baker woman was dead. They won't likely be hurrying none."

Rance said, "Yeah, that's what I figured. Probably took the wagon trail and hit the crossing for the South Loup River. They would be looking for a place to camp by then. If that's what they did, we should catch up to them by sunrise. Regardless, they will have to stop and sleep and rest the mounts sometime. Worst case, we find them in North Platte. I'm sure Abe Steele is still county sheriff. I was his deputy for three years and left on good terms. We can count on him if we have to call in the law."

"But we ain't going to wait for the law."

"Didn't plan on it. I'll take them to the law, though, if they allow it."

They walked their mounts out of the dusty farmyard, Whitehorse casting his eyes over the earth in attempt to pick up any disturbance. Rance left the tracking to Whitehorse, knowing that the Pawnee had no equal in such skills. Whitehorse helped Rance with cattle at the ranch when called upon, saving the Rising Sun Ranch the cost of a full-time hand. Whitehorse did not talk much, but over a three-year period, Rance had learned that the Pawnee had spent many years scouting for the United States Army during the Sioux and Cheyenne wars. When the Pawnee had departed their villages along the Platte for Indian Territory several years back, he and others just disappeared. He dressed like a moccasined cowhand, and most folks didn't know a Pawnee from a Sioux, or for that matter, a Mexican from an Indian. So long as he did not take up killing and scalping, nobody much cared about his ancestry.

They walked in silence on the perimeter of the farmyard for a good fifteen minutes before Whitehorse spoke. "Headed for the wagon road and the South Loup crossing."

Whitehorse stepped into the saddle of his bay gelding, and Rance mounted Rusty, and they reined their horses to a well-used trail west that would connect with the wagon road that snaked south toward the South Loup River. As they rode abreast through the drying grass that stood a foot high in some patches, Whitehorse continued to fix his eyes on the ground, although Rance could see nothing meaningful.

"Like we guessed, they're going to the wagon road," Whitehorse said. "Three riders leading two horses. Not in a hurry."

Rance said, "How about when we get to the wagon road, you move out ahead? See if they've pulled off for the night. Let me know if you find their camp. If you don't find anything, head back my way at sunrise, and tell me what you're thinking."

Whitehorse nodded. "Figured that's what you'd want."

A few minutes later, they reached the rutted wagon trail, and Whitehorse reined his horse south and quickly disappeared into the darkness. Rance headed down the trail at a leisurely pace behind the Pawnee. If they had stayed together, there was a risk that they would have alerted the pursued. Whitehorse had made his living scouting and tracking for a good number of years, and that was why Rance had hired him on. His friend would do better ferreting out the killers on his own.

It was not more than an hour later that the Pawnee appeared again riding his horse at a trot. Rance reined in and waited until Whitehorse sidled his mount up next to him.

"They're camping in some cottonwoods about a hundred feet off the trail, maybe twenty minutes down the wagon road," Whitehorse said. "Decided not to cross the South Loup in the dark, I guess."

"Guard posted?"

"No. Coals still glowing in what's left of the fire. They ain't worried none about being chased. I could slip in and cut their throats if you want. Be done quick and quiet."

"No, can't do that. Dead or alive, I'm going to turn them in to the sheriff in North Platte. See if there's a poster out on any of them. This wouldn't have been the first time for men like that. If they're dead, they've got to look like they were taken fair and square. Nothing that causes too many questions to be asked," Rance said. "We'll give them a chance to come peaceful-like."

"You're the boss. Was me, I'd kill them, take the horses and anything worth a dollar or more, and let coyotes and buzzards clean up the mess."

Chapter 6

RANCE AND WHITEHORSE rode their horses as far as the trail that branched off to the campsite. They dismounted and staked the animals before pulling their Winchesters from the scabbards and started walking softly on a deer path that twisted through grass and scrub trees. Clumps of fresh horse dung had no doubt made the trail easy for Whitehorse to follow, Rance figured.

They paused when they approached the cottonwoods where the men camped. Rance counted five horses, including Missus Baker's black mare, staked out in the meadow fringing the cluster of towering cottonwoods. The night had turned chilly as morning approached, but there seemed to be no effort to maintain the campfire. Rance hoped that did not mean that the killers were expecting company. He thought it was more likely they were too lazy to get up and feed the fire. Also, they had left their horses exposed, which they probably would not have done if they were worried about pursuit. Of course, most criminal types were short in the brain department.

With a voice that barely rose above a whisper, Rance said, "I'd like to move into the trees near the campsite but wait till the first light of sunrise to take them into custody."

"Don't want to shoot each other in a crossfire. How about you come in from the west on this trail? I'll come from the south," Whitehorse suggested.

"Okay by me," Rance said. "I'll step out and announce our presence and tell them to surrender their weapons. They can make the choice to live or die. If they decide to fight, start squeezing the trigger."

Whitehorse nodded, veered off the path and headed south to circle around and slip into the trees surrounding the campsite.

Later, when Rance saw the first tentative orange glow slip above the eastern horizon, he continued his deliberate walk toward the trees, his rifle clutched in his left hand and his right hand resting on the grip of his holstered Army Colt. As he approached the camp, he found himself agitated. Something wasn't right. Too quiet, too easy. He stepped off the path where he would make an easy target for a gunman waiting for him. He angled away from the path, staying on course to enter the camp from the west.

He was almost to the tree line when a rifle cracked, and a slug kicked up dirt at his feet. Another shot tore a hole in his hat before he hit the ground, rolled and then rose to his knees behind a young cedar tree that offered little protection but provided some cover. He fired a few wild shots, hoping to draw more fire and locate his ambusher. This time shots came from two locations about twenty-five feet apart. He returned fire at the ambusher to his right and heard a groan. He figured he must have got lucky and struck home. Shots came again from the gunman to the left. There should be a third man someplace, but, hopefully, Johnny Whitehorse was positioned by now to lend a hand.

"This is Deputy Rance Coldsmith," Rance hollered, using his former title. "I just want to talk."

"Go to hell," came the raspy voice. Shots came again from both men, so he guessed the wounded man was still in business.

"Drop your guns," came Whitehorse's voice from behind the shooters.

More gunfire, and the man to Rance's left broke from the trees and raced for one of the horses. He obviously was not thinking, Rance thought. The animals were neither saddled nor bridled. Rance got to his feet and charged after him. He drew his Colt from the holster and fired in the air. "Stop, or the next one goes between the shoulders."

The tall man stopped, tossed his rifle aside and raised his hands, but as he turned, his hands dropped and he crouched and went for his pistol. Rance's first shot hit the gunman in the belly and the second dug into the center of his chest. He pitched forward and fell to the ground. The man would meet his Maker shortly, Rance decided and wheeled toward the campsite, noting that all seemed quiet there.

"Johnny," Rance hollered, "are you okay?"

"Yep. Got me a dead one and another that's only got a lump on the back of his noggin. Come on in."

Rance returned to the path that led into the camp and followed its winding course through the cottonwoods that led to a little clearing where bedrolls were spread out around the remains of a fire. When he stepped into the clearing, he found Whitehorse standing not far from a man who was sprawled out, face-down in the dust, rivulets of blood dripping off the back of his head.

"He's alive," Whitehorse said. "Just got a twitch out of him. He'll be coming around. Gave him the butt of my pistol. The one in the trees was shooting at you, though, and I took him down. He's got a slug in the neck and another in the chest. Appeared you put one in his hip. Didn't want to backshoot him, so I had to let him know I was behind him, so he'd turn around. I take it you got the other?"

"Yep. He panicked and went for his sidearm. I'm not a gentleman who donates a free shot. I think he might be the one Missus Baker identified as the leader. Said they called him 'Tobe.'"

Whitehorse asked, "Now what?"

"Help me drag the other two in here. Then maybe you could fetch our horses up and stake them with the others. I've got some rawhide strips in my saddlebags. When this bird starts to wake up, we'll cinch his wrists to keep him from causing trouble, but I doubt he's going to feel like making himself a nuisance for us."

After they had dragged the two dead outlaws into the campsite, Whitehorse departed to collect their horses, and Rance commenced searching the pockets of the dead men. The britches of the younger man with the shaggy blond hair and beard surrendered one hundred forty dollars and some odd cents, which Rance figured included the money taken from the Bakers. The stocky black-haired man gave up fifteen dollars. A search of the saddle bags turned up ninety dollars in gold eagles. Rance wondered where they had stolen the money and whether anybody had died in the taking of it.

The older man with the drooping, white mustache was on his hands and knees now, shaking his head and obviously trying to clear his mind and figure out just what had happened to him.

"Sit down and stay put," Rance ordered.

The man did not need much encouragement to fall back on his buttocks.

"Who the hell are you?" the man asked.

"My name is Rance Coldsmith. I'm a friend of the woman you raped and murdered. Now, who the hell are you?"

"I go by Jeb Parsons. But I ain't kilt nobody, much less raped any woman."

"Who are your friends?"

"Tall, skinny one went by Tobe Gates. Won't miss him none. Meanest sumbitch I ever run into. The other feller is Sniper Holland. Don't know much else. I ain't rode with them more than six months. They claimed to be cousins. Scared to break off from them. Think they'd have kilt me if I tried."

Rance was pleased to find a man who would loosen his tongue so easily. The challenge would be to sift out the truth from the passel of lies Jeb Parsons would spill out. He sensed movement behind him and reached for his Colt and turned.

"Just me, Rance."

It was Johnny Whitehorse. He should have known, but old instincts did not die easily. "Your friend has joined us since you left," Rance said. "Meet Jeb Parsons."

Whitehorse looked at the man. "What are we going to do with him? String him up? Plenty of stout limbs here to do the job."

Parsons's eyes widened. "Hanging? What the hell you talking about? Are you the law?"

"As near to it as we got nearby," Rance said. "I'm not turning you loose, and I've got to take you all the way to North Platte to turn you over to the sheriff. I don't have time for that without good reason. Tell me why you killed those folks and set fire to the house." He asked Whitehorse, "Johnny, do you want to take a look at this man's head wound and see what you can do for it?"

"Yeah. I can do that." Whitehorse stepped behind Parsons and knelt to examine the wound he had delivered to the man's head. "Give me your kerchief," he ordered Parsons.

While Whitehorse staunched the bleeding and wrapped the hapless captive's head, Rance pursued his questioning. "So, Parsons, tell me what you were doing at the Baker farm."

"Well, we had been working at the Print Olive place. But Tobe kept having run-ins with the big colored man there and wanted to go out on his own again. Didn't take to bossing by a black man. A few months back somebody was talking about all the money the North Platte bank handled these days with the cattle market, railroad and all. Tobe decided we should help ourselves to some of that money."

"If you were going after all that money, why would you trouble with the Baker farm?" Rance asked. "Doesn't make sense."

"I knowed Baker from our days riding with Quantrill in Missouri and Kansas during the war. When the war ended, we headed to Texas together to look for work. Carl never was much of a horseman, though, and thought he'd try his luck at farming. I found a ranch job punching cows, and he took on a job with a pig farmer nearby. Neither of us liked our jobs—Carl hated pigs but he didn't mind the crop work. The carpetbaggers showed up and started squeezing the landowners, and both our bosses lost their properties to taxes. But Carl, he courted his boss's daughter who wasn't more than sixteen or seventeen years old and talked her into marrying up and going to Nebraska to homestead."

"So you and Carl split up?"

"Yeah, but we stayed in touch. He let my ma in Kansas know where he settled in and wrote me there once or twice a year. He was an educated man—finished eighth grade, you know. Almost made six myself, so I ain't no man's fool. I write good enough to get by."

Rance said, "But you haven't said how you and Carl Baker came to meet up here."

"Well, after Carl left Texas, I came across some of my old Quantrill's bunch and we started fighting the damn Yankee crooks that was trying to run Texas, raiding their places and the like. When things got too hot, we broke up into smaller gangs, started hitting some trains and banks. Folks came and went, and over the years the Quantrill riders disappeared. Tobe and Sniper showed up a while back and joined up with three of us. We lost my other partners on a train job and that's how I ended up with Tobe and Sniper."

"Just tell me how you ended up at Baker's."

"Well, like I said, we was wanting to hit the bank in North Platte but Tobe and Sniper both had paper out on them and couldn't go into town to scout out the bank. We thought it better if nobody seen me in town before a robbery, and I thought of Carl Baker. I went over to his place and made a deal with him to scout out the place and make drawings of where things was in the bank and outside on the streets. Promised to pay him a hundred dollars if he had it when we came by his place."

"I see. You went there to get his sketches."

"Yep. And he had them but wanted more money. That didn't set well with Tobe since we didn't even have the hundred dollars. That's why he shot Carl and helped hisself to the drawings. And then he'd caught sight of that pretty wife at the door. He'd never had no problem with taking a woman when he got the chance. I hated that. I didn't like seeing Carl kilt, friend that he had been, but taking his woman I didn't want no part of."

"But you didn't stop them," Rance pointed out.

"One man against two like that? I couldn't. I begged them not to burn her up in the house, but they wouldn't listen. Said she'd be a witness."

"She's alive, and she is a witness, so you'd better be telling the truth."

Parsons looked at Rance with disbelief. "You're sure? She was laid out on the floor when Tobe and Sniper started firing the place."

"She's alive."

"Well, that's not all bad for me. She can tell you I didn't touch her. I don't know how much she saw with Carl, but I'm telling the truth. I wouldn't have kilt him. Tobe done it."

Rance spoke to Whitehorse. "Johnny, we need a few hours of shuteye. We'll have to bind this man's wrists behind his back while we sleep a spell. Then, we'll wrap the bodies and pack them on their horses, and I'll take them and Mister Parsons to North Platte. I want you to head back to my place with Missus Baker's horses. I'll send her money with you, too. Tell her I'll be back in four or five days. Jake Rice will be looking after chores at my place, but he likely needs help checking on the herd. If you can back him up, I'll make it right with you."

"I'll check with him and see if he can use me."

Rance dug into the leather pouch he had been dropping the money in and plucked out two double eagles. He handed the gold coins to Whitehorse. Your twenty-five-dollar bonus and three nights on the trail. Forty dollars in all."

Whitehorse stuffed the coins in his front trousers pocket. "Should barely have two nights. Guess it's morning now. I ought to be back home by tonight or tomorrow morning at the latest riding at an easy gait."

Rance nodded at the bodies stretched out on the ground. "Those gents wanted to pay you a little extra." He gave Whitehorse the pouch. "This is for Missus Baker."

He had already pocketed forty dollars for his venture into North Platte, figuring he would need twenty dollars for the sheriff's contingency fund and that the remainder would furnish decent lodging and meals during his stay. He had less than ten dollars cash of his own and not twice that in the North Platte bank. He had already driven his steers to market and sold them in North Platte to meet his bank loan payment. He would grudgingly sell some breeding heifers and cull some cows to make it through the winter. That was on October's task list.

Whitehorse said, "I'll go unsaddle our horses and grab the bedrolls. You're sure you don't want to have a hanging?"

"As long as Mister Parsons behaves himself, we'll leave his fate to the law."

Chapter 7

LISBETH BAKER HAD slept only sporadically the previous night, but when she swung her feet out of bed at sunrise, she was pleased to see that Morgan and Marissa were still sleeping soundly on the feather mattress. The room was dusky, but the windows admitted enough light for her to find her way about the room without stumbling over something. Having no bed-clothes Lisbeth had crawled into bed naked, but a thick, down comforter had kept her cozy. It seemed odd briefly, sleeping in sheets previously occupied by a strange man, but she had shaken off the feeling quickly.

What she really hated were the garments—Carl's shoes and britches she was forced to wear. Coldsmith's shirt did not bother her so much. She figured she would be a piti-ful sight when she greeted Mister Rice. She shrugged and picked up the clothes and got dressed before making a quick visit to the outhouse, which she found surprisingly clean after living with a man who took no care with the aim of his pizzle. A small basket full of cornhusks was tacked to the wall within easy reach, and a stack of newspapers rested on a single wall shelf.

She had laid out the tinder and sticks for starting a fire next to the fireplace before she retired well after midnight, and she took the little hand scoop and gathered the embers that still showed life. Fifteen minutes later, she had a lively fire started, its warmth welcome in a room that had taken on a bit of a chill during the night. The stacked Dutch ovens near the fireplace seemed to trigger her hunger. She was suddenly starving and figured the kids would be, too, when they woke up. Perhaps she could find the fixings for biscuits and ferret out a jar of jam. After making a quick search of the cupboards and food storage crates in the kitchen area, she found a large tin canister of flour and another of cornmeal and an array of baking foodstuffs. No jam, but a near-full jar of honey would substitute nicely. It had been years since she enjoyed the stores of food she was uncovering in this place. Of course, city folk would not understand.

She had biscuits baking in the smallest oven by the time Morgan and Marissa awakened and rolled off the mattress sleepy-eyed and seemingly confused. "Morg, would you take your sister to the privy out back? Stop at the pump on the way back. There is a bar of lye soap and a pan for washing your hands. I'll have biscuits ready when you get here."

She could fill them with biscuits and honey for now. She would bring Rosey the milk cow and as many hens as she could capture from her place so they could add eggs and milk to their menu. She had potatoes and an assortment of vegetables, as well as some canned goods, in the root cellar. After they removed Carl, she would retrieve supplies for immediate needs.

She had no idea where she would be a week from now, but she was thinking seriously about returning to her own farm and taking up residence in the barn temporarily. There was something about this untamed, open country that had cinched her to it. Her unhappiness had never been about where she lived. It had been about the angry, sometimes violent, man with whom she lived. Without Carl, she might yet carve out a tolerable life at the farm. At her father's insistence, Lisbeth had finished twelve grades of school in Texas by the time she was sixteen, and she had been thinking she would seek a teaching job at a nearby country school to help with her father's money crisis. Fred Galbraith had been the patriarch of a thriving farm family less than five miles east of Austin before the war, but Lisbeth's mother, Rebecca, had died during the war's early months. Her two older brothers, fighting for the Confederacy, had both died at Gettysburg, or so it had been reported. The location of their burials, if any, were unknown.

Within six months after the war, Northern carpetbaggers were swarming over civilized Texas, taking advantage of new laws that effectively confiscated Southern lands via taxes or outright forfeiture. Fred Galbraith had held out for almost two years before his two-hundred acres of river-bottom land was foreclosed for delinquent taxes. A day after the Yankee sheriff served her father with notice of the foreclosure, Lisbeth had found Fred Galbraith's limp body, rope cutting into his pale neck, hanging from a rafter in the barn.

Carl Baker, the farm's only employee at the time, had helped her bury her father and care for the hogs and the few horses that remained until government agents claimed the animals for some nebulous obligations. During this time, he had sold her on his dreams of homesteading in Nebraska. She had never felt more than gratitude toward him, but she was naïve about love and romance and matters of the heart. Life had forced her toward pragmatism, and there was nothing but family graves now on someone else's land holding her there. She had agreed to marry him, figuring it could not get much worse.

Did she wish she had not married Carl Baker? No, for if she had not, Morgan and Marissa would not have come into her life, and their absence was unthinkable.

Morgan's appetite was unaffected by events of the previous evening. He ate three biscuits soaked with honey. Marissa, on the other hand, could not be persuaded to eat more than a few nibbles and sat silently and teary-eyed at the table, the fingers of one hand twisting the shoulder-length, copper-colored hair that was a near match to her mother's. The girl was obviously unsettled, Lisbeth thought, and with good cause.

"Mama," the girl asked, "is Papa in heaven now?"

Lisbeth thought Carl was more likely burning in hell but tried to assure her daughter. "He is in a better place." She had heard that statement countless times when people tried to console themselves after the death of a loved one.

The girl shrugged and seemed satisfied with her mother's answer for the moment. "But what will happen to us?" Marissa asked.

"Don't worry about it. We are safe here. I am going back to the house to get Rosey and some of the hens. Maybe we can move back there when we get the house repaired and stay in the barn till then. The important thing for you to know is that I will take care of you. And that we will be together."

"Are we going back to the farm with you?" Morgan asked.

"No," she said. "A young neighbor girl is coming to stay with you while her father and brother go with me."

Marissa's lips formed a pout. "I don't want you to leave. I don't want somebody else to stay with us."

"I'll be here with you," Morgan said. "Mama doesn't need us in the way."

Morgan obviously understood that burying his father would be high on the chore list, and he likely did not mind missing out on that task. He had never been a disciplinary problem. The discord and tension in their lives had forced him to bypass childhood and become Mister Responsibility early on. A rapping at the door startled her, and her eyes went to the rifle on the gunrack.

"Missus Baker?"

A female voice. She went to the door, pulled the iron bar from the slots and slowly opened the thick barrier. She was greeted by a smiling young woman with flawless, cinnamon-colored skin, her arms loaded with bulky gunny sacks.

"I'm Sue Ellen Rice," she said. "Daddy thought I should come up, so as not to scare you. He's at the wagon reins out in your lane. My brother, Jake, is with him, mounted on his spotted mare."

Lisbeth stepped back. "Come in, Sue Ellen. I'm Lisbeth." She gestured toward the children, "This is Morgan and Marissa. Just drop your load anyplace."

Sue Ellen placed the sacks on the floor, opened one and pulled out a beautifully crafted wood checkerboard. She stepped over to the table and placed it on top. "Do you play checkers?" She asked Morgan.

"No, ma'am."

"It's about time you learned. This board is yours along with a little leather bag of checkers I brought with me. Daddy makes them. Today you learn checkers. Next time, we will try chess, and you can come to our place and pick your own set of chess pieces."

Lisbeth smiled as she watched her son run his fingers over the smooth checkerboard. It saddened her to realize that her son had never engaged in simple pleasures like playing checkers.

"Thank you, ma'am. I've never seen anything like this," Morgan said.

Sue Ellen reached into another bag. "I hope you like dolls," Sue Ellen said to Marissa, and plucked a ragdoll from a sack. She handed it to the girl whose eyes widened as she took the doll into her arms. Lisbeth could not remember ever seeing her subdued little girl smile like this.

Some little white girls might have protested upon seeing the doll's black pigtails and brown face but for Marissa it was instant love. "Oh, thank you. I love her. I always will. Her name is Alice." She bounced out of her chair, reaching out to Sue Ellen, who bent over and received the girl's hug.

"Alice? That was a quick decision. Why Alice?" Sue Ellen asked.

"Alice in Wonderland."

"Lewis Caroll's *Alice's Adventures in Wonderland* and *Through the Looking Glass*, the sequel," Lisbeth said. "Among our few books outside of some McGuffey Readers. Unfortunately, we lost them all in the fire."

Sue Ellen released Marissa to dote on Alice and turned to Lisbeth, "We can share our McGuffey Readers. Mama has them for all grades as far as they go. We don't have the Alice books, but we can go book shopping in North Platte. We can have more books between us and trade."

"That sounds fun and practical," Lisbeth said, fearing she would have no money for McGuffey replacements, not to mention a library contribution. Of course, she and her children might be many miles from here when that time came, although she had no clue where that might be.

"We can talk about this another time," Sue Ellen said. "I brought some things for you." She opened the remaining two bags and began pulling out clothes, including some denim britches, a buckskin coat, several shirts, a pair of moccasins and assorted undergarments. "Rance told Daddy you didn't have anything to wear. He thought we might be near enough to the same size you could wear some of my things. I thought when I saw your children today, I might be able to figure out what we can put together for them."

Lisbeth almost cried when she saw the garments. "You are a godsend, Sue Ellen. I hate to keep your father and brother waiting, but I'd sure like to get into something that doesn't make me look like a circus clown."

"I told them it might be a short spell. They are well-trained. They're used to waiting on Mama. Let me help you put these things on the bed, and you can pull the curtain and try them on."

While Sue Ellen chatted with Morgan and Marissa, Lisbeth cherished the comfort of a soft pair of drawers over her hips and thighs. A green shirt, faded from countless washings, fit snugly but comfortably over her firm breasts. She did not think of herself as busty, but Sue Ellen, slender as a reed, appeared to be a small-breasted woman. She slipped into a pair of denim britches that were a bit snug but not uncomfortable. She guessed Sue Ellen to be about her own height at nine or ten inches over five feet, but as she had guessed, Sue Ellen was more on the leggy side, and the pant legs needed to be rolled up a few narrow folds. Her toes rubbed against the ends of the moccasins, but they were a luxury compared to the painful clod hoppers.

She pulled back the curtain and stepped out. "Everything fits fine," she said. "I feel like a human being again."

"You look like a beautiful woman," Sue Ellen said.

"Liar. I saw my bruised and swollen face in the mirror this morning."

"I can wash away the bruises with my eyes. You will turn any man's head, Lisbeth."

"Frankly, the last thing I want to do is turn a man's head right now or ever."

"I'm sorry. I should have been more sensitive," Sue Ellen said.

"No. You've been very kind, and I cannot thank you enough for what you've done."

"Mom, Sue Ellen's father and brother are waiting for you outside," Morgan said.

Morgan had moved the checkerboard to the center of the table and was separating light checkers from dark ones. Marissa sat in one of the rocking chairs with Alice cradled in her arms, carrying on a conversation with her new friend. Lisbeth decided her absence was going to be barely noted. She plucked a tattered straw hat from a wall peg next to the door and pulled it down over her head. It was a bit large, but her head was not swimming in the headwear, and it would ward the sun off a face that burned easily. She gave Sue Ellen a tentative wave and smile, gathered up the empty gunnysacks and slipped out the door.

Chapter 8

LISBETH APPROACHED THE buckboard hesitantly. She was by nature a shy person and uncomfortable meeting strangers, but the bearish man stepping down from the wagon put her immediately at ease, as had his daughter.

"Missus Baker, I'm Ben Rice." He gestured toward the lanky young man astride the black mare on the other side of the mule team. "That there is my oldest son, Jake. We're here to help y'all with any chores that need doing at your place."

She extended her hand, and he accepted it, gripping it gently with a huge paw that was no doubt capable of bone-crunching force. He gave her a warm smile.

"Thank you, and please call me Lisbeth," she said. "Your daughter wasted no time charming my children. That's a big worry scratched off my list."

"Let me take them gunnysacks and help you up on the wagon."

She could have easily climbed up to the wagon seat, but she took his arm and used his leverage to get onto the wagon. "Thank you," she said, as she settled into the seat.

The rutted wagon trail that passed for a road to the Baker farm offered the same bone-shaking ride that she had taken the previous night, but the journey to the unpleasant task ahead carried more foreboding for her than the escape. She was not in a mood for casual conversation, and Ben Rice apparently sensed it because he did not disturb her thoughts with small talk. Furtively, she studied her seatmate's face as he reined his plodding mule team toward her farm. His skin was a rich brown, not as dark as some colored folks she had known. His face was adorned with a thick, but well-trimmed, mustache, the ends of which arched downward to merge with a goatee on his chin. He was not fat, just big and amply muscled. He was not the least intimidating to her, appearing to be a gentle giant, but she suspected he could be fearsome in the defense of his family and their property.

Jake rode silently beside the wagon. She would not have guessed him to be colored but for some black kinks of hair that fell below his low-crowned hat. She supposed some might call him mulatto, but many might guess him half-blood Indian or Mexican from his pale olive skin. Sue Ellen's skin was of a lighter hue, but she was not near to passing for white. Could his mother be a white woman? Not that it mattered, but she did not think it unnatural to be curious.

When they reached the house, Ben spoke. "Y'all will have to tell us what you want done, Lisbeth."

"The burial first. We need that behind us, I think. We left Carl's body in the root cellar."

"We've got shovels. Show me where the root cellar's at, and I'll just head the mules that way."

Lisbeth pointed toward the east side of the burnt-out soddy. "Over there. It's not deep. You can reach him from the edge of the pit and just drag him out." It occurred to her that her words probably seemed callous, but she could not feign the grieving widow. She hoped that Mister Coldsmith had forewarned him that she might be less than sorrowful.

When Ben reined the mule team in near the root cellar, Jake dismounted and hitched his mount to the wagon bed. Lisbeth scrambled down from the wagon before Ben could come around and assist her. She hoped he would not be offended, but she didn't feel like a helpless old woman today. She knelt by the root cellar, slid the top off the pit and peered in. She turned her head away and began trembling when she saw Carl's eyes staring back at her, his pallid face contorted in a mask of anger.

"Y'all going to be okay, Lisbeth?" Ben asked.

"Yes, it's different in daylight somehow." She pointed to a lonely charred and twisted tree trunk some fifty yards east of the soddy and away from the building site. "Could you bury him next to that old oak tree? It got struck by lightning a few years back. It would mark his grave for now anyhow. I've got a horse blanket in the barn I guess you could wrap him in."

Ben asked, "Do y'all want to say any words over him?"

"No. You can say something if you want. I will be milking the cow in the barn and getting her haltered to go back with us. The chickens didn't get shut in last night— I'll have to see if the coyotes left us any and figure out how to move them. Just come to the barn when you've got him buried."

"However y'all want it, ma'am. Jake, help me get him into the wagon bed. Then you can go to the barn and fetch the horse blanket."

Lisbeth walked away, heading toward the barn to tend to milking and feeding Rosey. The poor critter would be needing some relief by now. Up until a few weeks earlier, they had shared her milk supply with a heifer calf that was killed and half eaten one night by a predator, possibly a cougar, they surmised. Only occasionally did they see wolves about, but they were included on the list of suspects. The children had been devastated at the calf's death, and it had been a financial loss as well, since heifer dairy animals sold at a premium in this country. Milk could be like gold to a family battling to survive.

Rosey would need to be bred soon. Perhaps, she could breed the cow to one of Coldsmith's bulls. They had led the cow almost three miles to a farm with a Holstein bull last time, because of Carl's feud with Coldsmith, a feud that her late husband's neighbor had been unaware of. A Hereford bull crossed with a Guernsey cow would not produce a great milking animal, but if the offspring were male, it would generate a better beef prospect. Her immediate concern was to keep Rosey producing milk and birthing any sort of calf would accomplish that.

Ordinarily, the cow would have grazed during the night in the pasture fenced off adjacent to the barn. This morning, however, Rosey occupied a stall and commenced bawling when Lisbeth appeared, demanding fresh hay and a bit of grain while the milker relieved the stress in the cow's udder. Lisbeth set about tending to her chores. After milking the cow, she poured the milk into two cream cans, and sealed the contents with lids. She wondered if the Rice family might be able to use some of the milk. She always had so much more than she could use that she had to throw some away, which seemed a sinful waste.

She corralled a half dozen hens and the rooster. She could not turn up three of her flock. She squeezed the birds into an old crate for the journey.

By the time Ben and Jake Rice returned from their burial task, she had collected most of the items she might have immediate need for. She would leave the remainder of the barn's contents behind because she might be moving back in a week's time.

Ben and Jake loaded the chicken crate and some nesting boxes along with the cream cans, the butter churn and a barrel of mixed corn and oats for graining her animals. Most of the other items were nonessentials.

"I have more milk than we can use," she told Ben. "Can you make use of the extra?"

"As a matter of fact, we can. One milk cow's dry and the other's starting to dry up. Till they calve again a few months off, milk's going to be in short supply."

"Well, I have plenty. You can take one of these cans with you and we'll work out transfer every day somehow as long as I am within a few miles."

Ben said, "We got lots of fruits and vegetables canned up. Maybe we can do some trading."

Chapter 9

RANCE RODE INTO North Platte, leading three horses on a rope line. Two carried the ripe corpses of Tobe Gates and Sniper Holland. His prisoner, Jeb Parsons, was astride the nearest horse, his wrists bound with rawhide strips and his hands clutching the saddle pommel.

Thanks to the Union Pacific Railroad, North Platte was a thriving town of some four hundred residents, large for a frontier community in the middle of nowhere. From the homes and businesses being constructed within his eyesight, Rance had no doubt the town was in the infant stages of its growth. He had spent several years here as deputy sheriff before departing to take up ranching. Since then, he had visited four or five times annually to market cattle or make major supply purchases.

His nearest source for provisions was "Arnold's Post," a small country store where the government had established a post office some ten miles south of his ranch. "Big Tom's General Store," a half day's ride to the southwest in the direction of North Platte was a more reliable source of supplies beyond foodstuffs. The store was operated by Tom Gunn, who also owned the adjacent saloon and the four or five houses that comprised the settlement that bore no name and had been carved out of the owner's homesteaded quarter section.

Rance led his procession down Main Street to the sheriff's office, tipping his hat when an old acquaintance would holler a greeting to him or when folks might stop to stare. This was not the first time he had performed the ritual, but he had hoped he was finished with those days. He reined Rusty in next to the county sheriff's office and dismounted. He was not surprised when Sheriff Abe Steele opened the door and stepped out onto the boardwalk. Steele, a barrel-chested man with snow-white hair and a brushy mustache, looked at Rance, then surveyed the line of horses.

"Good morning, Abe," Rance said. "Brought you some business."

The sheriff nodded. "Howdy, Rance. Don't take offense if I don't thank you. What in the hell is this all about?"

"Be glad to sit down over coffee and tell you all about it, but I got two back there on the rank side. I thought maybe you'd provide a cell for Mister Jeb Parsons here, and I'd take his friends down to visit Wally." Wally was Walter Weaver, proprietor of Weaver's Furniture and Funeral Parlor.

"County going to have to pay for this?"

"I'll make a deal with Wally. Ten dollars each, including a pine box and grave digging. No embalming or preaching needed. I'll tell him to take it or leave it. I can dump them in the Platte if necessary."

"He'll take it. Funeral business has dried up lately."

Rance said, "Take a look while I've got them here in case there are any posters out."

The sheriff stepped off the boardwalk and joined Rance to examine the dead men. Rance pulled the blanket back enough to reveal each face. Steele started coughing. "Damn, you weren't joshing when you said they was rank. This is outright stink." He gestured at Tobe Gates's corpse. "This fella looks familiar. Tell Wally to take some pictures of both men naked and another of their faces. County will pay for that. That's all I want to see of them. Now, get them the hell off the street."

Chapter 10

WHEN RANCE RETURNED from the undertaker's, Sheriff Abe Steele not only had a coffee pot on the corner table but a plate of sweet rolls as well. Rance commented, "What are we celebrating? I've never seen pastries served here before. Maybe I'll visit more often."

Steele said, "New bakery down the street. The lady calls it 'Grandma's Delights.' I'm trying to help keep her in business. Afraid it's not shrinking the old paunch, though. She has tables and all and serves breakfast in the place, or you can pick up what you want and take it with you."

"Well, since I didn't get breakfast, it's a welcome sight."

"I already gave the prisoner a cinnamon roll and cup of coffee. I hope you will tell me eventually why I am holding him."

Rance took a sip of coffee from his tin cup and plucked a roll from the platter. It was generously frosted, the way he liked such things. He took a bite. Peach filled. "Better than good. The lady shouldn't have trouble selling her sweets without your help."

"That's true enough. She's a good businesswoman, too. Very smart."

"Pretty?"

Steele flushed a bit. "Well, I suppose most men my age would think so."

"You are a year or two over sixty. What's age got to do with it?"

"Well, I'm guessing she's mid-fifties. A young buck like you might not see her through my eyes."

"Not many available females up my way. A man starts to expand his female requirements after a certain time. I'm thinking you might have a romantic interest in this lady."

Steele said, "Undecided. Martha's been gone five years now. I'd like to leave this job one of these days. But to go home to an empty house?"

"Well, I wish you the best, Abe. If the lady's looking for love, she won't find a better man around these parts."

Steele shrugged. "You going to tell me your story?"

Rance began with the fire he saw at the Baker farm, and, glossing over any details that did not fit his narrative, provided the sheriff with a run-down of events that had transpired since discovering Lisbeth Baker in the doorway of the burning soddy.

Steele spoke when Rance was finished. "There are a few holes in your story, but you're telling me what I need to know. What about this Jeb Parsons you drug in here? You would have saved me some trouble if you'd brought him in a package like the others."

"The lady said he didn't rape her, and we couldn't prove he pulled the trigger. Besides, I don't play executioner unless I'm forced to. You know that. I saw enough killing while I was fighting Comanches in New Mexico Territory and Texas, as well as during the time I worked here. I just want to be a cowman."

"A cowman, huh? Not a cowhand?"

"Nope. As you well know, a cowman owns the cows. A cowhand just works the cattle for somebody else. I had enough of that, too, after two drives north from Texas. That's why I'm headquartering my operation within a week's cattle drive of a railroad shipping point."

"Makes sense. But back to Parsons. I got to do something with him. The crime was committed in Custer County, not here in Lincoln County. I'm acting sheriff for you folks because Custer's just been a legal county for not even a year yet. Waiting on a county seat and a courthouse and most of the officials that go with it. Custer, which is no more than a house and post office is only the temporary county seat."

"Well, it seems you are telling me that Parsons is your problem if you're the Acting Custer County sheriff. Is Hank Pickles still the prosecutor here?"

"Yep. When he's sober or aint' doing private legal business. County pays a pittance, but still lets him do private work. I like Hank, but he's your age, and at the rate he's drinking, he won't see forty. Ain't a bad law wrangler when his head's clear."

"I wouldn't want to see Parsons strung up, but he ought to do some time in the penitentiary at the capital city. Suggest to Hank that the guy might plead guilty to an accessory charge of some kind, if Hank recommends a year or two in the pen to the judge. Hank won't want to spend time trying the damn thing." Rance dropped a double eagle on the table. "This is a donation for the sheriff's contingency fund but use five dollars of it to hire a lawyer for Parsons."

The sheriff said, "That would be Asa Wiggins, since Tobe Tisdale won't take criminal work anymore unless it's for one of his rich clients, and most of them got that way by staying out of trouble with the law."

"Well, I guess that's for the most part settled. The outlaws aren't going to be needing the three horses and their tack. I was thinking I might keep the piebald for the widow Baker and sell the other two to Bart at the livery. I would give the money to the widow, after deducting ten per cent for the sheriff's contingency fund."

"Guess nobody would be claiming the animals, and the county sure as hell don't want to pay stable rent. I assume you would be selling the tack, too, and that the contingency fund would receive a share."

"I wouldn't expect otherwise," Rance said. "Now, I am going to find me a room at one of the hotels, get me a hot bath and shave and pick up supplies for my extra horse to carry. I can't waste a trip to the civilized world, such as it is."

"You going to pay a call on Katherine?"

"I thought I might."

"I'll put a flea in your ear. She's been seeing somebody."

That triggered second thoughts about his plans. "Anybody I know?"

"George Oglesby."

"The weaselly bank clerk?"

"The bank clerk, whose father, Hiram, owns the Oglesby Bank and will someday anoint his son as his successor as president and eventually endow him with a small fortune."

"Well," Rance said, "when she broke off our engagement, she left open the possibility we might get back together. We were both free to see others, though—but that prissy, pompous ass. He's about as robust as a sick kitten."

The sheriff said, "I think I'm hearing more than a hint of jealousy here."

"I just hate to see her end up with the wrong man."

"And you are the right man? When was the last time you saw her?"

"Whenever I was in North Platte. Three or four months ago, I suppose."

"A woman can get mighty lonesome in that much time. She would expect that a man who was interested would try to see her before that much time run out."

"She could have been with me all that time if she had married me. She decided she couldn't live on a ranch that far from town. And it didn't help when she and her folks took a trip out to see my place. She was horrified of my soddy, but I told her we would build a nice new house soon."

"Sounds to me like you should talk to her, maybe get some things settled once and for all. But that's between you and her. Before you leave, I got one more thing to ask you about?"

"Yeah?"

"I've got a job—one that will let you stay on your place."

"I'm listening," Rance said.

"I told you that I'm acting sheriff for Custer County temporarily. It could go on for a few years, so I need a deputy over that way to keep an eye on things. I wouldn't need any patrolling or anything like that, but somebody who could act on information I might send out or who folks would know they could get hold of in case of trouble. It would pay fifty dollars a month. Put some food on the table between cattle sales."

Rance always needed money. The money well was always nearly dry, it seemed. And he would likely be borrowing from the bank again to get through the winter. Damn, he hoped he didn't have to deal with young Oglesby. "I'll think on it. I'll stop back tomorrow morning before I leave town."

Chapter 11

RANCE COULD NOT have avoided Katherine Anderson if he had tried, for she was a clerk at the Riverside General Store, which was owned and operated by her father, Josiah Anderson, a kindly, balding man in his fifties. There had not been open hostility from the man, but Rance always figured the father had been less than enthusiastic about the young deputy as a suitor for his daughter, in no small part because he did not want a rancher spiriting away cheap labor from the store.

Katherine, who was closing in on her twenty-fifth birthday, was nearly ten years younger than Rance, and there was no doubt talk among the local ladies about the young woman's approaching spinsterhood. Prospects of marriage were thought to be greatly reduced after reaching the early twenties, but Rance thought the notion preposterous. That might be true back east, but single men outnumbered unmarried women by well over three to one out west in cow country. Spinsterhood was a choice, not a woman's fate in the west. Given the quality of the crop of male prospects, he supposed, foregoing marriage might be a more than viable option.

Freshly bathed and shaved and wearing a clean cotton shirt and britches, Rance stepped into the store midafternoon. Flaxen-haired Katherine was waiting on a customer at the counter, but her sky-blue eyes flashed instant recognition when she caught sight of him, even though she continued with her business. He moved into the first aisle of shelves to wait for her to finish with the customer and feigned examination of the merchandise while keeping his eyes on the fair-skinned Nordic beauty.

They had little in common, and he had never been certain whether his proposal of marriage had been born of love or lust. He wondered if part of his attraction to her was triggered by the draw of the forbidden fruit. Katherine was a prim and proper church-going lady, and if she was not a virgin, the trespass on her virtue had not been his doing. A sharp rebuke when he had tentatively fondled her fully cloaked and bound breast once had told him it would be a hopeless effort to get the woman to remove her drawers. But her resistance had enflamed him even more, making him even more determined to get the woman in his bed. Besides, he was past due for marriage, and a cowman needed a wife to maintain the home and birth and raise a brood of kids to work the ranch.

When Katherine was finished with the customer, she stepped into the storeroom and returned momentarily with a fuzzy cheeked young man who took her place at the counter. Then she approached Rance.

"Are you shopping?"

"I will be. I wanted to speak with you first." Her grim face was not welcoming.

"Follow me through the storeroom. We will go through there and out the backdoor. There should be a bit of privacy behind the building. I have no more than fifteen minutes," she said tersely.

He was already wishing he had not approached her. When they went out the door, he saw that two buckboards blocked the view of casual observers.

"I did want to speak with you," she said. "There has been no official announcement, mostly because I wanted to tell you first. I am engaged to be married. It will take place late November."

"I see. Oglesby?"

"You heard. Of course. You stopped to see Abe Steele at the sheriff's office. He's a terrible gossip."

"I had business with him, and Abe is not near to being a gossip. He is a friend, and he knows that I still care for you."

"Enough to leave your dirt house and the godforsaken hell you call a ranch?"

Was she giving him a second chance? He replied quickly. "No."

"Then we're done. I will not risk visiting alone like this again. You will be just another customer in the store. Understood?"

"Understood. Do you love him?"

"I like him well enough. But it is none of your business. We make choices as we move through life. You made yours, and I have made mine."

"I guess so. We can go back in, and I will give you a list of the items I need. I will come by in the morning about ten o'clock. Maybe you can have the towheaded boy ready to help load everything on my packhorse. And Katy?"

"What?"

"I do wish you happiness. I really do. I won't forget you and what you were to me once."

She turned away and headed back into the store. To avoid scandal for her, he walked behind the buildings that lined the street and then slipped between two buildings onto Main Street. Then he took the boardwalk that lined the street on his return to the general store and re-entered through the front door.

Chapter 12

RANCE DID NOT bother seeking out breakfast, counting on pastries and coffee at Abe Steele's office. It had been a good decision. It was shortly after eight o'clock and the sheriff had a platter of rolls and a steaming pot of coffee on the desk when his former deputy arrived. Rance poured himself a cup of coffee and pondered his choice of the pastries. He noted that the platter had already been invaded, but he supposed the prisoner was getting the same breakfast, which would be charged to the county.

"I talked to Pickles," Steele said, plucking a frosted roll from the platter. "He won't be hard to deal with on the charges. Wiggins will take Parsons's case and will be in to visit with him this afternoon. I don't think it will go to trial, so Missus Baker won't have to deal with the unpleasantness of being a witness."

"Good. She doesn't need any more worries right now."

"You said you left her and the kids at your place. Where does she go from there?"

"I don't know. I hope she has got that figured out by the time I get home day after tomorrow. She doesn't have family or anyplace to go, but she doesn't seem a helpless sort, either," Rance said. "Ben Rice and his family are helping her out while I'm gone. You've met Ben?"

"I have. He helped me out when my horse tossed a shoe out that way. I got lucky to come across a man with blacksmithing skills. That was before you moved to the neighborhood. He's stopped by the office to say howdy a couple of times since. Seems like a good man."

"Better than good. Yeah, he's a skilled blacksmith, but I'm still looking for something Ben can't do. Anyhow, I'm counting on Ben's wife, Tillie, to find a way to push Lisbeth Baker and her kids out my door. With the horse money and the funds that are returned to her, I will probably be bringing them back here to put on a train to Lincoln or Omaha—or maybe she could find a place in North Platte for a while."

Steele got up and went over to his desk, picking up a sheet of paper and returning to the table. He sat down and flipped the paper to Rance. A wanted poster with

Tobe Gates's picture on it. Five-hundred-dollar reward, dead or alive. Bank robberies and multiple killings.

The sheriff said, "You made some serious money going after these guys, Rance. I can send the documentation and have the money deposited in your bank account in a week's time, if you like."

"Yeah. For now. I'll see that it goes to Missus Baker. I'm not a bounty hunter."

"It explains why they needed Carl Baker to check out the bank here. Gates had to be darn careful about showing his face anyplace. I'll check some more. I wouldn't be surprised to turn up this Sniper Holland's picture yet, maybe under a different name."

"That's up to you," Rance said. "That job you were talking about. Is it still open?"

"Till you close it. Are you in?"

"Yeah. I need the money. I could live on the salary easy enough. That way I could keep my cattle profits in the business."

Steele pulled a silver star from his shirt pocket and slid it across the table. "You've been sworn before. Consider yourself reinstated as a deputy sheriff for Custer County. Now, there is one other matter we need to talk about."

Rance said, "Holding out on me till I took the job."

"Well, I don't see it that way. I just didn't want to be starting rumors if you weren't going to be working for me."

"Sure," Rance said, not buying into the excuse.

"Have you ever met a rancher up your way by the name of Prentice Olive?"

"Once. He said his name was Print Olive. Tobe Gates and his partners worked for Olive but had a falling out according to Parsons. You can ask him about Olive."

"Yeah, most folks call him Print, I'm told," Steele said.

"Anyway, not more than a year after I settled in at my place, he came by and wanted to buy me out. He offered two dollars more an acre than I paid. Of course, I had no interest, and he seemed a bit insulted, like he was entitled somehow. His headquarters is about thirty miles from my place as the crow flies. On the east side of the county. He's close to ample public lands still available for grazing, but my place has a foothold on the edge of the Sandhills. Those hills are just starting to be recognized as prime cattle country. I could double or triple my investment if I wanted to walk away. I won't. I expect to die on the place, but not anytime soon. Seems like Olive's trying to buy up the whole county. He's certainly putting together a big operation."

Steele said, "Tax records say he's the biggest land-owner in Custer County, and he's got a good start in Logan to the east and Dawson and Buffalo to the south. He ain't been in Nebraska more than four or five years. Came from Texas. They pretty much ran him out of there. Spent a few years in Colorado till he wasn't welcome there no more. Wherever he sets up, his herds grow, and his neighbors' get smaller, if you get my drift."

"Rustling?"

"Strong suspicions of it. But stories are he's strung up more than a few men accused of taking his stock."

"I'm glad there is some distance between us."

"The man doesn't borrow money. He deposits. And old Hiram Oglesby at the Oglesby Bank will kiss the man's ass on demand."

Rance said, "Olive is president of the Custer County Livestock Association that was just formed. He was the instigator in organizing it. It was understood that membership was by invitation only. Small outfits like mine didn't get the invite."

Steele said, "I'll be collecting everything I can find on the man. I'll ride up your way or send a messenger if I've got something you need to know quick. Otherwise, you just stop by when you're down this way. Olive has a wife and kids and brought two brothers, Bob and Ira, with him. He's a Confederate vet and had plenty of killing experience. I'm guessing he's on one side of forty or the other."

"That's what I'd guess from my meeting with him. Likely on my side of it."

The sheriff said, "He has a man you might call a regulator or enforcer. Take him seriously. He's been with Olive since the war ended. A colored man, even a mite taller than you, at least six and a half feet tall, they say. His folks and him were slaves owned by Olive's family. They're about the same age, so they probably grew up together. He's saved Print's life more than once."

"I've heard of him," Rance said. "Jim Kelly, the enforcer for the Custer County Livestock Association."

"Yep. That's the man. Watch out for him. I'm hoping he will be a bit more careful with a man wearing a badge, but some lawmen who got too interested in Olive's affairs ended up dead. I'm not asking you to go after Print Olive. I just want you to keep your eyes open."

"I'm thinking I should have held out for more money."

Chapter 13

THE MORNING AFTER Lisbeth's visit to the farm to retrieve some of her belongings, she went about her morning chores. The barn had no stanchion, so she hitched the still haltered Guernsey cow to a post in a stall, glad she had thought to bring the milk stool as she set about milking the cow. She had explored the farmstead after Ben and Jake helped her unload the cargo the previous afternoon and had been pleased to find a nice chicken coop behind the barn, obviously taken over by mice and spiders for some time but in remarkably good condition. She had put the kids to work cleaning out the structure for occupancy by her hens, confident that her birds would quickly devour any spiders or insects that refused to vacate.

The chicken coop had no confining fence, so they would have to gather the hens in nightly or lose them to coyotes, foxes or other chicken-loving predators. The hens had been untroubled by the move to accommodations that were an upgrade from the Baker dirt-floored, cramped hutch. Coldsmith's coop could house thirty to forty birds with their chicks. What a waste that he did not make use of it, Lisbeth thought. She was certain eggs could be marketed to one of the trading posts or neighbors. She smiled at the thought of the tall rancher gathering eggs each morning. No, he was a cowman, not a chicken man. She supposed milking a cow would be beneath his dignity, also.

Lisbeth had told Jake she would look after her mule, Plato, and the two bluish-gray colored fillies, which Jake referred to as "grullas." Some horsemen called the animals "mouse duns," the young man had told her. Whatever they were called, the fillies were beautiful creatures, she thought. She saw other horses grazing on the ranchland and wondered why these were kept in stalls. Maybe they were being held for breaking, or he had special breeding plans.

Later that morning, leaving the chicken coop, she saw a rider leading two horses approaching the ranch from the west. A brief wave of panic struck her, and her first thought was to locate the children and grab the rifle in the house. She looked inside the soddy and found Marissa engaged in a serious conversation with Alice, providing a high-pitched voice for responses by her new best friend.

She pulled the Winchester down from the rack, stepped back outside and caught sight of Morgan standing on the corral fence near the barn, watching Plato and the horses for a bit before he opened the gate to release them into the fenced-in grass. He had asked to ride one of the fillies, but Lisbeth had not been comfortable giving him permission to ride another person's horse, especially when she was uncertain of their broken status. She swore the boy would sleep on horseback given the opportunity.

She started to call Morgan to the house but then recognized her black mare, Ebony, and her bay gelding on the lead rope behind the rider, who sat low in his mount's saddle leaning forward as he came into the yard. The man, his bronze-colored skin and aquiline nose suggesting he was Indian, raised his hand in greeting or as a peace sign. She was not certain which, but either was welcome. She relaxed and lowered the rifle and walked out to greet the stranger when he dismounted.

He was a small man with a friendly face dominated by dark, searching eyes that told you he did not miss much. He removed his battered hat revealing black, white-streaked hair that looked like it had been shorn with a butcher knife. She hoped he spoke some English.

Her question was answered when he said, "Ma'am. My name is Johnny Whitehorse. I'm Rance Coldsmith's friend. Work for him now and then and took a little trip with him a few nights ago."

"Mister Coldsmith's all right?"

"Oh, he's finer than frog hair, ma'am. He had to ride on to North Platte, though, and won't be back for three or four days yet, I'm guessing. He asked me to bring your horses back along with your tack that was stolen."

"I can't believe it. I thought I would never see them again. I can't thank you enough." She knew that the mare was probably worth nearly two hundred dollars and the gelding not far from that figure. The tack had been worn and needed repairs when purchased, but at least they would not be forced to replace it if they did not sell the horses.

"I'm glad I could help out, ma'am, but Rance thanked me with hard cash."

"I need to know. What happened to those men who killed my husband and . . . took the horses?"

Whitehorse said, "The older man with the mustache is alive. Rance was taking him to the North Platte sheriff. The other two rode along tied down over their horses' backs. I suppose somebody will bury the no-goods there."

"I see." She did not want to hear the details. She knew the scum had not died of smallpox. She was starting to realize that Rance Coldsmith was a man to be reckoned with.

Whitehorse plucked a leather bag with a rawhide drawstring from his saddlebags and handed it to her. "Rance said I was to give you this. He said to tell you it is your money with interest."

"All of my money?"

"I think so, ma'am. Now I got to get back to my place. My woman won't be worried none, but she lets me know if I been gone too long. Where do you want the horses?"

"My son's coming this way. He'll take them and put them up. Again, my thanks, Mister Whitehorse."

"Please, ma'am, make it 'Johnny.' That's what my friends call me."

"Okay, Johnny. And I'm Lisbeth."

Morgan raced up to his mother. "Ma, it's Ebony and Sleepy. This man brought them back."

"He certainly did. Now you take the horses and put them up in the barn and rub them down for now. They need a bit of rest, but you can probably ride tomorrow if you want."

Morgan took the horses and led them off, and White-horse pushed his hat down on his head and mounted his horse. "I'll be by now and then, Lisbeth. Rance don't go long without some work for me."

"Well, I hope to see you again, Johnny, but I likely won't be here for more than a few days yet."

"You'll be here when I'm by next." He reined his mount away and headed northeast, angling off onto the trail that ran along Wildcat Creek.

Chapter 14

LISBETH'S MORNING SURPRISES were not finished. First, as soon as Whitehorse rode off, she went into the house and emptied the contents of the leather bag onto the kitchen table. She could not believe her money had been returned. She counted the gold coins twice, confirming that she had $185 in front of her, not quite double what had been stolen. She guessed the extra eighty-five dollars was the interest Johnny had referred to.

The recovery of the horses and the money suddenly changed her options. And she had a farm she could sell for as much as ten dollars an acre, which would give her another sixteen hundred dollars. There were no bank loans because Carl had not been considered a good credit risk. That had become her good fortune now. She had ample funds to start up somewhere else or to stock her farm with a swine herd, "mortgage lifters," as her father had called hogs.

Some folks, especially cattlemen, looked down upon pig farmers, but because of reproductive rates and large litters and at least two litters annually, a person could get established quickly in the business with minimum capital. Her father had been a successful hog breeder until the war, and she had helped him with the money since she was eleven or twelve years old. She had tried to convince Carl to try hog raising, even offering to do most of the work, but he had always resisted, possibly because it was her idea. What would she do in a town or city someplace? She had serious thinking to do.

Her next surprise came while she was putting the coins back in the bag. Morgan opened the door and raced into the soddy. "Ma," he yelled, "we got company. It's Sue Ellen, but there's a lady and a couple other kids."

Oh, no. It was closing in on noon, and she was not finding food supplies to feed her own children anything but a skimpy meal of more biscuits and beans, let alone serve up something for a crowd. She took her bag of gold coins and stuffed it under her mattress, then rushed out to greet her guests.

The same buckboard that Ben Rice had driven to her farm was parked behind the same two mules in the lane in front of the soddy. Sue Ellen and a tiny woman Lisbeth surmised to be the girl's mother were unharnessing the mules like the visitors intended to stay a spell. Sue Ellen came toward her, leading one of the mules.

Evidently reading her anxiety, the girl said, "Don't worry. We brought dinner, and Mama packed some supplies that should tide you over a few days. Can we put our mules in the barn, steal a mite of grain and hay and carry some water for them?"

"Well, I don't own the grain and hay, but I'm certain Mister Coldsmith would be fine with that."

"We brought my brother, John, along. He will help me put up the mules, and I see Morg. I'll put him to work, too. The boys are within a month of the same age. I know they will be friends before we head home. My little sister, Louisa, is just six months younger than Marissa, so I thought they could play together."

Sue Ellen's mother came up with the other mule. "Oh, this is Mama," Sue Ellen said.

Tillie extended her free hand, "I'm Matilda Rice, but everybody calls me Tillie. I'm so sorry about all that's happened to you and your family."

Lisbeth accepted Tillie's hand, squeezed it gently and then dropped it and wrapped her arms about the woman in an awkward hug, almost knocking a surprised Tillie off her feet while she held fast to the mule's halter. The women both laughed. "I am Lisbeth," she said, "I didn't mean to be so rough. I'm just so thankful for all your family has done for me."

"Time for us to get acquainted, I'd say." She turned and hollered at her son, who still sat in the wagon bed. "John, you come and grab Charlie and help your sister get the mules situated."

The boy jumped out of the wagon and ran to do his mother's bidding, returning Lisbeth's smile as he led the mule off, following Sue Ellen toward the barn. Sue Ellen waved at Morgan to follow.

"My daughter is in the house with Alice, the precious baby you allowed us to adopt. Why don't you come in and bring Louisa with you? We'll see if we can get the girls to warm up to each other."

"Louisa brought her baby doll, too, and a little crib for Marissa to keep for Alice."

"You're doing too much."

"Just what we can. Now, I've got dinner packed and some food supplies to tide you over till Rance gets back. You can help me get things from the wagon."

Inside, Lisbeth was pleased to see that the girls had become instant friends. Lisbeth had worried because Marissa had never had a playmate, nor had Morgan for that matter. She had been aware of the Rice family residing less than three miles distant from the Baker farm, and she had spoken to Ben when he and Coldsmith were building the line fence, but Carl forbade any contact with colored neighbors. Of course, no interactions beyond commercial trades or sales were established with white members of the rural community, either. They might as well have been situated on an island.

Lisbeth watched as Tillie began to remove dinner from the huge picnic basket. Such a pretty, petite woman, she thought, with her flawless olive skin and dark eyes and long lashes, she did not appear that much older than her eldest children. It was hard to believe this little lady had borne eight children. Her energy and enthusiasm suggested that eight more would not have fazed her all that much.

Tillie placed an apple pie on the table. "We have an orchard that we started when we got here ten years back. We were the first homesteaders out this way. The trees are producing big crops now, enough that we sell surplus to the trading posts. I've got an extra pie and a sack of fresh apples I'm leaving for you. You can't imagine the things I find to do with apples."

"I wanted an orchard," Lisbeth said, "but it never worked out."

Tillie took roasted chicken from the basket and two loaves of fresh bread. "We'll likely eat most of one loaf. The other is yours. I brought half a ham and some bacon, too. I have some sliced potatoes we can fry up quick if you want to get a skillet out. I see you've got coals in the fireplace yet. I've got a small sack of potatoes you can use for baking or however you like later. Rance usually has a store of dried beans and flour and a fair supply of canned goods to fill in with. I figured you had probably eaten enough beans that I didn't bother to make any."

"You figured right. The man must live on biscuits and beans."

Tillie laughed. "We have him over for meals a lot, and I drop food by. He does so much for us, that's the least we can do. We've never paid for a beef, and our bunch eats a lot of it. Of course, we trade back and forth with labor and the like. We have a cookstove—Ben made me a bigger one as the family grew—and the old one is sitting there for Ben to put in, but Rance claims he would not use it. Likes cooking on an open fire."

"That reminds me," Lisbeth said, "I have a cookstove in my house that can probably be salvaged and sold if I don't fix up the place to move back in."

Later, Lisbeth felt like she would burst. She could not remember the last time she had enjoyed so much to eat.

She teased Tillie about the six-legged chicken that had provided all the drumsticks. Tillie said, "Ben's going to be grumbling tonight about the legless chicken I left for him and the other kids. They won't go hungry, though."

After they washed the dishes and cleaned up, the women sat down at the table to chat. Sue Ellen had given the children no choice about either going outside or to the barn to play, and Lisbeth had agreed the boys could ride the horses if they did not race the critters. It occurred to her that the horses had not carried riders on their journey to Coldsmith's Rising Sun Ranch and should not be overworked after just a half day on the move. She suspected that removal of the children from the house had been planned by Tillie, but it suited her. It was nice to have another woman to talk with.

"You are feeling okay?" Tillie asked. "I am a listener, if you need one."

"Your husband probably told you I am not a grieving widow."

"He did, and I have been given to understand why not. There are likely a good number of women who do not grieve the death of a husband." She smiled, "And I daresay more than a few men who are not heartbroken at the loss of their mate. I count myself among the lucky ones. I have adored Ben Rice since I was sixteen years old, and he has never given me a moment where I had second thoughts. That's not to say we don't have a fuss from time to time. He can be a stubborn man."

Lisbeth said, "He might say he has a stubborn wife."

Tillie shrugged, "Well, I do have strong opinions sometimes."

Lisbeth instinctively trusted Tillie. "Some good things are happening for me. Rance recovered my money and the horses. I will own the farm free and clear. I will have enough money to start over if I plan carefully."

"But?"

"The rape troubles me. Carl and I did not have—how should I put this? A loving relationship. Ever. I think he tired of me, and I don't blame him. Anyway, it was better when we no longer shared a bed. I liked the straw mattress rolled out on the floor better."

Tillie said, "That's sad. I am no expert on such things, but I am blessed to have a man I treasure in my bed at nights. But I did not always have such a man. I came here to listen, but if you like, I will tell you my story."

"Please do."

"I am thirty-six years old. I told you I have loved Ben since I was sixteen. He is almost ten years older. Twenty years ago, we were both still slaves. Ben was owned by Ezekiel Rice, a plantation owner twelve or thirteen miles north of Atlanta, Georgia. I was owned as a house slave by a preacher and his wife—Reverend Frederick Borden and his wife, Mary. They owned my mother, so when I was born, the couple owned me, too. My mother died when I was five, and they kept me and raised me as their own. The Bordens were in their early fifties by this time. The wife had been a schoolteacher and she taught me to read and write, which was illegal for a slave in Georgia. I received an education from her that was superior to that most whites were given. I will always be grateful for that. It has enabled me to educate my own children and to continue learning myself."

"I wondered about that. I hope you will not be offended, but I have never encountered colored folks, and not many whites, who speak with such excellent grammar as you and your children."

"I take it as a compliment. My husband is a brilliant man as you will come to learn, but I know it bothers him that he is the only member of the family who can do little more than write his name. I have tried to help him, but the frustration is too much. It has to do with his eyes. He does not see the letters in the correct order or something. I can't explain it. And, of course, we were never able to work on this for hours at a time. He has had a family to support."

Lisbeth said, "And he appears to be doing that well."

"Well enough, and he is an ambitious man. Back to my story. I took care of the house as I grew older, learned to cook and prepared meals for the couple, all of which turned out to be useful training for my future life. But around my thirteenth year, problems came into my life. The preacher began coming to my room at night. At first it was just touching and unwelcome kisses, but eventually he took my virginity, although I did not understand the term at the time. The visits were usually weekly, and I came to accept it as a slave's lot, although I hated it. He was not violent with me, but I fear he would have been had I resisted."

"That must have been awful."

Tillie shrugged, "That is the way it was then. Why do you think you see so many persons tagged as Negroes who are only slightly darker than those we call white, if at all? Anyway, Ben was doing repairs at the manse when I first met him, and we began talking at every opportunity during that time. After the job was over, we found ways to get together to talk, never anything beyond that."

Lisbeth asked, "Did you tell him what was happening to you at the manse?"

"No. If I had, he could have done nothing about it. Or if he had tried, he might have been beaten, or worse, sold and sent away. Finally, it was resolved. A month following my seventeenth birthday, I realized I had missed my monthly twice. I was naïve about such things, and I mentioned it to Mary. She immediately asked me if I had been having relations with Ben, and I insisted I had not, which was true. Then she asked if I had been having relations with any man, and I told her about the reverend's visits. I figured she knew. She exploded and became hysterical and at first called me a liar and a slut."

"I cannot imagine how that made you feel," Lisbeth said.

"She told me I was likely with child. Worse yet, she said, Reverend Borden would be the child's grandfather. This made no sense to me at first. I met up with Ben a week later. I told him about my dilemma. He was not angry and was very calm about it. He understood I had no choice. That was just the way things were. He said he was going to buy me and marry me if I would have him. Of course, that's all I dreamed of at that time in my life, being married to Ben. When I told him about Mary Borden saying the reverend was the baby's grandfather, Ben asked me what I knew about my mother and father. I explained that I knew nothing of my father, which was not uncommon during slave times. I only knew my mother to have been a young household slave for Reverend and Missus Borden at the time I was born. Ben nodded his head as if he understood something. A week later I was sold to Ben's master, Ezekiel Rice and placed as a house slave on his plantation."

"I thought Ben was going to buy you, but I didn't understand how that could be, a slave owning a slave," Lisbeth said.

"It was complicated. There were free Negroes who owned slaves, but Ben was not free. He had money saved up, because his master had foreseen the end of slavery and given his slaves the opportunity to learn skills and to keep a share of the money earned selling services to others. This happened more frequently than you might think. Ben tried to buy his freedom as was done occasionally, but his master said he needed him too much to release him. They made a bargain. Ben would loan Ezekiel Rice the funds to buy me. Ben would never be sold, and we could be married. In ten years, Ben and I, along with any children, would be granted our freedom and the loan would be cancelled."

Lisbeth said, "I never heard of such a thing. And he kept his promise?"

"Ezekiel put it down in writing and gave the paper to Ben. Of course, he couldn't read it, but I could. I still have it. Ezekiel was a good man. He would have kept his word, but the war intervened, and a few years later Lincoln's Emancipation Proclamation. Jake and Sue Ellen were born slaves, but the others were born free. I finally came to understand before Jake was born that Reverend Borden was my father and that Jake was a product of incest. Thank God, he was a healthy and intelligent boy, but now you understand his light skin coloring. My mother's skin, as I remember it, was not as dark as that of many Negroes, and mine is lighter. Jake would be at least seventy-five per cent European, probably more."

"Does he know all this?"

"No. You are the only person I have ever told. Ben knows, of course, but he has always insisted Jake is his son, and he does not want Jake or anyone else to think otherwise. What concerns me is that Jake has probably figured out that he is different from the other kids. I have educated him as best as I could, and he reads everything he can find. He and Rance share books all the time. I dread the day he asks me about it."

"Maybe he won't."

Tillie said, "He will. Someday, it will become important to him. I have said much more than I intended, but somehow it feels right, and it has given me comfort to share my story. I really set out to say that we all bear crosses, carry histories we would rather forget. We cannot bury such things, but we can put them aside and make life good again. And friends can help with that. Count on me as your friend."

"I will. And count on me as yours."

They talked for several more hours before Tillie rounded up her family and headed back to the Rice farm. Lisbeth felt she had formed a special bond with Tillie Rice that day, one she would not easily surrender. Sometime during their conversation, the critical question about her future was answered. Plans had yet to be laid and incidental decisions made, but she and her children were remaining in the Nebraska Sandhills.

Chapter 15

DEPUTY SHERIFF RANCE Coldsmith, astride his sorrel gelding, rode into the Rising Sun Ranch early afternoon encountering more activity than he had anticipated. A half dozen white hens and a big rooster were just outside of the soddy's front door pecking at the ground and devouring insects or some other seemingly invisible objects. Morgan Baker and John Rice were near the old chicken coop, going in and out with shovels full of something and piling it not far from the little building. He assumed it was the decayed chickenshit that came with the place and was three or four inches deep on the coop's floor.

He dismounted and hitched his mount and the piebald gelding he had on a lead rope to the hitching post in front of the house. He heard girls squealing and cast his eyes toward the ancient cottonwood that stood about fifteen paces south of the barn. Somebody had put up two rope and board swings from one of the low hanging limbs, and Louisa Rice and Marissa were swinging so high it made him nervous. He could not help but smile, though. How long had it been since he had sat in a swing, clinging to the rope as he pumped his legs and flew into another world? And he was stricken by a few moments of melancholy as he remembered those idyllic days in Missouri when he had pushed his precious daughter in a similar swing. He could not begrudge the girls that.

Rance entered the house to inform Lisbeth Baker that he had returned. He was also eager to tell her that he had brought her an additional horse and that reward money would be arriving soon. He was surprised to find it unoccupied. He wheeled and returned to the horses, untied the diamond hitches that held the canvas-wrapped load on the piebald's back and eased the supply-filled canvas to the ground. Most of the contents were foodstuffs and house supplies, and he left everything on the ground for later transfer to the house.

He led the two horses to the barn, where he would rub them down and give them a bit of grain before turning them out on the grass. When he led them into the building, he found Lisbeth Baker, attired in snug britches and a green cotton shirt that betrayed the lithe form that had soft curves in the right places. She had a pitchfork in hand and was cleaning the stalls and tossing the straw-manure mix into the back of his handcart. She was unaware of his presence and humming a song he recognized instantly, Stephen Foster's *Virginia Belle*.

She had a pleasant voice, and he paused to listen, his eyes misted up. He wondered if she knew the words. He did, particularly the fourth and last refrain: "While her life was in its morning came a sad and solemn knell. She was taken without warning—sweet Virginia Belle." And the chorus: "Bright Virginia Belle! Our dear Virginia Belle! She bereft us when she left us—sweet Virginia Belle."

Only his three-year-old daughter's name had been Tessa. Her mother, Rachael, had died with their infant son during childbirth almost six months later. A quick four-year chapter of his life had ended abruptly and without warning. After that, it had been three years with the Army, several years wrangling and driving cattle, the hitch as a sheriff's deputy, and finally his own boss again as a subsistent rancher chasing an elusive dream.

Missus Baker turned to toss a fork full of waste into the cart which was in the runway between the rows of stalls, five on each side. Their eyes met and she nodded and surrendered a tentative smile before finishing her task and setting the pitchfork down.

He led the horses toward her and she said, "I am glad to see you are back safely, Mister Coldsmith. Your Pawnee friend said you took a prisoner to North Platte."

"I did. His friends weren't so lucky."

"Johnny told me when he left the money and horses here. I can't thank you enough for what you have done for us."

"This piebald is yours, too, to sell or keep. It's up to you."

"He's not my horse."

"After all the losses you've taken, that's part of the killers' reimbursement for damages. And there was a five-hundred-dollar reward on the guy with the shaggy, long hair and beard. His name was Tobe Gates. That will be yours."

"No, Mister Coldsmith, I think not. The horse will cover my financial damages. I have my money back, with 'interest,' as you called it. My horses were returned. I have no claim to the reward. I did not capture or kill the man."

"Please, call me Rance. I would be uncomfortable taking the money."

"I will call you Mister Coldsmith, and I am Missus Baker," she said, her voice was firm but did not seem angry or hostile. "And you and Johnny earned any reward money," she added.

So Johnny had earned first name status. Ben likely had, also. It annoyed him some, but he would not make an issue of it. Missus Baker would be out of his life in a few days. He would split the reward with the Pawnee. Johnny Whitehorse would see $250 as a fortune, and Rance could not deny that his share would be welcome in his bank account. It would keep him from selling off a dozen Hereford heifers to get through the winter. He hated to give up breeding stock when he was trying to build a herd. With the salary from the deputy's job, things were looking up.

"Well," Rance said, "I'll see to the horses and then turn them out in the pasture with the others."

Lisbeth said, "I'll finish this work later. I will go up to the house and make some coffee and fix something to eat. You haven't had any dinner, I'm sure."

"That would be welcome, ma'am. I'll be along shortly."

When Rance went back to the soddy, he saw that the supplies he had left on the ground had been removed and apparently carried into the house. He felt a twinge of guilt but was glad for the task's disappearance. When he walked into the house, he entered a heaven of aromas drifting from the kitchen area. Coffee, of course. He guessed ham and potatoes were in the mix. There had been an apple smell when he was briefly in the house earlier. Suddenly, his appetite was that of a starving man.

"Come in and sit down, Mister Coldsmith."

The table was set for him, and he obeyed. Lisbeth spooned several heaps of what looked like a mix of fried potatoes, chopped ham and cheese on his plate, then a big spoonful of green beans.

She nodded toward a loaf of bread. "I heated it up in the Dutch oven. Fresh butter is in the butter dish. Eat all you want. The kids and I have eaten, and I just rewarmed this. Do save room for apple cake, though. Tillie's apple trees are bountiful this fall. I've promised to help her can some on shares. It's none of my concern, but you really should take Ben up on his cookstove offer. It would make your life so much easier."

He tried to ignore her, but it was nice having a woman in the house. She reminded him of Rachael. Probably the red hair and freckles. The little girl, Marissa, too. Her mother's hair and features, like Tessa. Too much nostalgia today.

He ate ravenously. Missus Baker had sat down across the table and was studying him with those coffee-brown eyes. At least her eyes were different. Rachael's eyes had been sky-blue.

"This is delicious," he said. "I've never eaten ham and potatoes like this."

"Not much to it. Tillie furnished the cheese. I just chopped up the ham, sliced the potatoes, mixed in the cheese and seasonings and let the Dutch oven do the rest. I like to cook, especially when it is appreciated."

He suspected Carl Baker had not appreciated her culinary efforts. "I guess we should talk," he said.

"We should," Lisbeth agreed. "Let me pour myself a cup of coffee and slice some cake." She got up and soon returned with two small plates with slices of unfrosted cake on them. One slice was twice as large as the other, and she placed that in front of Rance. After finding herself a cup, she sat down again and poured coffee for herself and warmed Rance's cup. He pushed his dinner plate, nearly wiped clean, to the end of the table. Abandoning his fork, he picked up his piece of cake and took a bite, savoring the taste before he swallowed. "A man might kill for this," he said.

"Not the cook, I hope."

He chuckled, "Definitely not the cook. Thank you for this meal. When I rode in, I was thinking I might scrounge up a plate of beans."

"I am not leaving the Sandhills," Lisbeth said, with an abrupt change of subject.

Taken aback by the sudden switch of the conversation's tone, Rance was silent for a few moments before he spoke. "I see. I guess that is a start for decisions you will be making."

"I intend to keep the farm. I know something about hogs. My father raised them, and I helped him. I am going to become a pig farmer."

As one who thought the most noble of a man's aspirations was the title "cowman," Rance could not grasp the notion of someone choosing to be a pig farmer, a woman no less. "Have you really thought this out?"

"Most of it. I won't try to obtain breeding stock till spring. I want to start with Hampshires. My father always wanted some. He said they are a meaty, muscled breed that produce good-sized litters, nine to a dozen piglets. You need to raise seven or eight to make a decent profit."

The woman was talking nonsense. "I confess. I don't even know what a Hampshire looks like."

"Black with a wide white belt over the back and shoulders."

"I saw such beasts in Missouri a few times."

"I know we are imposing on your hospitality here," she said. "I need to go over to our farm and see what I can salvage and do some rearranging there."

"You don't even have a roof on what's left of your house. You can't live there."

"I am thinking we can live in part of the barn until the house is repaired."

"Lis . . . Missus Baker. Winter is coming on. You can't have a fire in the barn. It would be a danger to you and your children. And that old plank barn can't be heated. Besides, a good stiff wind could bring it down."

"I've been thinking. I have a stack of old boards in a corner of the barn. I can construct a small sleeping area and cover the tops and side with straw. I would leave a small opening to cover with a cowhide flap. It would be far cozier than an Indian tipi."

"You have a little money now. Why don't you move to North Platte for the winter? Rent a room or small house?"

"I need to stay at the farm, so I can work on hog facilities through the winter."

"You will need to find help to do the construction unless you are a carpenter."

"The tools are still in the barn, and I am reasonably competent with a saw and hammer. Jake said he would help me. I am grateful for everything you have done, and I would appreciate it if you would put up with us for another week, but I will leave tomorrow if you prefer.

Frankly, Mister Coldsmith, you are acting as if you have some say in this. You do not."

Her tone annoyed him, but he had to admit she was right. She could do whatever she chose. And he had not offered an alternative. He sighed heavily. "I have a proposal."

Her eyes narrowed, and she looked at him suspiciously. "I'm listening."

"Stay here for the winter. Take some time to think this out. This is a business proposition." Her eyes were storm clouds now, anger threatening to strike like lightning. After her recent experience, he guessed he could not blame her for thinking he had carnal business in mind.

"Hear me out. You would pay rent, say five dollars a month. I would buy the food supplies, but you would do most of the cooking. I would get Ben to install the cookstove he has been nagging me to take. That would give us another heat source, too. You can work over at your place, or maybe you can use the barn here for some of your projects. I don't know what you have got in mind."

"I don't know," she said doubtfully.

Rance sensed that her attitude was softening. He plucked his deputy sheriff's badge from his shirt pocket and held it out for her to see. "I haven't told you about this. I have been hired to act as deputy sheriff for Custer

County. I was deputy for Lincoln County for several years, and the sheriff there is acting sheriff of this county as well. He offered me the job, and I decided the extra money would help and took it on. It is not a full-time position, but I may need to be gone for several days at a time on occasion. I need somebody here to look after the place while I'm gone. Morgan's old enough to help with the horses, if it is okay with you, and I would pay him a little something. Jake would check once a day to see if anything is needed here."

"What are you proposing for sleeping arrangements?"

"Just like now. I'll lodge in the barn. I've had a lot worse."

"Do you know how I would feel with you doing that when the temperature is below zero and the wind is blowing outside?"

"I can get another mattress and roll it out on the floor at night, just like we're doing for the kids."

"There wouldn't be a place to walk."

He had known from the beginning that the sleeping arrangements could be the deal breaker. He did not care to spend the winter in the barn. Lisbeth Baker was not his wife or even his lover, and she had just been through an experience that he supposed could be life-changing for a woman. She might never want a man to touch her again. He could not begin to understand how something like that might affect a woman. He supposed it would be like other terrible experiences women and men faced. Some came out scarred and broken. Others eventually turned out stronger. But he did not know this woman or any woman well enough to guess what might be going on in her head.

There was a long silence, and then Lisbeth spoke. "A bundling board. We will share the bed, but like brother and sister."

"A bundling board? I don't have a notion what you are talking about." Brother and sister? Maybe she had already lost her mind. He doubted he could share a bed within a short arm's reach of a handsome woman and think of her as his sister for more than an hour.

"I accept your business proposal, Mister Coldsmith, subject to your approval of my sleeping rules and arrangements, which I shall present within a week's time. I am sure that as the days pass, we will have other things to negotiate, but I cannot foresee anything else that would be an insurmountable problem. For now, you may sleep in the barn or on the floor, or it might work well for me to share the mattress with my children."

"I would prefer the barn for now, unless the weather turns before we have the bundling board thing worked

out. And the cookstove is fine. I will talk to Ben sometime."

Chapter 16

THE RISING SUN Ranch fell into a comfortable routine during the week following his return from North Platte. That was Rance's viewpoint anyway. He would be hard pressed to volunteer to take over cooking responsibilities again. He could not remember eating so well since shortly before Rachael's death.

He had not been given time to contact Ben about putting in the cookstove. Lisbeth had ridden her black mare over to the Rice farm after breakfast the morning following their conversation. Ben had arrived the same afternoon with the stove and had it installed and vented out the roof in time for supper. His neighbor had also accompanied Lisbeth to the barn to consult about one of her projects. Missus Baker had also made it clear that Mister Coldsmith was not invited.

Rance had also invited Morgan to ride with him on the outings to check his herd and make head tallies. He found that he enjoyed the boy's company. Morgan was a quick learner, and each day in the saddle improved his riding skills. Tall for his age and built like a slender willow tree, Morgan, like his sister, had his mother's auburn hair, freckles and brown eyes. He also had a winning smile that instantly melted any of Rance's black moods. He could not judge his mother's smile, since he had not yet seen it. It was not that she frowned all the time. Missus Baker was generally just expressionless. Of course, implementing this living arrangement with the woman had not triggered many of his own smiles in her presence.

Missus Baker had forged a tight bond with the Rice family during her short stay. She and Tillie visited almost daily, apparently with some understanding that visits between their homes would be alternated. Their calls were usually brief, but it was clear that they had established a female alliance of some sort. Whatever was going on, he knew instinctively to keep his distance. He was grateful that the woman's presence would not fracture his friendship with this special family.

One afternoon after he rode into the yard with Morgan, Missus Baker came out of the house and followed the riders to the barn. When they had dismounted inside the wide doorway, Lisbeth said, "I have finished my project. If you will help Morg unsaddle the horses, perhaps he can finish up with them and you can help me."

Rance looked at Morgan and the boy said, "I'll take care of it, Rance. Take my word, it's better to do what Ma wants."

Rance smiled, and Lisbeth tossed her son an aggravated look. Rance helped the boy unsaddle the mounts and left the horses in his charge, while he followed Lisbeth to the far end of the barn, where she had set up a private workshop in one of the stalls.

"Have you been looking at it?" Lisbeth asked.

"Your project? No. You had it covered with a blanket. I took that as a message that it was private."

She looked up at him, her eyes searching for something in his own. "I think you are telling the truth. You do have self-discipline, don't you?"

Was that a trace of a smile he saw on her lips? Couldn't be. "I have been told that," he replied.

They entered the stall, and Lisbeth tugged the blanket off her project, which was propped against the wall. Rance did not know what to make of the thing or what to say. With his permission she had salvaged scraps of cedar planks from a pile that had been left over from the original homesteader's construction of the barn. She had built a panel that was about seven feet long and two feet wide with support boards every few feet along the length. There was no space between the boards, and a strand of barbed wire hugged the top of the board from one end to the other.

"This is your bundling board?" he asked, although the answer was obvious.

"Yes, of course. I am certain it will fit." She pointed to two longer, narrow boards with holes drilled in them. "Those will rest upright on the floor and be bolted to the bed frame at the head and foot. Then I will bolt the bundling board ends to the upright posts. The partition will set four inches above the mattress, so blankets can slip underneath. I hope it will be okay with you if we share blankets."

"Uh, yeah. I guess it makes sense." At first, he had been offended by the barbed wire, but now he decided that it might help defend him from this lunatic female.

"Now," Lisbeth said, "we need to each take one end of this and carry it to the house. If we each take one of the support posts, with your help, I can install this quickly. The pliers and bolts are on the bed. I will need you to hold the pieces in place, but it will only take a short time and then you can go about whatever other business you have."

They carried the bundling board to the soddy. Missus Baker had everything organized, Rance had to admit. In minutes, everything was in place, and a sturdy partition several feet in height divided the bed. Maybe it was a practical solution for joint occupancy of the house. He had not looked forward to spending the winter in the barn. Neighbors would figure out soon enough that they were sharing the house, but there was plenty of distance between neighbors, and he did not care about the talk if she did not.

Lisbeth said, "There appears to be plenty of room at the foot of the bed for you to get to your side. I notice there is a chamber pot under the bed."

"I never use it. On the rare occasions I have the urge I step outside." It felt strange to be talking to a woman who was still pretty much a stranger about such things. "I hereby grant you exclusive use of the chamber pot."

She did not seem to appreciate the humor he was trying to interject. "I won't have much privacy if I should need it during the night."

"I will keep my eyes below the bundling board."

"I guess I will just need to get accustomed to some things. I must remember we are brother and sister for purposes of our arrangement."

"Well, sister, I have things to do. You did nice work on your project. I leave you in charge of our sleeping area." He turned and started for the door.

"Oh, Mister Coldsmith, Tillie said I could tell you. The barbed wire was her idea. She thought you would find it funny. Let's just think of it as a symbol of our commitment."

He stopped and faced her and grinned sheepishly, "I just thought it was a mite on the crazy side."

Missus Baker smiled. She truly smiled, her eyes crinkling and her cheeks revealing soft dimples. He had not been unaware of her lithe figure and other attractive features, but it only now struck him that he was going to be sharing a bed with a very pretty woman. He suddenly saw great frustration on the horizon.

Lisbeth said, "You may come to think I am madder than Alice's March Hare."

Chapter 17

ISOM PRENTICE "PRINT" Olive stood in front of the partially completed headquarters house between the Middle and South Loup rivers in eastern Custer County. He was getting impatient with the pace of progress on the structure, but the pool of craftsmen was shallow in this sparsely populated country. This was his second attempt to establish a Nebraska headquarters, having initially placed his first herds along the Dismal River north of the county line and into the Sandhills country.

His wife, Louise, had informed him, however, that she and the four children would be remaining in Plum Creek, which had been intended as a temporary stop. His brothers' wives had joined her in the rebellion. They wanted no part of that lonely, isolated country to the north. Plum Creek, located in Dawson County to the south, was set not far from the Platte River and enjoyed railroad access, the key to the civilized world.

Olive had found this spot in Custer County not more than fifty miles north of Plum Creek and begun buying out homesteaders. There were ample public lands to the north for the twenty thousand head of cattle he planned to run here. The bonus was railroad access only fifty miles distant. The wives had unintentionally furnished a perfect financial plan, and now the Olive men would be near enough to visit their families with some frequency.

Print Olive loved Louise as much as he supposed he could love any woman. She had been an orphan and had brought nothing of monetary value to the marriage. He had provided her with a life of relative luxury and considered her a satisfactory wife. She ran the household competently and was a good mother to the children. She was compliant in bed and, outside the recent resistance, was generally obedient and supportive, so he thought he had chosen his mate well enough. With a few exceptions he tried to be faithful when within a hundred miles from home. Beyond that, well, a man had needs.

He had the funds after liquidating the Texas herds to finance his ambitions without becoming unduly beholden to bankers. His eyes scanned the bunkhouses, stable and barns nearing completion. Life was good up north. He vowed that it would get even better.

"Print, Deacon rode in just now. He's down at the stable."

Olive recognized Jim "Nigger" Kelly's raspy voice and turned to face the ruggedly handsome Negro strolling across the dusty yard in his direction. Olive stood a good six feet in stockinged feet, but Kelly towered a good half foot above him. He carried his nickname with good humor and even introduced himself to strangers with it. Olive and Deacon did not address him with it, however. Kelly and Deacon Scruggs, both in their late thirties, were about Olive's age and his best friends. He trusted few others, not even his own brothers without some reservations; Bob, the youngest, least of all.

When Kelly reached him, Olive said, "About time. Deacon's been out at least a week. Hope he learned something worthwhile."

"Yeah, thought you'd want to know he made it back. It takes a spell to call on all the Livestock Association members, them being so strung out and all. You told me yourself, Custer County is over twenty-five hundred square miles. Lands claimed by ranchers goes beyond those borders to public lands not mapped out yet."

"Let's go see what Deacon's got to say."

They met Deacon limping out of the stable with his bedroll and saddlebags tossed over his shoulders. He was a short, stocky man with a week's growth of blondish whiskers cloaking that part of a ruddy face that was not covered by his brushy mustache.

"What happened to you?" Olive asked, nodding at the gimpy leg.

"Horse got spooked by a rattler and threw me. Got a knee swelled like a watermelon, but I lived to tell about it. Boss needs to give me some rocking chair time."

"You got it," Olive said, "if you got any useful information."

"My gut says it's past noontime. How about we go over to the chuck house and get me some dinner, and we'll sit down for the story?"

Shortly, the men were seated under a canvas canopy that extended from the little chuck house and covered four tables with benches for ranch hands to dine at. Because of shifts and riders coming and going, the cook and his assistant kept the facility open throughout the day. Scruggs had a tin plate of roast beef and beans on the table in front of him, as well as a bowl of apple cobbler and a cup of steaming coffee. Olive took pride in feeding his cowhands well. Having eaten earlier, the other two men settled for fresh coffee.

"Talked to ten of the association men," Scruggs said. "That's all but two. Explained there won't be no meeting called till March unless somebody asks for one. Not many cattle losses reported. Hard to get a count till spring roundup anyhow."

Olive said, "We don't want to stir up association members. We got a rough count on herd numbers when we set up the association. I don't want us cutting out more than ten percent of any man's herd between now and spring. Everybody expects to lose some during winter. We'll take small bites spread out over the next months."

Scruggs asked, "What about the non-members?"

"No limit. We want them out of here, and the sooner the better. How many small operators in Custer County and near its borders?"

"Thirty, at the most, with less than three hundred head. That don't count homestead operations that don't have more than a dozen."

Jim Kelly had been silent to this point. "Time for a few to disappear?"

"I think so," Olive said. "Deacon, I want you to make a list of the small outfits, where their headquarters are and family status. Bachelors, wives, kids and whatever."

"I'll need a few days, but I took notes and I've got a county map. I'm guessing half of the ranchers are young and unmarried. Women are hard to come by out here. Some got a female waiting to come out in the hills once they got decent living quarters."

"We want to pick those off a little at a time over the winter. Owner disappears and we set up a few wranglers on his place and take over the herd. I can claim we bought the works. Most won't question. We ought to be looking in North Platte for a lawyer to fix up deeds. Then we'll work out the details of the dead man signing before a notary public. We'll move a little slow with that."

"And if the real owner disappears, is it going to be like Texas?" Kelly asked.

"You could get to be a busy man," Olive said.

"You're making it sound damned easy, Print," Deacon Scruggs said before scooping a chunk of roast beef into his mouth. "It might not be."

"You haven't told me everything," Olive snapped.

"Wanted to get my dinner mostly down before I lighted your fuse."

"Well, what the hell is it?"

"There's a deputy sheriff working Custer County now. He lives northwest of here almost into the Sandhills. He has a small operation he calls 'Rising Sun Ranch.' Ain't much to the place. Lives in a soddy. Hundred to 125 cows, no more. Owns a full section, grazes a few head on public land in the Sandhills. Perfect location if he wants to grow."

"Name?" Olive asked, shaking some tobacco from his pouch into a paper to roll a cigarette.

"Rance Coldsmith."

"Never heard of such a name. What kind of man would have a name like that?"

"Isom Prentice Olive ain't all that common," Deacon said, digging into his cobbler. Only Deacon Scruggs and Jim Kelly could get by with such sarcasm.

"What do you know about the guy?"

"A fair amount. Picked it up in bits and pieces from social calls on a few neighbors. Most was glad to talk about him—except the one nearest by." He looked at Jim Kelly. "One of your people, Jimbo. Big Negro with more kids than I could count running about the place. I think him and this deputy are cozy. He got suspicious right away when I started pressing for information. Maybe you would like to make a call there, Jimbo. I saw a pretty, young lady come out of the house while I was getting a drink at the well."

"I just might do that," Kelly said. "Not any colored women to speak of around here. Not like Texas. The white ones about piss their underpants when I get within ten feet."

"Ain't just white women," Deacon said. "It's any human. You are one scary bastard. Anyhow, they seem to be dirt farmers pretty much. Name's Rice. Does blacksmithing and a bit of everything else. Not much he can't do according to folks in the neighborhood. White men don't see color near as much if a black man's got a skill they need."

"Damn it, Deacon," Olive said, "spit out what you know about the deputy. You're wasting time."

"Used to be a deputy in North Platte. Some Army in his background. A few years younger than you. Nobody knows a lot about him. Seems to keep to himself. Took in the woman and two kids from that place that got burned out. Woman's husband was kilt, and Coldsmith snatched up the widow fast as lightning. He'd be poking her by now. Of course, that was all Tobe Gates's doing—his and Sniper's and Parsons's."

"You haven't told me much of anything that helps. Has he got any smarts? Is he handy with a gun?"

"Handy enough that him and some Injun killed Tobe and Sniper. He took Parsons in to North Platte and turned him over to the sheriff. Like I said, folks don't know a lot about him, but most are glad they got law nearby in case they run into trouble of some kind."

Olive did not like the idea of a deputy sheriff working in the area. He had never killed a lawman but had been at odds with a fair number. It was a combination of a sheriff's persistence and a community uprising that had motivated him to move his cattle operation out of Texas and north to the Nebraska Sandhills. He had made the mistake of killing the wrong people.

He said, "Keep your ears open for more information about Coldsmith. Now, I remember meeting the man once when we were starting to settle by the Dismal River. I stopped by his place and offered to buy him out. He wasn't outright hostile about it but made it clear he wasn't interested. I didn't push since his property wasn't in our path—not yet anyhow. Figured he'd likely go broke, and I'd buy it for a dime later. That was a year ago maybe. I wasn't there more than a half hour. I remember I did most of the talking."

"Sounds about right," Deacon said.

Olive ignored the sarcasm. "Make it clear to the crews that we don't touch the Rising Sun herd. That would be an invitation for a visit. Come to think of it, I might visit him first and take his measure. Maybe I can talk to the lady friend and see if she would like to sell her farm. She's got to be hurting for money."

Ron Schwab

"Wasting your time, Print," Scruggs said. "If the woman's in his bed, Coldsmith's all but got the place bought."

"We'll see. Anyhow, Deacon, you dug up some things we need to know. Go ahead and take a few days to let that knee mend." He turned to Kelly. "Jim, I want that Crowell place that sets next to ours to the southeast. Half section, I think, nice set of buildings, decent house. I'm thinking I might set my little brother, Bob, and his wife up there. An old timer owns the place. I'm told he has no wife or family. He needs to start missing some cattle. Then we'll go over and see if he might like to sell the place and his herd cheap. If he won't by spring, he might have to disappear."

Kelly said, "I'll take a few of the boys out to scout the place and find likely spots for cutting out four or five head of cattle at a time. From there, I just might ride south and pay a call at Ben Rice's farm just to get acquainted, us being of the same kind and all. I might be gone a day or two."

Olive said, "From what I've heard, we could have a month or six weeks before serious snowfall in these parts, or a blizzard could roll in from the Wyoming Rockies west of us tomorrow. You can't count on anything here, and none of us have been through enough Nebraska winters to have much idea what we're in for. We're for damn sure not in Texas, though. I don't want too many cattle added to our herds too fast. With brands to change and all, we don't want more at a time than we can handle, and we don't want to cause suspicions."

Chapter 18

November 1877

RANCE CLIMBED OUT of bed at six o'clock. The maneuver generally gave him a challenge to start the day, since his side of the bed was pressed against the wall, and he had to crawl off the foot of the bed. It was early November, and he was sleeping in his long underwear now, partially for the warmth but more for the sake of modesty, even though his bed partner slept on the opposite side of the bundling board.

Another wall joined the bedside wall to form a corner, giving him about two feet clearance between the wall and the foot of the bed. He grabbed his denim britches, folded haphazardly and placed on the floor on top of deerskins that served as a rug to cover the cold stone floor.

He slipped into his pants, almost tumbling to the floor before he got both feet through the legs and pulled them up. His flannel shirt hung with his sheepskin-lined coat on the wall outside the curtain, and he had left his boots and socks next to the fireplace.

He smelled the sweet aroma of coffee drifting through the curtains, and the soft rattling of pans and dishes was music to his ears. He did not know what time Lisbeth Baker rose from bed each morning. He only knew that the cookstove was heating and a fire was crackling in the fireplace when he got out of bed and that coffee was waiting with breakfast not far behind each morning when he got up. He had offered to get up and get the fires started and help fix breakfast, and she informed him that she preferred alone time first thing in the morning, and she did not want him in the way when she was preparing breakfast.

He felt a bit guilty at first about the spoiling he felt he was receiving but not more than a bit and not for too long. He stepped through the curtain and retrieved his shirt. "Good morning," he said. "Coffee smells good." He slipped on the shirt, unbuckled his belt and tucked it in his britches. Familiarity had removed any inhibitions about such things.

"Good morning to you, Mister Coldsmith. I hope you slept well."

"I did."

"I'm glad you don't snore," she said. "I had worried about that some. Carl snored like a big grizzly and kept me awake. I have been sleeping quite well here, although I'm a light sleeper. Part of that is being a mother, I think. Listening for the baby to cry, that sort of thing."

Rance pulled the rocking chair up to the fireplace and began slipping on his socks and boots. "I would wake up instantly if I heard a noise outside that didn't fit. It wouldn't matter how deeply I was sleeping. Somehow that sound would get through. Do you know what I mean?"

"I think so."

"Maybe it comes from soldiering with Comanches covering the countryside. I don't think I was so much that way before the Army."

"I'm pouring a cup of coffee. I'll set it on the table. Flapjacks and eggs in five minutes."

Rance said, "I haven't eaten like this since . . . never mind."

"Since you lost your wife?"

"You know then?"

"Tillie told me. And I take your words as a compliment. I'm not accustomed to a man's appreciation."

"I've liked having you and the kids here, Missus Baker. The place feels like a home, and you've given me time to get my work done. I just want you to know that this is working out fine. No complaints."

He got up and stepped over to the table and sat down, blew on the coffee and took a sip. "Perfect," he said. "You know, it always seemed to me that coffee should be coffee. It should all taste the same. But that isn't the way it works. Mine was always like muddy water and bitter. This is smooth and soothing, not quite sweet, but just a gentle bite."

Lisbeth smiled—she had been doing more of that lately—and set a plate of three big flapjacks with two fried eggs draped over the top in front of him. She nodded toward a covered butter dish. "Fresh butter from yesterday. The little pitcher is full of hot maple syrup. It's a luxury, but Tillie and I dickered with Homer at Arnold's Post and bought a three-gallon jug to share. She needed two, of course, so we poured ours into an empty gallon jug."

She put her own plate on the table, which he noticed included two eggs and a single hotcake. She should eat more, he thought, but it was not his place to suggest. As they ate the two spoke softly, so they would not wake the children, about plans for the day.

Rance said, "I'm taking the buckboard and meeting up with Jake and Johnny Whitehorse along the creek. Johnny found a place where a lot of trees washed up during flooding last summer. We're going to try to cut us each a wagonload. We're not short yet, but I'd sure hate to be looking if winter turned nasty and we ran out."

"I have plenty of ham and bread. I'll make sandwiches for all of you and send along a batch of cookies."

"They'll probably bring something."

"You can share. It will be like potluck. I haven't done that since I was a kid. But I loved potlucks. Bring back what you don't eat."

He said, "I won't turn it down, and I do thank you for it." He finished off the last hotcake. "And this was delicious. A perfect way to start the day."

She said, "I have plenty of batter. I can make more if you want."

He chuckled. "If I keep eating like this, I'll soon be waddling to the barn mornings. No, thank you. The kids will have to do the best they can to finish the rest. What's your day bringing, Missus Baker?"

"The usual chores, milking the cow and so forth, but Tillie's bringing her McGuffey Readers over, and we're going to see what we can do about schooling the kids. Mine all burned up, so I might have to find a way to get some from North Platte. Tillie's better at some things than I am, and I'm better at others, especially numbers, so we're going to organize a school and split up teaching duties. If it works out, we might offer a private school for other families next year. It would take a day's ride to get to the nearest public school. Some folks are boarding their kids in one town or another. That's not good, and it's costly. We'll see."

"I hadn't even thought of that. Those kids need to get all the education you can give them. Besides, if you get Morg busy on schoolwork, maybe I won't have to play checkers every night. He's starting to whip me more than half the time. He's not there on chess yet, though." He admitted to himself that he loved playing the board games with Morgan, and he liked reading to Marissa from the books they borrowed from the Rices. He would have to buy a good supply next trip to North Platte. He told Lisbeth: "I need to go to North Platte soon to report to Sheriff Steele. I can try to locate the books you need then. Or maybe you could go along. But it would involve at least one overnight trip on the trail with an early start." He added, "Perhaps, Morg and Marissa could stay with Tillie and Ben, and Sue Ellen would come along as a chaperone, so to speak."

Lisbeth seemed to be at least considering the possibility. "We can talk about this later," she said. "I do have something else I thought I would bring up." She hesitated. "We have agreed to live as brother and sister. It occurred to me yesterday that brothers and sisters call each other by their first names, not Missus Somebody or Mister Somebody. This is starting to seem silly. I'd be pleased to have you call me Lisbeth if you wish."

He did not tell her he thought the formality was silly from the first day. "I wish. And, Lisbeth, I hope you will call me Rance."

She extended her hand across the table, offering a handshake, and he accepted it. "Rance and Lisbeth," she declared.

Chapter 19

RANCE RETURNED TO the soddy with a heaping wagonload of firewood not yet sized to the fireplace or woodstove, much of it consisting of thick trunks and limbs of hardwood oak and ash that would require splitting as well. The real work had only begun, but at least he had a supply nearby in the event a serious storm struck.

He pulled the wagon next to the woodpiles that already stretched some twenty feet in double rows and a good five feet high. Perhaps addition of the new wood harvest would take them through the worst of winter. At least they were running ahead of Old Man Winter for now. With Lisbeth and the kids settled in with him, however, he felt a greater responsibility to be prepared for the worst that the season might bring on.

As he led Plato the mule to the barn, a stiff wind started to bite at his ears and nose. Darkness had settled in quickly this evening, and he looked up to confirm that clouds covered the moon and stars totally now. It felt like snow could move in, but usually the Sandhills would be spared a life-threatening storm this time of year.

After putting up the mule, Rance headed for the house. It was a good feeling to see lamplight glowing through the windows. The pleasant smell of smoke in the air told him that he would enter to a warm fire. Lisbeth would have saved some supper for him. Likely, she would have fed Morgan and Marissa and held off her own supper until his arrival. Eating together when he came in late had become a ritual a few weeks earlier. Sometimes, nary a word passed between them at those times, but he found her presence a comfort. He hadn't shared a home with family since the deaths of Rachael and Tessa. It had not taken him long to get accustomed to it. Even the sleeping arrangements were more than tolerable.

Lisbeth was already dishing out two bowls of stew when he came into the house, hung his hat on the wall peg and placed the Winchester on the rack. He shrugged off his sheepskin jacket and fitted it over the back of his chair. "Smells good," Rance said.

She smiled, "Beef chunks and a little of everything. My dad used to call it son-of-a-bitch stew."

Rance said, "The old-timers will tell you it's got to have tongue, liver, kidneys and brains to be true son-of-a-bitch stew, but I know your version will suit me fine."

"I've got biscuits in the Dutch oven at the corner of the fireplace and apple dumplings warming in the cook-stove oven. I feed you a lot of apples because Tillie's got a surplus."

"You know by now that I love apples, as well as anything made with them."

She lifted the Dutch oven lid with a steel hook Ben Rice had given her for that purpose and forked out four biscuits, putting three on Rance's plate and keeping one for herself. "Butter in the dish. Surprise. The jam is apple."

He grinned. "Like I say, I love apples."

He poured a cup of coffee from the pot, and while it cooled, tore into the stew. "Scrumptious. I'm going to have to loosen my belt a notch, if you keep feeding me like this."

"I'd bet against it," Lisbeth said.

He stopped his spoon mid-bite and looked at her, realizing suddenly that something was different. "You're wearing a dress."

She laughed. "Tillie said you wouldn't notice for two weeks."

"I admit this dim light in my brain was slow figuring it out, but I'm not that blind. It's nice. You look very . . . very nice." What does a man say to a sister?

It was a simple light-green, high-necked cotton garment with long sleeves, set-off perfectly by the long auburn hair that flowed over her shoulders tonight in contrast to the usual practical ponytail. A stunning woman sat across the table from him.

"Tillie and Sue Ellen made me two dresses. The other is pale blue. They are cut the same, nothing fancy, but Tillie said I should start looking like a woman. I don't know why it matters. Anyway, I'll be back in britches for outside chores and riding horseback. I wouldn't even know how to ride sidesaddle. It always looked scary to me. I don't think of myself as that kind of a lady anyhow."

Rance felt tongue-tied and decided it better to stay quiet than to say the wrong thing. He returned to his meal, quickly downing another bowl of stew and demolishing the three biscuits. He barely had room for an apple dumpling, but he did not waste a crumb.

"Leftovers for one meal tomorrow," Lisbeth commented.

"I'm thankful for that. I can't wait for the repeat. Do you know I have never eaten an apple dumpling before? I've heard of them. It would have been a tragedy if I had missed this opportunity."

"Well," she said, "I hate to change the subject, but I must turn to business."

"Business? I see Morg's got the checkerboard out. I thought this would be a good night for checkers or chess."

"Later. I promised to deliver a message."

"Go on."

"Deputy sheriff's business. A young man who goes by the name of Clem Snyder stopped by early afternoon. Do you know him?"

"I recognize the name. Small rancher. He's got a half section about fifteen miles east of here not far from the Middle Loup. Does some farming, runs a small cow herd."

Lisbeth said, "He asked me to tell you that a friend of his has disappeared. Another younger man. The friend's name is Trapper Wollenberg."

"I know Trapper. He worked for me during roundup the first spring I was here. Hard worker. Good head on his shoulders. He had inherited a quarter section next to public lands up that way. He hoped to borrow against the land to buy a foundation herd of cows, maybe fifty or so. He stops by a couple of times a year just to talk and ask me for a little advice, which is worth exactly what he pays for it—nothing. Where does he think Trapper went?"

"He has no idea, but he says a few of Print Olive's men are staying in the house and acting like they own the place. Apparently, one of Olive's men, a tall colored man, that some call 'Nigger Jim' to his face, if you can imagine, came to Wollenberg's and Snyder's places and made offers to buy them out. The man said they could extend their lives many years by taking the offers and moving on. Snyder and Wollenberg both turned him down flat."

"Sounds like a serious threat."

"Yes, but the young ranchers didn't take it seriously. Of course, Snyder does now since his friend disappeared. When he found out Olive's people had taken over Wollenberg's house and buildings, he headed home, turned all his horses out of the barn and left to find the law. That's you, deputy. He's not going back till he knows it's safe."

"I need to talk to him."

"He said Archibald Tufts would know where to find him. Do you know Tufts?"

"Yeah, not well, but I talked to him a few times when I was deputy in North Platte and I'll run across him here during roundup on public lands. He runs a herd of a hundred cows or so—about the size of mine. He would own close to a section of land, too. He comes from Texas, and

Sheriff Steele says he used to have a big operation down there. He's an old codger—well almost sixty, I'd guess. He keeps to himself and doesn't talk much, but I always had a feeling there were a lot of smarts under that Stetson he wears. His place wouldn't be more than two or three miles north of Snyder's."

"I suppose you will be heading over to his place in the morning," Lisbeth said.

Rance sighed. "Afraid that's my job—if weather permits. Feels like snow in the air."

"I know it's none of my business. But do you think you should do this alone?"

"I don't think it's that serious. Olive probably just bought Trapper Wollenberg out."

"Clem Snyder was scared. He was convinced something terrible had happened to his friend."

"Maybe I will drop by Johnny Whitehorse's and see if he will ride along to back me. I can pay him and put in a claim with Abe for reimbursement." Lisbeth nodded her head approvingly—not that it mattered, he tried to convince himself.

The kids were asleep on the floor mattress and Lisbeth was still working in the kitchen area when Rance readied himself for bed. He stepped outside to relieve his bladder and was glad to see that snow had not started yet.

Hopefully, he had guessed wrong. When he reentered the house, he shucked his boots and shirt and went behind the bedroom curtain to peel off his britches, which seemed an unnecessary gesture of modesty given that his long underwear fully covered vital parts.

When he started to crawl into his side of the bed, he noticed a change. The barbed wire had been removed from the top of the bundling board. Now what did that mean? Lisbeth had called the wire a symbol of their commitment. With the symbol removed, had the nature of their commitment changed?

She must have been reading his mind. From outside the drawn curtain, Lisbeth said, "The wire being gone doesn't change anything. I just decided it served no purpose but to suggest that somebody couldn't be trusted. Still no fence jumping by either of us."

"I wouldn't think of it," Rance lied. It was getting so that was all he thought about. He wondered if he might not get more sleep if he moved back to the barn.

Chapter 20

TILLIE AND LISBETH had McGuffey Readers and other books spread out on the table and in front of the fireplace. Louisa and Marissa with dolls nearby were doing chalk drawings on a big slate board laid out on the floor and John and Morgan, absorbed in a chess match, were only a few feet from the girls and vainly trying to keep their respective sisters hushed so the chess masters could concentrate.

Tillie said, "I do okay with the reading and writing, but I can't take the kids far enough in arithmetic. You've had more formal schooling. Here's what I've been thinking. Ben is walling off a corner of the stable into a small room. He's even planking the floor and putting a wood-stove in it, making some real school desks and benches. I'm thinking that if you could bring your kids over four days a week, you could stay and teach school two days, and I would do two days. That would give us each time to take care of home chores. Maybe sometimes we would have to be at school part of another day to help the other on special things. What do you think?"

"What?"

It was obvious to Tillie that Lisbeth was not totally engaged in their project. "Were you listening to me? Your head's someplace else."

"I heard you. Ben's making a school room, and we'd take turns teaching."

"What's worrying you?"

"I guess it's Rance. He went out on a deputy's job this morning. He said he might not get back tonight, that it could be a few days."

Tillie said, "We only got a dusting of snow. It's on the chilly side, but it's not bitter cold. Sun's out bright and clear. He'll be fine."

"It's not the weather I'm worried about. There may have been a killing. I don't know what he might be walking into."

"Oh, my Lord."

"What?"

"Are you starting to care for this man?"

"Well, he's been good to us. I care about what happens to him. I wouldn't want him to get shot or killed."

Tillie said, "I've seen him look at you. There's lust in the man's eyes, but it's more than that."

"Oh, no. That's not what I want. I'm not ready for a man. I'm not sure I ever will be. That's the last thing on my mind."

"Maybe you just think that's the last thing on your mind."

"What have I got myself into? I knew it was a bad idea, my staying here. I don't want to hurt him."

"Don't get yourself all worked up. Is it what those men did to you that's closed your mind?"

"Not really. I'm getting past that. You told me about your experiences before you were with Ben. You told me to just think of that night as one of hundreds of nights we have in life if we're lucky. You told me not to give those animals the power to decide how I live the time that is hopefully left for me. I have thought about that every day, and that experience is starting to turn into just a bad dream for me."

"Then why close your mind to possibilities? Don't rush to judgment."

"I did that once and thought I was in love before I came to hate the man who became my husband."

"Are you saying you are in love with Rance?"

"No, no. Absolutely not. I like him. We seem to work together like a team pulling a wagon. He is wonderful with my children. But we have only really known each other for a few months or so. I think a woman should know a man for a good year or two before she even considers the possibility of committing to him. And I don't really know how he feels about me."

"He's a handsome devil, isn't he?" Tillie noticed that Lisbeth flushed some.

"I suppose you could say that. In a rugged sort of way."

Tillie said, "I notice you stripped the wire off the bundling board."

"I was afraid one of us would accidentally get cut on it."

Tillie laughed, "It could be kind of dangerous going over that board."

Now Lisbeth turned scarlet. "That is the last thing I'm interested in. I did not enjoy that part of marriage with Carl. I just tolerated it from the beginning, and I hated it as time went on."

Tillie shook her head. "You poor thing. I guess you do have some heavy thinking ahead of you. Just give yourself time."

Chapter 21

THE TUFTS RANCH house was set back in a hill-side like some soddies and dugouts Rance had seen. The difference was that it was constructed of limestone and the roof was laid out on solid oak beams and covered with red tile reminiscent of Spanish structures Rance had seen during his time in Texas. When he and Johnny Whitehorse entered the house behind a gimpy Archibald Tufts, they stepped onto a solid oak floor that women in Sandhills country would kill for. Even though many folks had to settle for dirt, Rance thought he would like more than anything to get Lisbeth off that damned stone floor and onto something like this. That would be a priority in the house he had in mind.

Navajo rugs, leather chairs and couch, paintings hung from plastered walls. Tufts had spent serious money on the house. Rance figured there was none finer within a hundred miles. It was not imposing size-wise, but everything about the house was high-grade. And the interior was immaculate, not a hint of dust that Rance's eyes could pick up, certainly not what one would expect of an old bachelor.

Tufts seated his visitors on a couch that faced the warming fire in the fireplace, and the old rancher took a stuffed chair that was angled toward the deputy and his friend. The man was dressed appropriately for his home, with shiny brown boots, string tie and buckskin jacket. He was a slim, fit man of average height with a mane of white hair and matching, neatly trimmed mustache, otherwise clean-shaven. Rance guessed the man's age to be somewhere on either side of sixty.

"I wasn't sure when to expect you," Tufts said. "Clem thought it could be today. It's almost noon. Snowbird will have a nice beef stew and fresh-baked bread for us in an hour or so. Cherry pie, as well."

The aroma was already drifting in from a room that had to be the kitchen, making Rance suddenly ravenous. "We don't want to impose on you, Mister Tufts. We have food in our saddlebags."

"You are not imposing. Save your beans and hardtack. And call me 'Arch.'"

Rance said. "We appreciate your hospitality, Arch. As I told you, I came here at the request of Clem Snyder, who is worried about his friend, Trapper Wollenberg."

"Trapper's dead. I wasn't quite so blunt with Clem. And he is right to be frightened. I'm hoping you can help with that. I will tell you how to locate him after we eat."

"How do you know Trapper is dead?"

"Because I knew Print Olive back in Texas. I sold my ranch there to escape the son-of-a-bitch. I had a big operation, made a lot of money even with Print's outfit out there skimming off my herd for a good ten years before I pulled out. He owned the law there. I'm gambling with you, but Abe Steele is a good man. If he says to trust you, I'll take the chance. Before he hired you, he told me he was going to try to get you to take this on. But you can bet Print has paid off a good number of the badge holders around these parts. Don't get me wrong. There are good lawmen who can't be bought, but you can't be sure which ones they are. There won't be many willing to take Print Olive on."

Rance found himself somewhat miffed at Abe Steele. The sheriff had warned him about Olive in a casual sort of a way, but Rance now realized that Print Olive was his real mission. He and the sheriff would have a chat about that soon. "Has Olive been around to see you?"

"His enforcer has. Jim Kelly, a tall colored man—make you look like a runt. Says folks can call him 'Nigger Jim,' and he don't mind none. Not me. Don't want trouble with that hombre. Anyhow, I'd run into Kelly in the Texas days. He mentioned that Print was interested in my place here, wondered if he might make a visit to see if it would fit for his family. Of course, I knew Kelly was saying I should sell cheap and move on if I valued my life."

"Or you would end up dead?"

"He didn't say as much, but I know how it works, and he knew that I understood. But I got money to set me for life, and I came here to run a small herd and enjoy this beautiful, lonely country. I got no ambitions to grow, but I ain't about to move again either. I've got some security."

"Security?"

"Snowbird. She's my wife under Dakota Sioux law, and she is the daughter of one of the chiefs, Many Horses. Her band is on the Pine Ridge Reservation north of here, but they go out on hunting parties and help themselves to a few head of cattle and a horse now and then. Olive harms us, and he will have a Sioux war to keep him busy for a spell. I told Kelly that. When he left, he said he was sure we would be good neighbors. Print won't want Indian troubles. He's too smart for that. He'll let us be."

"You are convinced he will kill to take more land and cattle?"

"In a blink of his eyes. His mind works funny. He's just taking what he thinks should be his. Back home, if somebody rustled his cattle—or even was suspected of it—they never made it to the law. He and his outfit strung them up right there. Ever hear of 'The Death of the Skins?'"

"Can't say that I have."

"I think the Mexicans came up with the name, but most give Comanches credit for the idea. That's what Print did to two rustlers back home. He caught two men who were killing his cows for the skins—sort of like the old buffalo hunters. Him and his brother, Bob, along with Jim Kelly and Deacon Scruggs came upon two men who had just killed and skinned two cows. They were loading the skins on their wagon when Print and his bunch rode in. They didn't have their weapons and they were caught dead to rights. Print took his Winchester and shot one man in the knee, and Kelly roped the other and drug him around a bit. Then they took the green skins, still wet and bloody, wrapped them tight around the two men and tied them tight. You know what fresh skins do in the hot sun?"

"Yep," Rance said, "they start shrinking. By the end of a day, they'll be a third the size of what they were. It would be a slow death. Eventually they would suffocate, but I can't imagine the pain and agony getting there."

"Well, that's what they did. Just left the men there. I heard the story from Bob when he was bragging about it in a saloon. He thought it was hilarious. These are our new neighbors."

"So the Olives steal neighbors' cattle but hang the neighbors when they rustle Olive cattle?"

"That's about it in a nutshell. Lord knows how many men Print Olive and his thugs killed in central Texas."

A pretty woman quietly entered the room, and Rance reflexively stood. Her skin was the color of rich copper, and her black hair, tied back, dropped to mid-back. Indian blood obviously ran in her veins notwithstanding the yellow cotton dress and slightly lifted leather shoes she wore. Rance suspected that this was an outfit reserved for entertaining white guests. Perhaps she felt less a curiosity in the attire.

She extended her hand to Rance. "I am Snowbird. You are Deputy Rance Coldsmith. Welcome to our home." She turned to Johnny Whitehorse, who was on his feet now. "Hello, Johnny. I am pleased to meet you. I know Primrose. She is Dakota, also. Give her my regards. I would love to see her sometime if you would bring her for a visit."

Whitehorse said, "Uh, yes. That would be nice, ma'am."

Rance could tell that Johnny was a bit overwhelmed by the hostess and the environment. They probably could not exit soon enough for him.

Tufts intervened. "Follow me to the dining room, gentlemen."

Chapter 22

AFTER ENJOYING A delicious meal with pleasant company, Rance and Whitehorse saddled their mounts. The horses had been fed and watered by Tufts's only visible ranch hand, a sinewy man dressed as an ordinary wrangler, but whose high-cheeked, aquiline features and dark coloring left no doubt about Indian heritage, likely Sioux. Rance wondered about the rancher's connection with the Sioux. It was none of his concern, but he would not mind hearing the story either.

Tufts had sketched a map of where they should find Clem Snyder, the location of the Wollenberg and Snyder properties, as well as the Olive ranch headquarters further south. Rance thought the map almost reached the status of artwork. He had understood why when he saw "A.Tufts" inscribed on two of the wall paintings.

The Tufts ranch house had several spare bedrooms, and Arch Tufts had urged them to return for an overnight stay if they remained in the vicinity. Rance rather liked the possibility, but he was betting Johnny Whitehorse would prefer the stable.

They slowed their horses to a slow trot when they approached the meeting place, a cluster of cottonwoods near a limestone-lined spring which formed a stream that eventually snaked its way southeasterly to the Middle Loup River. The location was well hidden behind brown, grass-cloaked hills, but soaring turkey vultures, the ugly, black harbingers of death, a few hundred yards distant sent a sinking feeling to Rance's gut.

They reined in their mounts for a bit to ponder what might lie ahead. "Could be an animal carcass," Rance said.

"Could be."

"But you don't think so?"

"I don't know. But if there was anything alive over there, the vultures wouldn't be swooping down like they are. Don't think we're riding into a trap."

"Well, we can sit here all afternoon and guess at it," Rance said, "or ride on and find out the facts." He nudged Rusty forward and the men rode at a slow trot in the direction of the vultures.

They angled between the highest hills and when they broke through, they instantly saw the cottonwood cluster ahead of them, with the buzzards decorating the branches like Christmas ornaments. Rance could make out the body, suspended by a rope from a heavy tree branch with feet nearly touching the ground. Most of the birds scattered as they rode up and dismounted, but a few bolder ones surrendered no ground until shooed off. Rance walked over to the naked corpse.

The body had not been terribly mutilated yet, he supposed because it had not fully ripened. The hanging had likely taken place earlier in the day. There was torn flesh about his pizzle and testicles, as well as his cheeks and nose, all soft targets. His left eye had been tugged from its socket and apparently carried off.

Rance pulled his penknife from the front pocket of his trousers and began sawing the rope that had dug deeply into the flesh covering Snyder's neck. Soon, the rope strands fell away, and the body dropped to the earth. Rance had seen more corpses than he could count while serving as a cavalry sergeant during the Comanche wars and his earlier stint as Abe Steele's deputy, but he had never grown callous to the sight of a human body taken down by violence. He vowed to bring the perpetrators of this atrocity to justice.

He knelt beside Snyder's body and examined it. No gunshot wounds. The neck and face were bluish purple, grossly swollen and distorted. The young man had no doubt been strangled. Rance's guess was that the rope had simply been looped around Snyder's neck and the other end tossed over the tree limb. The executioners had then pulled him off the ground and let him kick and choke. It appeared they had not even bothered to tie his wrists, probably enjoying the sight of the flailing hands trying to tear the rope loose. He hoped the struggle had been a brief one but feared it had not.

He turned away and noticed that Whitehorse was walking a circle around the site, kneeling, sometimes with nose almost to the ground like a hunting dog sniffing out an animal's trail. He waited, not wanting to destroy sign with his own footprints. The snow had disappeared with a few hours of sunshine, but the sandy soil was soft and left discernible trace for someone who knew what he was looking for. Rance had never fancied himself much of a tracker.

After he completed his study of the area, Whitehorse joined him. "Three men rode in with three horses. Left with four, one without rider. One man has big feet. One horse is missing piece of right back shoe. Find that easy enough if I see it again."

"According to Arch's sketch, Clem's house is about two miles down the main trail from here. I'll pull a blanket from my bedroll to wrap him in and then maybe you can help me get this poor devil slung over the back of my horse. Once I get him tied down, I'll lead Rusty to the young man's ranch house. I'd like you to ride on ahead and scout it out and be sure the place isn't occupied. It seems unlikely anybody would have moved in just yet."

A half hour later, less than a mile from Snyder's house, Rance saw Whitehorse headed his way, his bay gelding moving at an easy gait. When they met and the Pawnee dismounted, Rance instantly read the grim look on Whitehorse's usually stoic face. His friend was not bearing good news.

"What is it, Johnny?" he asked.

"Find Trapper."

"Dead?"

"Dead."

"How far?"

He nodded toward the corpse slung across Rusty's back. "His place."

"Clem's house? But Clem was out looking for him."

"Didn't look close enough maybe."

"What happened?"

"Couldn't tell."

Darn Johnny. He loved to string out a story. A man had to dig words out in bits and pieces. "You did see the body?"

"Nope. In the well. Lowered the bucket to get water for my horse and me. No water. Bucket stops. Looked down the well and seen a man blocking it. Got to be Trapper."

Rance decided it would be hard to argue otherwise. It made a certain sense. Maybe the body was a final warning to Clem. But Clem left his place without using the well or the body was dropped during his absence. "Well, that's where we're going, anyway. Let's get whoever is in the well out. Any critters about the place?"

"Two mules in a lot outside a lean-to shed that looks to be a barn. Hungry, so I throwed in some hay from a stack. Need water."

"If he had any other horses, the visitors probably helped themselves."

They led their horses on to the small ranch. It would be a miserable place to spend a winter, Rance thought when they walked into the yard. The ranch house consisted of a one room log shack exposed to wind on all sides. The logs were caulked with mud that had mostly crumbled away, leaving cracks that would welcome icy winds.

They hitched their horses on a crude hitching post in front of the house. Rance retrieved his lariat from the rope strap on his saddle, and he and Whitehorse strolled over to the well. Rance leaned over the stone walls of the well and peered down. He could make out a hazy form, but it was too dark to confirm much else. Still, he knew it was Trapper Wollenberg. "Do you think he's near bottom, or is he wedged in higher up?"

Whitehorse said, "Hit bottom, I think. Well's not deep. Springs and creeks like spiderwebs here. Man can hit water at twenty feet."

"Well, I guess I'll hitch a rope to Rusty's saddle horn and let myself down. You'll have to help with the rope on this end."

"No. I'll go. The little guy goes down. The big guy stays up. If you get stuck, we got more trouble."

Rance had hoped the Pawnee would volunteer. He did not like closed-in places, and with his large frame he had long ago accepted he was far from being a contortionist in tight places. "No argument from me."

Whitehorse removed his moccasins and lowered himself into the well, grasping the rope and leveraging his feet against the rock walls of the narrow tunnel to the water. Rance marveled at the older man's agility. In a matter of minutes, his friend called for him to hoist the body from the well. Rance let the horse do most of the pulling until the corpse's head appeared at the well's rim. Then he pulled the body, covered with half-soaked clothes, over the top and eased it onto the ground. He dropped the rope end back down to Whitehorse, and he scurried like a racing lizard to the top.

Rance knelt beside the body. The cold had helped with preservation, but he guessed Trapper Wollenberg had been dead three or four days. He had been spared the agony of a hanging. A single bullet in the right temple had killed him. Appeared to be an execution.

Whitehorse asked, "We gonna bury them here?"

"No. I thought I'd take them back to the Tufts place. If we use those mules, we can get there well before dark. Maybe we can bury them on his land someplace. I'd like another impartial witness to identify the bodies and be able to say what he saw. With it being winter, the corpses should last longer, and if the sheriff wants, they could be dug up again and moved someplace."

"I get the mules. They haltered. Got rawhide rope if you need."

Rance said, "I want to take a quick look in the house before we go."

He entered the shack. It did not look any more livable inside than it did from the outside. A straw mattress on the floor with a pile of dirty blankets on top. An old woodstove, apparently used for cooking and heating and a warped cedar table with a single chair. Rance noticed a stack of addressed envelopes on the table and picked up the missives and riffled through them. All contained correspondence and were addressed to Snyder, and the return addressee was one Nancy Whittier of Cedar Rapids, Iowa. It was a contact name if they could not come up with any other, likely a sweetheart or betrothed who would be devastated by the news he would be writing her about. He took the envelopes with him. He would read only as much necessary to elicit the information he needed, and then he would burn the letters. Even in death, folks were entitled to their privacy.

He met Whitehorse back outside and they anchored the bodies to the mules. As they rode out of the yard and turned up the road that led back to the Tufts ranch house, Rance said, "I should have just told Arch we would return to his place tonight. It will be near dark when we finish our work there, and I hate surprising him that late."

"Won't be surprised."

"Why do you say that?"

"Sioux warrior from Tufts's ranch has been following us. Now he rides ahead. He will tell Tufts what he seen us do. Sioux fool. I fought Sioux all my life. Scouted for the Army in the Sioux wars. I can smell them for many miles."

"Why didn't you tell me before?"

"No call to. He's not an enemy. Not now. I even took a Sioux wife. Primrose is okay most times."

Chapter 23

LISBETH AND TILLIE sat on the bench at the school desk in the barn schoolroom at the Rice farmstead. The desks were more tables than anything else, approximately two feet wide and five feet long, crafted to furnish ample elbow room for two students. Ben Rice had somehow snugged two boards together for the top and planed them to a smooth, splinter-free finish so a person had to give serious scrutiny to find the juncture. It was set on sturdy, crossed and braced legs that made the thing nearly immovable. The bench required a single, thick board and was just as sturdy.

Tillie, as always, took pride in her husband's craftsmanship. "Ben wanted you to see this before he makes the other four," she said. "Will they do?"

"Do? They're perfect."

"Ben will make any changes we want without complaint," Tillie said.

"I couldn't imagine changing anything Ben made. We will have seating for ten children. That will more than cover our families. We could add a half dozen easily enough if we ever wanted to offer a neighborhood school."

"I don't think we could handle more students ourselves."

"We could hire a schoolteacher to take over instruction if we don't have time, somebody who might be able to take the children further."

Tillie said, "Maybe we'd better handle what we've got first." She paused a moment. "You don't sound like you're going anyplace."

Lisbeth said, "Well, I told you I was going to stay around here, go back to my farm when the house is repaired."

"You don't like it with Rance?"

"I . . . I, well, it's not that. It's worked out well enough. The kids adore him. Frankly, we've lived better than I ever did during my years with Carl. No fighting and fussing. We're comfortable together, I can say. For my part, anyhow. I can't speak for Rance, but he doesn't seem unhappy."

"Have you thought about marrying him?" Tillie asked.

"Marry him? Tillie, I haven't been a widow three months."

"Some folks remarry even faster in these parts. Sometimes it is the practical thing to do. The market for women—white ones, anyhow—is always healthy. You move into town, and you would have men lined up at your door. Finding a man would be the least of your worries."

"My experience with men has convinced me that I can do without one just fine. Besides, Rance hasn't asked me."

Tillie burst out laughing so hard she could barely catch her breath.

"What's so funny?" Lisbeth asked.

"What you said. That sounds like a door part open."

"Oh, Tillie, I guess the door is not closed. There are just things I'm not certain about."

"Like what?" Tillie saw Lisbeth flush a bit.

"Being intimate with a man again. I'm still haunted about what happened that night."

Tillie thought about Lisbeth's words. The slave woman's world was different. She had no choice about such things and had to come to terms with it in her own way if she wanted to escape a beating or being placed on the market. And the visits made by her master were not of her choosing. Yet she had never thought of herself as scarred by what had happened. It had never affected her marital bed. She could not advise another how to come to terms with such experiences, but she knew how she had dealt with it.

Tillie turned toward Lisbeth and reached out and took her hand, fastening her dark eyes on Lisbeth's own. "Listen, sweet girl. I don't know how to patch your wounds, but I told you what happened to me, night after night. Not the same. One man, not two. But I told myself, "Tillie, it doesn't count for anything. That old man is stealing something from me that isn't his to take. But he doesn't have my heart, and he's not going to make off with all the good things I'm going to have in a life with my Ben. He can go to hell."

"You've put it behind you, truly?"

"That man has never for a moment come between Ben and me. Of course, I can't forget him entirely because of the child he sent with me. But that part has been a blessing, more so because of the man I married who accepted him as his own flesh and blood."

"You are a wise woman, Tillie."

"Tell my husband that the next time you see him."

Chapter 24

IT WILL TAKE the better part of a half day to get to Print Olive's headquarters in the Clear Creek valley about halfway between the North Loup and the Middle Loup. You likely won't need my map after you hit Clear Creek," Tufts said.

"Arch, I truly appreciate all your help."

"My pleasure. I just hope I can help bring Print Olive to justice. You just watch your back. I'll help Johnny and Coyote Man with the burying, and when that's done, they'll stay on your trail till you get back here. Count on supper at the Lazy T and a soft bed no matter when you show up."

Rance nodded and reined his big sorrel out of the yard. It was barely past sunrise, but he wanted to allow plenty of time to confront Print Olive. Arch Tufts had filled him in on the rancher's Texas shenanigans the previous evening, providing invaluable insight into his adversary. Tufts was a fascinating man and he felt he had formed a fast friendship with the old cowman.

It seemed Tufts spent most of his time painting these days and the cattle were just a part of his past he could not let go of. During a tour of the man's studio, Rance had encountered a room with walls nearly covered with paintings of the American West. Some were what the artist called landscapes, but most were scenes depicting Indians, cowboys, soldiers and the like. Those subjects and their horses and cattle seemed to come alive on the canvas. Tufts told him he had retained an agent to market his work, and he was just beginning to receive revenue from sales. He did not mention the price of his works, but Rance hoped he could afford one or two for his new house when the time came to furnish it.

They had agreed that he would ride ahead on his own to meet with Olive and that Whitehorse and Coyote Man, who happened to be Snowbird's brother, would follow or pass him by to be available if trouble arose. Rance did not have any notion of making an arrest. He had no evidence, and his authority was limited. It was essential that he confer with Sheriff Abe Steele soon for instructions on how to handle the situation that was developing in Custer County and adjoining counties and public lands. There were legal matters that needed clarification.

The Dismal River, where Olive still maintained a camp, lay a short distance north beyond the boundaries of Custer County in territory that had not yet been organized into county subdivisions of the state. There were miles of such lands that bordered Custer, not to mention parts of five or six other organized counties. What authority did a deputy operating in Custer County and appointed by the sheriff of Lincoln County have there? The killings of the young ranchers, however, clearly had taken place in Custer County.

Rance headed north toward Clear Creek on a narrow trail Tufts had marked on his sketched map. The trail snaked between hillocks carpeted by dry grass. Rance observed that the grasses, consisting of a variety of types including switchgrass, Indiangrass and patches of the shorter buffalo grass, showed no signs of pasturing by animals, domestic or wild, the past season. He assumed this was public land not yet homesteaded or surveyed by the government for claims. There was plentiful grass and water in the Sandhills north and west, and cattlemen were just beginning to discover it. The area had been largely ignored for years, having been dubbed by earlier explorers as a part of the "Great American Desert" based upon the seemingly endless sand dunes and hills that appeared unsuitable for farming or pasturing even though they were obviously covered with grass.

He took some comfort from the dearth of trees and bushes on the trail, figuring it would be difficult to set up an ambush here. On the other hand, it would be easy enough to follow a rider without discovery by moving through the breaks between the hills and ridges. He would be cautious, but he was not greatly concerned. One man headed toward the Olive headquarters should not cause serious concern. It would make more sense to hear his story before killing him.

Midmorning he reached the Clear Creek, a narrow ribbon of water that twisted its way eastward through the hills where it would eventually flow into the Middle Loup River as the river angled south. An hour downstream he should find the Olive Ranch headquarters site. He reined his mount southeasterly, following a well-travelled trail along the winding creek's edge, figuring it would lead him to his destination. Later, he was forewarned by spirals of smoke climbing skyward and feathering out above the hills. He found a break in the hills lining the creek and turned his horse away from the trail and worked his way to the top of a craggy bluff.

The bluff overlooked the Olive headquarters that was laid out in a natural hollow on the near side of the river. He dismounted and took the telescope that Tufts had sent with him from his saddlebags. He could make out at least two bunkhouses and a cook's building with an attached covered eating area that had temporary canvas walls on the sides. There was a barn in progress, a separate stable already completed and a maze of wood fences. A substantial house had been started, but work would be halted by winter's onset before occupancy.

Tufts had told him that the wives and children of Print Olive and his brother, Ira, had settled in nice homes in the village of Plum Creek south of the Custer County border in Dawson County on the north side of the Platte River. Rance had made supply trips to the village a few times. He guessed the population at no more than two hundred his last visit, but with rail access it was growing rapidly. Tufts had speculated that with the ladies now planted in civilization, a castle could not lure them further north to the vast, sparsely occupied plains and hills. Residence there would leave them two or three days from any store beyond a trading post with mere survival inventory.

Rance thought that the activity on the site gave the appearance of a colony of ants with men scurrying from one place to another, usually with lumber or tools in their arms. There were a few men with rifles strolling the perimeter of the headquarters tract, but they did not seem too interested in their tasks. It would require an army to threaten this sanctuary, and Rance would bet another sentry or two were roaming the hills at this moment, prepared to give warning of any threat. He would not be surprised to learn that someone was watching him now.

He spotted a wagon trail below his location where the rolling terrain flattened and made a natural entrance to the headquarters complex. He decided to descend the bluff and connect with the trail for his approach. He dropped the spyglass back into his saddlebags and started to mount Rusty when a voice with a thick southern accent spoke from behind him, "What's y'all's business, mister?"

Rance was not foolish enough to reach for his Colt. He lifted his hands above his head and turned slowly. Some twenty feet distant stood a very tall, lean, colored man holding a pistol in his left hand, dark menacing eyes peering from beneath a low-crowned black hat. The man's full dark mustache arched downward past the edges of his lips, like a big frown, to make his appearance more imposing, He was wrapped in a lined canvas duster that dropped to his knees.

Rance said, "My name is Rance Coldsmith. I am a deputy sheriff assigned to this area. I am going to slowly lower my left hand and pull back my coat to show you my badge."

The man gave a barely perceptible nod of his head.

Rance tugged his sheepskin coat front back enough to reveal the deputy's badge pinned above the pocket of his gray flannel shirt.

The man he had already guessed was Jim Kelly lowered his pistol and holstered it. "Y'all still ain't stated your business."

"I'm here to visit with Print Olive. Just to talk." He paused. "For now."

Kelly's face was as impassive as a cardsharp's. "Follow me." Without a word, the man turned and headed down the path Rance had taken to the top of the bluff. Rance led his own horse behind. When Kelly reached the base, he clutched the reins of an enormous black stallion that had been waiting, led the animal out into the flat and swung easily into the saddle.

Rance followed suit, assuming from the stranger's demeanor that talk was not welcome. They rode out to the trail Rance had spotted from the bluff and, once there, turned toward the ranch, continuing to ride in silence, with Rance holding Rusty a respectful distance back.

When they reached the ranch yard, they continued to the chuck house, where they dismounted. They tied their horses at a long hitching post that ran the length of the attached shelter.

"Wait here," Kelly said before he disappeared behind the canvas wall.

Rance gently stroked his horse's muzzle while he cast his eyes about the ranch headquarters. It would be an impressive place upon completion and equipped with everything a cowman might desire. He could not aspire to half of this, he supposed. Or if he had that much, would he still want more? And was that good or bad? Was there a point at which the power that accompanied such wealth inevitably corrupted the holder of such influence?

As a novice Missouri lawyer in a life not quite forgotten, Rance had considered venturing into politics, but with reference to those of the political class he encountered, he had found himself put off by the bloated self-importance of many and the casualness with which they dispensed their favors with taxpayer dollars. He did not want to be that kind of man. Was it possible not to succumb to the temptations offered by power?

His reverie was interrupted when the canvas tarp was pulled back and the tall colored man appeared. He waved Rance to the opening and stepped out and held the can-

vas back while the deputy entered the improvised dining area. Rance stepped into the dusky box-like room
with billowing walls, lighted only by the sunlight that
sifted through tannish canvas and openings between the
draped tarps. Two men sat on benches across from each
other at one end of a table in a corner nearest the chuck
house.

One man, clean shaven with thick brown hair, stood
up, and weaving between tables, approached Rance. It
was Print Olive, with his fake politician's smile, wearing
a suit and string tie out in the middle of endless hills.
Rance accepted the outstretched hand.

"Print Olive," the rancher said. "We met once when I
dropped by your place. A pleasure to see you again, sir.
Welcome to Olive ranch headquarters."

"Thank you, Mister Olive."

"No, Print. Call me, Print."

Rance did not respond. "I'm here on business, sir. I'm
investigating two killings. I just wanted to see if you or
some of your people might be able to help me out."

"Two killings. Why, I haven't heard a thing. Come on
over to the table and sit down and we'll talk. Can I offer
you some spirits? Coffee?"

He waved Rance toward the table, and the deputy followed. He sensed that the man who had to be Jim Kelly

had slipped in behind him, moving with the silence of a cat. Rance sat down at the near end of the table, Kelly claiming a seat at his side.

"You didn't answer about the drink or coffee," Olive reminded him.

"No, thanks," Rance said. "I just want to take care of my business and I'll be on my way. I thought we might talk privately."

Olive said, "No secrets from Deacon and Nigger Jim. They're my right and left arms. Couldn't say which is which."

"Deacon?"

"Scruggs," the stocky, bearded man sitting across the table next to Olive said. "I go by Deacon Scruggs."

Rance decided that was all the name he was going to get. He looked at the colored man. "And you are Jim Kelly?"

"Whatever suits you."

Rance shrugged. "Any of you gentlemen acquainted with Trapper Wollenberg and Clem Snyder?"

Olive said, "Never met Snyder. I know Wollenberg. Seemed like a nice enough fellow, but I heard he and Snyder have been rustling cattle in these parts. I'll have twenty thousand head when they all get here from Texas and that concerns me some. I bought out Trapper's herd a few days ago just to get him to move on. I hope to drop by and make a deal with Snyder, since they seem to be partners in the rustling business."

Rance said, "I haven't heard anyone else suggest they were rustlers."

"Well, it's not like they would advertise it."

"They won't anymore. They're dead. Both of them."

Olive said, "You don't say. Accident?"

"Murdered. I'm looking for the killers."

"Gunned down?"

The rancher was answering too quickly, Rance thought. Olive had already rehearsed for an occasion like this. Play dumb. That was the smart thing to do. "One was hanged. The other was shot in the head."

Olive said, "I see. Somebody must have seen them running off their cattle. Rustling's a hanging offense where I come from."

Rance said, "In these parts, the cattle owner doesn't serve as prosecutor, jury, judge and executioner. The owner brings his evidence to the sheriff and the law takes it from there. Hanging a man is murder if it's done outside the law."

"That can be a waste of a lot of time and the taxpayers' money."

"It's hard to understand why Trapper Wollenberg would be rustling cattle if he had already sold his herd to you. Where are the cattle you bought? Was he still living on his place?"

"We are buying his land, too, so we kept the cattle on his land, and moved a few men over there that needed a place to bunk until we've got everything finished here. He packed up and left. Didn't know where he went. I guess not far."

"Do you have a bill of sale for the cattle?"

"No paperwork needed. We trusted each other, I gave him fifteen dollars a head, and he gave me his word that he owned the critters."

"You took the word of a man you thought was a rustler?"

"I had Deacon and Nigger Jim here as witnesses. They will testify to the transaction. No recorded titles on cattle, so I don't need paper."

Olive sounded like a man of experience when it came to such things. Rance said, "A land deal requires paper. A deed must be recorded with the county clerk, or the purchase is worthless."

"We had a lawyer from Plum Creek come up with a deed he made out. He's a notary public and witnessed the signing. He's having it filed and recorded."

"May I have the lawyer's name?"

"You're getting a little personal, deputy. Are you accusing me of something? Oh, what the hell. His name's Luther Bedlow."

"Never heard of him."

"Came up from Texas with me. He's a notary public in Nebraska. Not technically admitted to the Nebraska bar yet but neither are half the lawyers in the state from what I've been told."

Rance could not argue that point. A good number of lawyers, especially outside Omaha and Lincoln, were self-declared. As to the deed, it would be easy enough to check with the county clerk at the courthouse, which consisted of a three-room log cabin set in the middle of the prairie in the south-central part of the county. "Well, you folks don't seem to have any more information I need right now. I will likely be out to chat with you again about the case. If you come up with anything I should be aware of, I suspect you know where my place is."

"I do," Olive said. "We take a road only a few miles from there when we travel to and from the Dismal River camp. I could use a good man down that way to look after my interests. I'm looking for properties in your neighborhood. I'd pay you fifty dollars a month to keep your eyes open for rustlers or other troublemakers that might cause the Olives any problems—and to let me know of any land that might be for sale. You wouldn't need to give up your deputy's job. This would just be a sideline, so to speak."

So this was how Olive sucked lawmen into his clutches. "No, not interested. There could be a conflict there. What if I found that you were the one who broke the law? I'm afraid that would compromise me some. Besides, I'm already being paid to track down rustlers. If you think somebody's skimming your herd, get word to me, and I'll take care of it. Vigilante justice is the same as no justice as far as I'm concerned. Hanging a man, guilty or innocent, without his day in court is murder, pure and simple, and I'll do my best to bring in anybody who is a part of it."

Print said, "You can't fault a man for trying to give a fella an opportunity."

Rance stood, "I guess I'll be on my way then. I've got my work cut out for me, it appears. But I'll find the killers. It may take time, but I'm a patient man. I thank you. I'm sure we will be talking again."

Chapter 25

"I DON'T LIKE the idea of killing Coldsmith. It might bring more law interest than we want up this way," Olive said.

"But . . ." It was Deacon Scruggs who spoke. Kelly, sitting across the table preening his mustache, appeared only mildly interested in the conversation, and his unwavering calm frequently annoyed Print Olive.

"But he may push me to it. There's something about that man that says 'watch out.'"

Scruggs said, "He ain't no bumpkin. He's already got us pegged for the Wollenberg and Snyder killings."

"He can't prove anything, can he? No witnesses."

"That we know of," Scruggs said.

"Damn you, Deacon. I've never seen the likes of you for raining on a picnic."

Scruggs shrugged, "We're friends, Print. But I told you back in Texas that you might want to think twice before you go stomping into a nest of rattlesnakes."

Olive respected Deacon Scruggs's judgment and valued his loyalty. That's why he paid the man well to stick around. That did not mean he liked Deacon's advice or that he always listened to it. He did not, however, like to be reminded when his actions turned sour. He looked at Jim Kelly. "What did you think of the deputy, Jim?"

"Honest man. Got grit. Not sure, but he might be smart. If so, that's a mighty dangerous man that just rode away from here. We'd best take him serious."

Print was not hearing what he wanted. "I think we need to know where Rance Coldsmith is at and where he goes. You got a few men you can send out to keep track of him and got enough sense not to get caught?"

Kelly said, "No guarantees. Muskrat Webb and Ramiro Vasquez. Webb blends in anyplace. Won't catch anybody's attention. Just an ordinary cowpoke. Ramiro might get noticed if there aren't many Mexicans about, but he can move in close and make hisself near invisible. The two get along good enough."

"Okay. You make arrangements. I want one of them to report to you every three or four days to let us know where Coldsmith's at and if he seems to be up to any-thing. Would they kill the man if you gave the order?"

Kelly said, "Ramiro would. Muskrat, I can't say. We ain't used him for elimination work. He's a wrangler and don't mind cutting out a man's cattle if he's paid for it. I wouldn't use him for killing yet."

Print said, "Well, we only need one man for that. And if you didn't think Ramiro was right for the job, we could send in somebody else, or you could take care of it per-sonally."

Scruggs interrupted. "Print, you've bought a good number of them, but you ain't killed a lawman yet. If you're trying to start over in Nebraska, that wouldn't be a good way to do it. I doubt the lawmen you paid would stand for killing one of their own, most of them anyhow."

Print said noncommittally, "We'll see how this plays out and do what we've got to do."

Chapter 26

RANCE HAD ENJOYED an extra night of luxury at the Tufts ranch house. Arch was a fascinating, intelligent man, and Rance hoped Lisbeth could meet Snowbird soon. The Sioux wife, he learned, had been educated at one of the first Indian schools in the west, spoke near flawless English and was a delightful conversationalist once she emerged from her natural reserve.

Nevertheless, he found himself anxious to get home after several nights away, and when Johnny Whitehorse split off to head for his cabin, Rance pushed Rusty a little harder toward his own soddy. When he neared the house, he paused on the rise above the house and studied the ground there for a few minutes. This is where he envisioned building a house someday. Nothing as extravagant as the Tufts' residence, but a solid structure with limestone a possibility. Two stories and wood floors, of course. A big porch overlooking the ranch yard would be nice.

Before he headed downslope into the ranch yard, he cast his eyes about for the men who had been following him and Johnny ever since they left the Tufts place early morning. It was midafternoon now, and before they parted Johnny insisted that they were still being trailed. Rance took the Pawnee's word for it. He knew better than to question his friend. If Johnny said they were being followed, they were being followed. There were two, he had told Rance, hanging loose and out of sight, likely because they knew Rance's destination. When they split, Johnny said he would circle around and see what he could learn about the unwelcome pursuers. He would go home and check on Primrose and then slip over to Rance's afoot after dark to report. "Should I kill them?" Johnny asked Rance, who had firmly said "No."

He rode down the gentle slope into the ranch yard and dismounted. He heard the rapping of a hammer from the barn. It piqued his curiosity, so he did not bother to check in at the house but led Rusty directly to the barn. A radiant sun warmed the back of his neck, but November promised that darkness just several hours distant would deliver a chill that would make a fire welcome. He was less than five paces from the barn entrance when Marissa appeared in the wide doorway. "Uncle Rance," she yelled and darted from her spot and raced toward him. He bent over with his free arm and scooped her up. She wrapped her arms about his neck and kissed him on the cheek, and from that moment, she owned him.

Lisbeth and Morgan came out of the barn, the latter with a big grin on his face. Even Lisbeth, wearing her baggy britches and a bulky sweater he recognized as his own, showed traces of a close-mouthed smile. "Welcome home, Rance. We were starting to worry," she said.

"Never any danger, but I collected a few things for us to talk about later. Maybe you can bring me up to date on what's happening here."

"Uncle Rance," Morgan said, "if you will help me with the saddle, I'll take care of Rusty." He took the reins from Rance's hand and led the horse into the barn.

Rance gave Marissa a gentle hug and let her down before he followed Morgan to help with the saddle. Lisbeth walked beside him. "He's saddling his own horse now," Rance commented. "Of course, Rusty's a big critter."

"He just wants to claim a few extra minutes of your time. Sorry about the 'Uncle Rance' business," she said. "Morg said he felt funny calling you just 'Rance.' We agreed on adding 'uncle' if you approved. The kids didn't wait, obviously."

"I'm fine with that. Has more of a family sound to it. And we're living like brother and sister, so that sort of makes me their uncle."

As Rance helped unsaddle the sorrel, he said, "I heard hammering when I came into the yard."

"I will show you," she said, motioning him to follow her to the far corner of the barn, where a small A-shaped building had been constructed. He guessed the structure to be about four feet high at its peak, perhaps about the same width at its base and a few feet deeper.

Lisbeth looked at him expectantly.

"My new bedroom?" he asked.

She rolled her eyes and gave him a vexed look. "Not funny. Try again."

"Back home in Missouri, I saw some farms that had hog houses like that."

"Better. I have got to finish the front and make a door opening yet. I had never built one, but my father used something like this for his hogs. Quite cozy and the angled sides leave space along the edges to help shelter piglets from being crushed by the sow when she lies down. This is just an experiment. I won't build any others here. We'll move this over to my place when we go back in the spring. The bottom just fits into the buckboard—I measured. We will need Ben and Jake to help load."

"I am impressed. You really are serious about the hog business, aren't you?"

"Absolutely, as Dad always swore, they are 'mortgage lifters.' I need to make a living if we are staying in the Sandhills area, and I know something about hogs. I talked to Ben, he might be willing to get in the business, too. We could build a smokehouse and market the processed product locally, ship out any pigs we couldn't butcher ourselves."

Rance frowned. He just could not envision herds of hogs running around this rolling prairie. This was cattle country.

Lisbeth said, "Don't say anything. Just let it soak in. You are a cowman. The idea takes a little time to get used to. Don't worry. I will keep my hogs penned up on my place. They won't soil hallowed cow ground."

He knew she was teasing him. What she did not know was that the thing bothering him most was the thought of her and the kids moving out. "I'm not worried," he lied.

Lisbeth said, "Tillie shared a ham with me that Ben brought back from a trip to Plum Creek. I was going to make ham and bean soup when you got back. As soon as I put the tools away, I'll head up to the house and get at that and bake some cornbread for supper. Maybe we can eat early, since I'm betting you haven't had much to eat today. I have an apple pie I made this morning, so I should have supper ready by six o'clock."

"Is there anything I can do to help?"

"You could see to your chores here and keep an eye on Marissa. Morg has taken over the evening milking now. He might like some help getting the cow up from the fenced pasture. Tell him I want the milking done early tonight."

"I can do that." In other words, he thought, he was to stay out of her way.

"I'll have a kettle of hot water and a bar of lye soap if you want to wash up and put on a fresh shirt when you come up." That used to be Rachael's way of telling him he stank.

Chapter 27

WHEN RANCE SHOWED up with Morgan and Marissa, Lisbeth placed the kettle of hot water on the hearth with a towel and wash cloth and bar of soap. She wondered if she was starting to get a bit bossy. Her father had always chided her about her bossy side, and it had evidently come out with Carl. A few harsh slaps and tirades had buried the tendency for some years, however. She did not worry in the least about Rance turning violent, but he had been kind beyond measure to her and the kids, and she did not want to annoy him—not more than a little, anyhow.

She watched furtively as he peeled off his shirt and fetched another from his box of folded garments. Modesty had gradually faded during their weeks together, and she had viewed his naked torso before, but this evening she found her perusal less casual as her eyes traversed over the muscle-sheathed shoulders and chest, the lean tight abdomen. She was struck by a stirring she had not felt before and did not understand. She shook it off when her curiosity started to travel to nether regions.

After supper, Rance helped her with the dishes as he did occasionally when he was not called to pressing chores outside. It was different tonight, she thought as she rinsed dishes he had washed in a pan of hot water. He was quiet, obviously preoccupied, but she knew him well enough now not to press. Let him work it out unless he asked her opinion about something.

When the dishes were finished, Morgan was ready for chess. Lisbeth sensed that Rance was not in the mood, but he would not deny the boy his pleasure. She suspected this was more Morgan claiming time with Rance than the chess game. She worried that Rance had replaced Carl, the father who had always been aloof and absent in the boy's life in any meaningful way. What would happen when she and the kids moved back to their own farm? They would still be neighbors, she told herself, and Rance would not disappear from their lives. But it would not be the same.

Later, she and Rance sat at the table drinking coffee. Thank heaven, she now was no longer shy about using the chamber pot in the middle of the night. Of course,

Rance's view was blocked by the bundling board as she squatted next to her side of the bed to relieve herself, but the thought of him listening had inhibited her greatly in those first days. It occurred to her then that they had become almost a married couple, absent vows, in all the ways except physical intimacy. Her decision to share the house had possibly not been a wise one.

Her thoughts were cut off by Rance's soft voice. "You know, of course, that I was married before."

"Yes. Tillie told me that you had lost your wife and daughter. I am very sorry."

"A son who lived only a few hours after his mother died, also."

"It had to be a hard time."

"Yes, and I thought at first fate was picking on me, but I finally reminded myself that many persons suffer great losses and somehow go on. I guess I did, too. But I ran, and I'm not sure that's a good thing."

"This was when you lived in Missouri?"

"Yes. We were happy there. I truly loved Rachael and my Tessa—and little Chance, the son I never got to know. Rachael and Tessa had auburn hair like yours and Marissa's. That bothered me some at first, but you really don't look that much alike. Rachael was a tiny thing with bright blue eyes."

Lisbeth conceded she would not be judged tiny. She supposed she was more like a tall gangly scarecrow. "Were you a rancher in Missouri?"

"Would-be rancher. We had a small cowherd—never more than twenty cows—just outside Oak Hills in the northern part of the state. I was a lawyer in a small firm in the county seat town. I practiced with my father-in-law. Gale and Coldsmith. I didn't go to a fancy law school or anything. I clerked for Tom Gale and read the law, passed the bar exam and was admitted to the bar. I was a hometown boy, grew up there. Rachael and I went through school together in the town. Can't remember when I didn't know her."

"Did you come from a ranching family?" she asked.

"No. We kept a few cows on the edge of town, but my father, David Coldsmith, was county sheriff till he died. I was fourteen then." His voice cracked. "I saw the mob hang him when I was coming to the jail to try to help."

"Oh, my God. I don't know what to say."

"The mob had come for his prisoner at the jail. The prisoner was a young man accused of raping a girl. Dad's two deputies deserted him when the mob showed up after dark. He refused to surrender his prisoner and when the jail was being overrun, he leveled his shotgun into the crowd and took down a few men, although they did not die. This infuriated the attackers and they strung up Dad along with the prisoner. I will never forget trying to get him down from the big limb of the tree on the courthouse square while his feet kicked in the air, and he was being strangled by the rope. I climbed the tree to get him and the prisoner down, but I was too late. I learned later that the so-called victim had tried to stop the hanging. The prisoner had been her boyfriend, and she had lied about him in a fit of anger."

"How awful."

"Someone said 'a mob has many heads but no brains.' I hate mobs more than anything. If there is a mind involved, it is that of someone who knows how to manipulate the mindless to achieve their own evil ends."

"Your mother?"

"She died a year later and the Gale family took me in till I finished school. Thrown together like that, and already caring for each other, it was inevitable that Rachael and I would end up as a couple. We were married at eighteen. My father-in-law had been kind to me and liked me well enough, but he insisted I would support his daughter properly and put me to work clerking in his office with the thought of preparing me to join his firm."

"So you were kind of an accidental lawyer?"

"I was still a kid when we married, and I had a wife to support—and a child six months later. I really wanted to be a rancher, although I didn't have any capital. I had worked on a cattle ranch near town when I was growing up and I loved working with cattle and being outdoors. That's why Rachael and I bought a small parcel near town and started a herd once I got established in the legal business. I liked what I was doing well enough until diphtheria hit Tessa and took her in a matter of a few days. Only six months later, Rachael and our newborn son were gone."

"And you joined the Army?" Lisbeth asked.

"I ran. My parents, Rachael, Tessa and little Chance are buried at Oak Hills. I left them behind. After I was discharged from the Army, I returned home, thinking I would take up my place in the firm again if Tom Gale would have me. I learned that he had died suddenly two years after I left and that his wife and the younger two children had moved to be near relatives back east. I stayed a few days, spending some time at the cemetery, and then headed back to Texas where I had done my Army service, thinking I might re-enlist. I had advanced to First Sergeant before my discharge, and the commandant at Fort Concho had told me he could obtain a second lieutenant's commission for me if I re-enlisted for four years.

"But the cattle business always called me and, before I connected with the Army, I found a job driving cattle north. It was hard, miserable work, and I loved it and stayed with the outfit for several years—got more education, you might say. That triggered sort of a re-birth of my dream to be a cowman."

"But you became a lawman first," Lisbeth observed.

"When I came in with a herd for delivery to the North Platte cattle market, I learned that Abe Steele was county sheriff there. He had been one my father's deputies in Missouri—several years before Dad was lynched. I used to hang around the sheriff's office when I wasn't in school and got to know Abe there." He chuckled. "Abe's the one who taught me to play checkers and chess. On county time. Of course, until Dad was killed, we were a sleepy little town with weekend drunks and neighbor fusses being the sheriff's main problems. Anyway, I dropped by to say hello to Abe. When I told him about my cowman ambitions, he invited me to take a few days and join him on a ride into the Sandhills to the north. I accepted, and I came back convinced I had found home. Abe even showed me this parcel where the house sits and introduced me to the homesteaders who lived here. The place was not for sale at that time, though, but they were thinking about a move. I asked them to contact Abe if they put the farm up for sale. I would be sure he knew where to find me."

"You must have ridden past our house that day."

"Yeah, but Abe didn't recommend stopping there. He said that the man didn't welcome strangers."

"I guess Carl's reputation got around."

Rance said, "Abe didn't say more than that, but that's probably true. Anyway, when we got back to North Platte, Abe asked me if I wanted to stick around these parts for a spell. I said I was sure interested, but I would need to find work. That's when he told me he had an open deputy's job, and it was mine if I wanted it. I thought all of ten seconds before I took it."

Lisbeth decided to change the subject. The nutshell version of Rance's history was more than enough for her mind to digest. Rance Coldsmith was a complex man, and he carried wounds that had not yet healed, possibly never would. She found it a bit strange that out of the blue he had revealed so much of his past.

"You told me before you left that you needed to report to the sheriff in North Platte. When do you plan to do this?"

"Two or three days. I can't wait long. Things have happened that make the visit more urgent." He told her about the killings and visits to the Tufts and Oliver ranches.

"And two men are following me. They're likely camped not far from here tonight, maybe not far from the river."

"Are you in danger?"

"I doubt it. I'm thinking they just want to know what I am up to. Johnny will scout them out tonight and stop by later."

Lisbeth said, "You talked about me going to North Platte with you. I need a lot of supplies. Ben said we could take his mule team. Tillie and he have a list of things they need, too. But a wagon will slow you down."

"I guess if we left early morning, we could get by with one night on the trail and get to North Platte by the following evening. Two nights there and another on the return trip. With a team we could move at a good pace. Almost all flatland on the wagon road. Have you talked to Tillie about Sue Ellen being a chaperone?"

Lisbeth smiled and rolled her eyes. "Tillie just laughed at me. She thought the whole notion was silly since we have been sharing a bed for three months now. I had to agree with her. Just another person to haul and lodge and feed. She's glad to take the kids, though, and Morg and Marissa are excited about it."

"I suppose it's okay."

She could see that she had left the poor man speechless. "I am long past worrying about any gossip. I don't even know anybody around here but the Rice family."

"Well, I thought we might cause a stir in town, but I suppose if we get separate rooms at the hotel—or I could even get something at one of the rooming houses."

"That would be a waste of money. You are not going to get anything for less than a dollar a night. Two nights. That's two dollars." She paused. "Tillie said you had a lady friend in North Platte. Is that what's worrying you?"

"No. Katherine Anderson is engaged to marry George Oglesby, heir apparent to the throne at the Oglesby Bank, where we will be doing some business. She wanted no part of a cattleman's life and was revolted by the mansion you and I are presently sharing." Rance sighed. "I will just leave the sleeping arrangements to you."

"An excellent idea."

Chapter 28

THE TWO STALKERS, presumably Olive men, had remained nearby, camping in a little clearing in the woods downstream on Wildcat Creek about a mile from the Sunrise Ranch building site. Rance did not like the idea of the two men trailing him and Lisbeth to North Platte and was pondering a confrontation. He had brought Ben's mules over to his place that morning to be ready for an early start the next day. He and Lisbeth had not had time to talk seriously since the first night of his return from the Olive investigation when his tongue had gone on a frolic. He could not explain what had got into him that night.

Rance was striding from the barn toward the rider who was coming in from the south. It was early afternoon, and he was pleased to see that Johnny Whitehorse had come to report on his daily scout to determine the whereabouts of the Olive spies. Whitehorse reined in and dismounted and said, "Still at the same camp, playing cards now. Morning and afternoon, they take turns riding over to see if you are here but they play cards and sleep most of the time."

Rance said, "Missus Baker and I are leaving for North Platte early tomorrow morning. I think it is time for me to ride over and have a chat with those fools. Back me up?"

Whitehorse grinned and said, "Don't want to miss that. Maybe we'll have some fun."

"I don't want to kill anybody, but I am not going to have these yahoos following us all the way to North Platte and back."

Rance went to the house, peered in the door and told Lisbeth he would be gone an hour or so. She smiled and gave him a quick wave as she continued with some kitchen project. Again, it struck him that a life without Lisbeth in that home, and Morg and Marissa, too, looked damned bleak. He and that darn woman had to have a serious talk.

He retrieved Rusty from the barn and soon Whitehorse was leading him to the camp. When they were within easy walking distance, they dismounted and staked out the horses in a wide draw that offered ample dry-grass grazing. Again, Whitehorse led the way, taking a course that followed a deer trail that weaved through cottonwoods and oak that fringed the riverbank. Rance could see smoke drifting above the trees and feathering out into the wind. Now he could hear loud laughter. The idiots were certainly making no effort to hide their presence. On the other hand, he supposed they had conjured up a story that would explain to anyone questioning their visit to the vicinity why they happened to be there. That made a certain sense, he figured. They would be assuming that Rance was not aware he had been followed to his place.

When they reached the edge of the clearing, Rance gestured for Whitehorse to remain hidden in the trees. He opened his coat for easier access to his Colt and stepped into the campsite. "Howdy, gents," he said.

Both men dropped the cards in their hands, and a young Mexican he instantly read as a gunslinger reached for his sidearm. Rance, who had already slipped his own weapon from its holster said, "Don't make me kill you."

The Mexican looked up and saw the pistol aimed at his chest and extended his hands away from his waist, signaling he had received the message. The other man, an Anglo with a walrus-like mustache had made no move and just sat on the tree stump that served as his bench with a perplexed look on his face. He did not appear interested in a gunfight. Rance said, "I won't take much of your time. My name is Rance Coldsmith. I am a deputy sheriff serving Custer County. Of course, you both know that. Just stay seated. I want to have a little talk and then I will be on my way."

The men remained silent; the Mexican, a wiry man, glared at Rance and sent a message that he was still interested in challenging the interloper. Rance said, "I want each of you to take the grip of your pistols between your thumbs and forefingers and toss them on the ground in front of me." He stepped closer so he stood slightly more than five feet distant.

The mustachioed man's weapon dropped at Rance's feet almost immediately. The Mexican hesitated a few moments before better judgment won out.

"I would like your names." He nodded first at the Anglo, a stocky man Rance placed in his mid-thirties.

"Frank Webb, but most everybody calls me Muskrat."

Rance suspected that the two protruding front teeth had something to do with the nickname. The man either had what his late father-in-law called an affidavit face, or he was telling the truth. "And you?" Rance asked, turning to the Mexican, who was probably ten years younger than his partner.

"Ramiro Vasquez."

Rance could not tell if the man was lying or not, but it made no difference. "What are you doing here?"

"Just passing through," Vasquez said. "We're both cowhands laid off for winter. Hoping we might find work up this way."

"Are you from Texas?" Rance asked.

"We are," Vasquez replied.

Apparently, Vasquez was the spokesman. He was obviously not Mexican-born. The accent detected was decidedly Texas twang.

Rance said, "I was just curious about what you would say. Let's not waste any more time. I will tell you why you are here."

The two men looked at each other.

Rance continued. "You both work for Print Olive. You have been following me since I paid a call on Mister Olive. I am guessing that either Deacon Scruggs or Jim Kelly gave you your instructions, but it could have been Olive himself. It doesn't matter. You have been watching my place, checking it a couple times a day. I have been tolerating it, but no more. I want you out of here today. And if I catch you around here again, I'm hauling you into North Platte to jail. I'll figure out some charges. Do you understand?"

Muskrat Webb nodded his head vigorously. "I do, sir. I'll be packing up."

Vasquez did not respond.

Rance said, "I have a message for your boss. Tell him I will be meeting with the sheriff within the next few days, and I will give him all the information I have about the Snyder and Wollenberg murders. I know who did the killings. I am gathering evidence, and we will bring the bastards to justice. Tell him I will see him soon."

Rance was bluffing, but he wanted to stir the pot some. Olive would not be inclined to believe the story, but he could not be certain. At least he might pull in his horns some. Maybe the rancher's unease would save a life or two. Without another word, he wheeled and walked away.

A rifle fired nearby, seeming to explode in his ears and deafening him temporarily. He turned, with the Colt back in his hand.

Vasquez lay on the ground next to the pistols, blood soaking the front of his shirt. Rance went back and knelt beside the man as Whitehorse, with his rifle cradled in his arms, emerged from the trees. Rance felt Vasquez's neck, searching for the pulse he knew he would not find. Whitehorse had been carrying a Sharps, and that weapon would have taken down a buffalo. The hothead Vasquez just had not been able to resist the temptation of Rance's back. He stood and spoke to Muskrat Webb. "Take him back to Print Olive with my message."

Chapter 29

SUNGLOW WAS JUST inching over the eastern horizon when Rance and Lisbeth, sharing the buckboard seat, pulled out of the yard with Rance handling the mule team's reins. A chill had descended on the Sandhills during the night, and an unwelcome wind made it seem even colder. The sky was clear, however, and not threatening. The possibility of snow worried Rance when traveling this time of year. Winter was drawing closer, and the Rocky Mountains of Wyoming to the west usually quit paying attention to the seasons by November and might send a snow their way anytime.

Sue Ellen had stayed at the house the previous night to be with Morgan and Marissa when they awakened. She would move the children to the Rice house later in the morning after Morgan milked the cow. After that, Jake would accompany the boy morning and evening to see to chores. Jake and Morgan would also check on the cow herd daily.

Rance had left his Stetson behind and wore a heavy, red stocking cap that Tillie had knitted for him a few years back. When winter's icy bite came, he quickly abandoned the cowman look. His sheepskin coat was more than ample to thwart the wind. Lisbeth wore practical trousers and a hooded wool mackinaw that covered all but nose and eyes. He had tossed in two flea-bitten buffalo robes in addition to their bedrolls. He also had three canvas tarps with which to fashion a shelter for the overnight layover between the Rising Sun Ranch and North Platte.

The wagon bounced along the trail at a brisk pace, and, barring a broken wheel, Rance figured they should make the twenty-five miles, possibly somewhat more, that they needed for their planned North Platte arrival the next evening. The road would twist like a writhing snake along the creek bottom for a spell for the first ten miles, and he had made allowances for the slowdown that would require.

Neither spoke for the first hour or so, but he knew that Lisbeth, like himself, tended to disappear in her own world from time to time, and he rather liked that they could be comfortable in long silences together. He needed some time to compose the right words for the subject he was about to broach. Finally, he summoned up the resolve. "I've been thinking, Lisbeth, about you and the kids moving back to your place. Why don't you just stay on at mine?"

Her head turned toward him, and astonished eyes peered out from the hood and looked at him with suspicion. "What are you saying exactly?"

He was not certain where he was headed with this. He did not want to embarrass either of them. "Well, the kids seem happy enough there. I like your living at my place. If it suits you, why be in such a hurry to move? I'm thinking that in the spring it's time to start the new house I mentioned. I showed you where I had in mind to build it. We would have plenty of space and you could help with the plans. Get you off the stone floor."

"I'm confused. How long is this arrangement to go on?"

He thought about her question. With the way he was fumbling for words, nobody would have ever guessed he had once made a living as a law wrangler. "As long as you wanted."

She cocked her head to one side and squinted one eye like she was trying to see into his head. "Are you talking about us living like brother and sister?"

"I'd be willing for us to have a go at husband and wife, if you were interested."

"Is this a proposal?"

"Yeah, I guess you could call it that."

"Damn poor excuse for one." She turned her head away and looked straight ahead as they continued down the trail.

They were both silent for another half hour or more. Rance did not have a clue what she might be thinking. Had he offended her? Was the notion of their marriage absurd? He realized there had been no courtship and that he had not told her that he loved her. He was fond of this woman—more than that, he thought. But it was not the all-consuming fire he had felt for Rachael, and he was nagged by what he knew was an irrational feeling that it would be an act of disloyalty to Rachael to tell Lisbeth that he loved her.

He saw it as a practical arrangement for an unattached man and woman. At least it was not like all the mail order bride business that was going on these days, where a couple made the arrangements by mail, got married at first meeting and hoped that love came along. If not, they just partnered through life. Love was just a word anyway, wasn't it?

Finally, Lisbeth broke the silence, continuing to look down the road. "I might be interested."

"That's a start. I guess there are conditions."

"Yes. We will have no relations until we are legally married, at which time the bundling board comes down. Come spring, I just would not be comfortable sharing a house with a man to whom I was not married. I do not want my children to grow up with such an example."

"Agreed," Rance said.

"We would each keep our properties in our own names for now."

"Agreed."

"I would be entitled to have my own projects. I am dead-set on raising hogs and intend to try it. It would be more convenient to do this on your place. I would want to carry on the business there. They don't take a lot of space."

Rance said, "I'm a cowman. Could we set up the hog buildings and lots back from the road, maybe north of the barn where folks couldn't see the hogs so easily."

She turned toward him. He could not see her mouth, but the sparkle in her brown eyes said she found his remarks funny. "I could live with those conditions," Lisbeth said.

"Then, agreed."

"A final condition, and I realize this may be a deal breaker. Morg asked me a few weeks ago if we were going to get married. I told him that we were not. I did not see your lame proposal coming. He said he wished we would because he wanted you to be his father and he would like to be a Coldsmith. In a few months' time you have been more father to him than Carl ever was. He feared Carl, never shared as much as a game of checkers. I would have to ask that you adopt my children . . . legally."

"Agreed," Rance said immediately. "I love the kids, and I would be honored to claim them as my own."

"Then, I accept your proposal. When do we do this thing?"

"How about when we are in North Platte? We could stay an extra night or two and call it a honeymoon. We can find a judge or preacher there. There will be a lot of business to take care of. I need to see a lawyer about a new will, and we can talk to him about adoption procedures. I don't know how long that takes in Nebraska but probably six months or more. You probably need some advice on clearing title to your homestead and getting it in your name."

"Yes. And I have never had a will."

"Don't leave the pigs to me."

She gave him a gentle punch in the arm. "Okay. I suppose we had just as well go ahead and get this done."

Chapter 30

LISBETH WONDERED IF she had lost her mind, negotiating marriage like she was entering into a business transaction. Last night they had spent the night sleeping on the ground under the wagon bed, their separate bedrolls wrapped in the buffalo robes and canvas tarps draped over the sides of the wagon box to block the wind. They had not exchanged so much as a soft kiss, although they had extended mutual "goodnights."

Darkness was just coming on when they reached North Platte this evening. They had checked into the Cattlemen's Palace as Mister and Missus Rance Coldsmith since that would be true soon enough. She had protested the extravagance since room rates were $1.50 per night. They could easily have found something for a dollar or less. Rance had assured her he was paying the bill, however, and insisted they needed something decent for the honeymoon. That was about as close as they had gotten to romantic words since departure from the Rising Sun Ranch.

The room was on the main floor, which was nice, and there was a water closet at the end of the hall with one of the newfangled flush commodes and a sink with water that appeared at the turn of a faucet handle. The hotel offered a nice dining room where they had enjoyed steaks, although she had felt self-conscious wearing her dusty riding clothes. To the rear were separate bath accommodations for men and women, as well as a barber and hairdresser. She thought that a dollar for bath and hairdresser was a bit pricey. The facilities were closed for the evening, so the best they could do was wash up in the water closet, but even that was a luxury that made her feel spoiled.

Lisbeth was sitting on the edge of the double bed, when Rance returned to the hotel room after using the water closet. He sat down on the stuffed settee which furnished the room's only seating except the bed. He pulled off his boots and then got up and tossed another log in the small fireplace that heated the room comfortably. He sat down again and looked at her with those translucent steel-gray eyes. She suddenly felt like a nervous school child reciting in front of an audience.

"Almost ten o'clock," he said. "Ready for bed?"

"Soon. I'm very tired, and I didn't sleep well last night."

He stood and walked toward her, extending his hand. "Come sit with me, so we can talk a bit about tomorrow."

She accepted his hand and held it as he led her back to the settee. She wondered if he could feel her shaking. She did not know what had come over her.

When they sat down, Rance continued to hold her hand. "I do remember our agreement," he said, "and by now you should know that I am a man of my word. If you are uneasy about the bed situation, I would be glad to spread my bedroll out on the floor."

"No. I don't want you to do that. I really don't. I am fine with our sharing a bed. We have been doing that a while, you know."

"Tomorrow, I will stop at Asa Wiggins's office. He is a lawyer who handles anything that comes his way. He's a pleasant gentleman in his mid-forties with a good amount of experience under his belt. I will see if I can make an early afternoon appointment for us both to see him if you are comfortable with us both having the same lawyer."

"Of course, I have nothing to hide from you," Lisbeth said.

"Nor I from you. I think that is a good start for us. After I stop at the lawyer's office, I will report to Abe and bring him up to date. I'll tell him about our plans and see if he can help find someone to marry us. Do you prefer a judge or preacher?"

"It doesn't matter, but a preacher would be fine if someone is available to bless the marriage of a couple of heathens."

"I'll see what I can do. Try for late morning day after tomorrow? I thought we would have breakfast in the Palace dining room tomorrow and meet at noon someplace to eat together and bring each other up to date. You said you wanted to find a dress. I would like to wear something a little more presentable for the occasion, so I would appreciate it if you would keep your eyes open for something for me to look at later."

"I will do that. I want to check out lumber for the hog buildings and find a livestock agent to help me arrange for shipping some pigs here in the spring."

Suddenly, she felt his fingers on the back of her head turning it toward his. He lowered his face and his lips found hers, touching softly until she responded with a lingering kiss that sent a tingling down her spine and awakened the indefinable need that she had experienced a few days earlier. Damn that agreement she had insisted upon.

Chapter 31

RANCE SAT AT Abe Steele's desk, across from the old sheriff who leaned back in his chair with one leg perched across the corner of the desktop, each holding a cup of coffee in his hand. Rance had just finished reporting on the hangings of Snyder and Wollenberg and his confrontation with Print Olive's spies. The sheriff had remained silent while Rance gave his narrative.

"That's about it," Rance said when he was finished. "My investigation won't scare off a man like Olive. With winter coming on, I look for things to be calm enough. Anything could happen come spring, though, and I'm going to have my own ranch to run. I can't give full time to herding that renegade, Abe."

"This Johnny Whitehorse, do you trust him?"

"Absolutely."

"Custer County has offered to reimburse Lincoln County more money for law protection. I can up your wage to seventy-five dollars monthly. If you want to sign on Whitehorse as a deputy, I'll pay him fifty dollars. But you have got to commit 1878 to me. Custer should have their own elected sheriff by the beginning of the next year and you can go back to full-time ranching—unless you want my job."

With a new family, Rance figured he had better grab every sure dollar that he could. "I'm sure Johnny will take the job, and I'll feel better if he's got my back and legal authority. See, I've got some new responsibilities coming on."

Steele lifted his wiry, white eyebrows. "I'm waiting. I ain't good at suspense, you know."

Rance grinned sheepishly, "I'm getting married."

That got the sheriff's attention. He swung his leg off the desk, placed his coffee cup on the desktop and leaned forward. "And who is the lucky lady?"

"Lisbeth Baker."

"The widow you took in? She still living at your place?"

"Yes. And it's all perfectly proper."

Steele rolled his eyes. "So you've been sleeping in the barn?"

"Well, no. We're sharing a bed, but . . ."

The sheriff started laughing. "Spare me the details."

To hell with him. Let the old fart think what he wants, Rance decided. "Anyway, we want to get married before we leave North Platte. I was hoping to get some help from you, if you would start taking this seriously."

The sheriff swept his hand across his lips as if wiping away the smile. "Of course, I'll help. Tell me what you need."

"A place to have a quick wedding. I thought you might be best man."

"I would be honored. Place depends on who's performing the marriage."

"She would like a preacher, but a judge would do. We want to take care of this tomorrow morning if we can."

"Son, I'd say calico fever hit you fast and hard."

"It's not like we're out of our heads in love. It just seems like the practical thing to do for us. We get along well enough and don't want to split up, so we figured we could make things work out if we both tried hard."

"Dear Lord, how could she resist such a romantic cuss? But you do need a woman out there. You'd better get hitched before she gets cold feet like Katy."

"She's not anything like Katherine, I guarantee."

"Well, we got a Methodist preacher now. Franklin Locke. He's been riding the circuit all over Nebraska for a lot of years. But the Methodists have enough folks to support a minister now. They don't have a church building yet, but Reverend Locke has set up shop in the abandoned building where Tully's Tavern used to be. You know where that is. You and your intended be there at eleven o'clock tomorrow morning. If that won't work for the preacher, I'll let you know. You're staying at the Palace aren't you?"

"Yes. How did you know?"

"I'm the sheriff. Got to know what's going on hereabouts. I heard you checked in there with a pretty, red-headed filly last night. One room, they say."

Rance stood up to leave. "I'll see you tomorrow morning at the Methodist Church."

Steele walked with him to the door and asked, "I was just thinking, does the bride-to-be have anybody to stand up with her?"

"No. But it isn't a legal requirement."

"How about I bring Martha?"

"I don't see that would be a problem. Might be nice. This is the 'Grandma's Delights' lady? You still sniffing around her, you old dog?"

"We're seeing more of each other. I thought if she took part in a wedding, it might set her thinking in the right direction."

"It just occurred to me. You didn't have any pastries for my coffee this morning."

"You got here too late. Besides, you had some of Martha's pastries with your breakfast at the Palace."

"How in the hell did you . . . never mind."

When Rance stepped out the door, he almost tripped over a medium-sized dog. The animal was eating meat scraps from a big tin pan next to the entrance. He had noticed the pan when he entered but had seen no animal about. He turned back to Steele who stood in the doorway. "You got a jail pet now?"

"Nope, he's a stray. He knows I'm good for a morning meal. He doesn't bite, but he shrinks away when I try to pet him. Look at the scars on his face and about the head. He's been beaten more than once. And look at those darned eyes, one dark brown and the other pale blue. He seems to see okay, though."

Rance said, "Australian Shepherd. One of the ranchers I worked for in Texas had two of them. Natural cattle dogs. They have some Australian ancestors, but they are a mix that somebody in California came up with. They will cost as much as a horse—two hundred dollars for a good one. I wonder if he jumped a train when it stopped here."

"Or somebody dumped him because he didn't do his job right."

Ron Schwab

"Handsome cuss even with the scars," Rance said. "Marked like a calico cat I saw once—brown, gray and black patches over the white. A little bit of everything. The dogs I saw were black and white, but I guess they come in different colors." He knelt beside the dog, taking care not to make a sudden move, and examined the animal closely while it gulped down the scraps. "He's not much more than a pup, I'd guess. Maybe a year or year and a half old. He's half starved."

"He's been hanging around town a week, but some of the businesses have been setting food out. You say you are a cowman. Shouldn't a cowman have a cow dog?"

"I'm taking on a whole family, Abe. Not a good time to add a dog."

"Think of him as another hand."

"There's something to that but maybe those scars mean he wasn't a very good hand." Rance slowly reached over and touched the dog's head and spoke in a voice barely above a whisper. "Hey, Tag."

The dog turned his head toward Rance, who began stroking him. The dog raised his head and gave Rance's face a few licks.

"I'll be darned," Steele said. "He didn't shrink away."

"I've got to go," Rance said, "got a lot of business to tend to today. I'll need to talk to Lisbeth before I take on

{242}

a dog. If Tag's still around and unclaimed in a few days, well, I'll see."

Steele said, "You're old enough to know that if you stamp a critter with a name, you're done for."

Chapter 32

RANCE AND LISBETH dined at the Cattlemen's Palace again that evening, both preferring the familiar after an exhausting day. At noon they had both eaten to near bursting at The Grease Joint, one of Rance's favorite eateries, that mostly offered stews, biscuits and cobblers. Tonight, they both ate prudently choosing the smallest steaks and dividing a serving of fried potatoes. No dessert.

The dining room was occupied by only a few customers, so they did not feel rushed as they sat at the table nursing their coffees. After leaving the The Grease Joint, they had gone directly to the courthouse and completed the marriage license paperwork for the County Judge's Clerk. The church pastor would complete the certification and see to the filing. After that there had been a lengthy meeting with the lawyer, Asa Wiggins, a congenial balding man with a clean-shaven face and modest paunch from too many hours at the desk. He had pleasantly surprised Rance with his high level of sophistication on property and estate settlement matters, and he had left the office feeling that their legal matters were in good hands.

"I liked the lawyer," Lisbeth remarked.

"I was just thinking about that," Rance replied. "I hope you are satisfied with the provisions I made for you and the children in the will."

She smiled, "How can I not be since I am the sole beneficiary with the kids to inherit if I don't survive? You had better watch your back."

"You will be my only family. We can sign our wills before we leave town, so everything is in place."

"And you are truly okay with my leaving my property directly to the kids?"

"I wouldn't expect otherwise. Besides, I will be their trustee until they are of age. Asa seemed experienced in these matters. He said he will prepare the affidavits for Ben and Jake to sign to prove Carl's death, and they can go to his office when they are in North Platte and sign. He will take care of the county clerk's filings in Custer County, and that's all there is to transfer of Carl's interest in your quarter section. The official adoptions can't take place till summer, but as far as I'm concerned, I am their dad."

"Then, I can tell Morg he is a Coldsmith? He will be thrilled."

"Sure. Maybe we can do that together when we tell them we are married."

"I suppose some folks will talk. Carl has not been gone close to a year."

"Do you care?"

"No, not really."

She paused, wrinkling her nose slightly like she tended to do when she was thinking about something. He found the mannerism endearing. He watched her, thinking how striking she looked in the green dress she had worn today, one of those Tillie had made for her. Not that it mattered, but he had enjoyed showing this lady off around town today. Since they had set up new accounts at the bank—a joint account and separate ones for their respective business enterprises—he assumed Katy would have heard about his impending marriage by now. Her own wedding was only a week or so off. He hoped he did not encounter her while he was in town.

"I was thinking," Lisbeth said. "I can't believe Hiram Oglesby would loan us five thousand dollars to build a house."

"The land is all free and clear. I was glad he would settle for a mortgage on the quarter section where the house will be. He will advance the funds as we need them. Maybe it won't take that much."

"It seems like an extravagance. I would be fine to live where we are at."

"With the kids on the floor? Us in the same room with just a curtain between us?"

Lisbeth said, "Lots of folks have worse. Think how crowded Ben and Tillie are."

"Tillie didn't tell you? They are going to build a house, too. We'll work together on the projects. Of course, Ben will be in charge. We'll have to hire some help, too."

"Tillie didn't tell me. She probably was afraid it would sound like she was bragging. And she didn't know about the marriage when I saw her last. Of course, I didn't either. Anyway, I am hoping we can do the house for half of what Mister Oglesby is willing to loan."

"You like to deal with numbers, don't you?"

She shrugged. "I have had to."

"Do you want to be the family bookkeeper?"

"Are you serious?"

"I don't like messing with the details. I just want to see the monthly numbers."

"Yes, I could do that. I'll bet you are behind for this year."

He grinned sheepishly. "Only six months. That job goes with it."

"I will try."

"What about your pigs?"

"Mister Samuels at the livestock agent's office is sending some telegrams. I will stop by tomorrow afternoon after the wedding and see what he found out."

"That's the start of the honeymoon?" he teased. Rance had been hoping that the marriage might sidetrack Lisbeth's plans for the hog business. However, she had set up her own account at the bank for the enterprise and had deposited her share of the reward money and some of her recently collected funds to start with a four-hundred-dollar balance, giving her ample capital to commence the business. She had also deposited two hundred dollars in the joint personal account, which he felt obligated to match but left him shorter than he liked for the cattle account. Perhaps he had spoken too quickly about Lisbeth handling the bookkeeping. He might be embarrassed to have her see how tight things were sometimes.

Lisbeth said, "I went with you to the haberdashery and got to see you with your wedding jacket and trousers and the new boots on, but you haven't seen my dress. Before you come up to the room, I would like to have time to put it on for you."

"I would see you in the morning after baths and clean-up. I didn't think I was supposed to see my bride before the wedding."

"That's rather difficult when we are sharing a room and bed, isn't it?"

"I suppose."

"Besides, you have something you want to do anyway."

"I do?"

"You want to see about that dog that's waiting on the boardwalk outside. Take him some scraps, talk to him."

He flushed noticeably. Tag had been following from stop to stop all day, and Rance had wangled some scraps from the restaurant owner for the dog at noon and planned to strike the Palace kitchen before he left. The woman was a mind reader. And she was emerging with new assertiveness since they made the marriage bargain. Maybe he should have thought about this a bit longer. Still, he rather enjoyed this new side of her he was see-ing. He had always warmed up to challenges. "Well, I had thought I might check on Tag. It's chilly out there tonight. I might see if I could put him up in a straw pile at the stable."

"That sounds like an excellent idea. I assume he will be coming home with us since he has a name."

Chapter 33

ISBETH SPREAD HER yellow dress out on the bed. She hoped Rance liked it. Strange that she was starting to care. She was a mature woman entering into a marriage that seemed more business agreement than romance, but ever since the seemingly reluctant proposal, she had begun to feel more like a teenage bride.

The dress was a simple cotton garment that would be functional for household wear after serving its initial purpose. It had puffy shoulders, which was the style, she had been told by the dress shop clerk, and the neckline swept low enough to reveal just the slightest cleavage between her small, but full, breasts. After she disrobed, Lisbeth put on the camisole, bloomers and white stockings and then wormed into the dress. She had rejected any notion of a corset, and the clerk had conceded that it would serve no purpose on her slender form. Finally, she eased her feet into the leather slippers she had selected for comfort, figuring her height did not necessitate the torture of high-heeled shoes.

Suddenly, she found she was trembling. It struck her that she was stepping onto an unmapped trail with the tall rancher, possibly too quickly. She had made an impulsive decision with her first marriage and descended into hell. Yet, she could not wish it had not happened, because she would never have known her diamonds, Morgan and Marissa. They had more than made the battle worth it. Sometimes, she guessed, life became a series of trade-offs.

She stood in front of the dresser mirror while she pulled back her hair and bound it with a yellow ribbon. She released her red mane and let it cascade over her shoulders. When she returned to the ranch, she would ask Tillie to give her a serious trim. She wished she had a pendant or necklace to accent her dress. Her mother's, the only one she had ever owned or worn, might still be recovered from the fire's rubble. She studied her face in the mirror. She supposed she would not be thought ugly. Just an ordinary woman. She felt silly now, though, with her plan to model the dress for her groom. Her giddiness was fading, and she wished she could hide someplace.

She started when she heard the two taps at the door. "It's okay. Come in."

Lisbeth swallowed hard and turned to face him. He closed the door behind him and set the bolt before he looked at her, and then he seemed to freeze, staring at her like she was an imposter in the room. "Did you find a place for the dog?" she asked.

"Uh, yeah. Stable boy will look after him. He sleeps there." He continued staring at her, while he took a few steps nearer. "You do know, don't you," he said, "that you are incredibly beautiful?"

"I fear you overstate. But I have never been told that by anyone other than my father before, and he was more or less obligated. It's kind of you to say so. Thank you."

"The dress is stunning. It's perfect."

She flushed. Carl had never spoken such words. "I'm glad you like it."

"I have a few things in my coat pocket. Just a minute." He shrugged out of the sheepskin jacket, laid it on the chair and began rummaging through the pockets. His fingers emerged with an unwrapped tiny box. "One box, two items," he said. He opened the box and plucked out a small gold band. "I almost forgot. Abe ran me down this morning. His lady friend, Martha, said he should be sure I had a ring. She knows men, I guess. I did not, so I went to the jewelry store and picked out a wedding band. The jeweler will let you exchange it, and he will size it since it likely won't fit."

"I hadn't thought about that, either. Shall I try it on?" she asked.

"Of course, but I have something else, too." He handed her the ring and drew a pendant and gold chain from the box, holding it up so she could see.

The gold pendant was circular in shape like a small coin, slightly more than an inch in diameter. While he held the chain, she took the pendant and held it closer. Clasped hands in sculpted relief appeared on the surface. "It's beautiful," she said, "I've never seen anything like it." She looked at him. "For me?"

"With a soon-to-be wife standing in front of me, it better not be for a lady friend. The hands represent ours. From now on we're riding the trail together, for better or for worse as the parson will probably say. I saw this, and I thought it made a nice symbol for what we're taking on. I hoped you would agree."

"I love it, and it is perfect. But the money . . ."

"Hush. Turn around and we'll see if I can put this around your neck. It's been a long while since I fought one of those darn clasps."

While he struggled with fastening the chain, she slipped the ring on her finger. It fit perfectly. She took that as a good omen.

"The ring should be fine. I'll give it back for tomorrow."

"Keep it on for tonight, so I don't lose it. You can give it to me in the morning, and then I'll give it to Abe, who will return it to me at the appropriate time. Seems silly, but we ought to keep a few traditions, I suppose." He moved back. "I think you're good on the chain."

She stepped to the mirror and stared at the face of the woman with the stunning pendant resting above her bosom. The plain woman she had seen earlier had disappeared. She was looking at a princess. She wiped the tears from the corners of her eyes before she turned back to Rance, stepped into his arms, pressed her body to his and held him tightly. She raised her face to his, and their lips met in a soft kiss that lit a raging fire.

She woke before sunrise, strangely comfortable with his naked form spooned up against hers. She was sated and relaxed from the frenzied lovemaking of the previous night. Rance had been gentle and patient and brought sensations to her that were totally foreign to her experience, and she had welcomed his second approach and, finally, third with enthusiasm. With Carl, she had merely tolerated intimacy, eventually hated it. She wondered if Rance was going to turn her into a shameless hussy.

Rance was still sleeping soundly, snoring very lightly, more like a cat's purr, which she found soothing. It was warm and cozy under the blankets with his flesh pressed to hers, but she knew the room was cold for neither had fed the fire during the night. She slipped away from Rance and slung her legs over the side of the bed. She was freezing, and the room was pitch-black. She would awaken him if she lit the kerosene lamp, so she could see to find some clothes. The fireplace was located a half dozen feet from his side of the bed and the firewood box was next to that. She inched her way around the foot of the bed and was relieved to find some hot coals still radiating in the fireplace.

She reached into the firewood box, felt for some smaller logs and laid three on the coals to see if they would ignite. She turned away to start back to the bed when her toe caught on the chair, toppling it over and launching her backward so that she lost her balance and dropped to the hard oak floor, landing on her butt.

"What the hell?" Rance said. "Lisbeth. Are you all right?"

She could hear his feet hit the floor and saw a flicker of light when he lit the lamp on his bedside table. She was still lying on the floor when the light came up.

"I was trying not to wake you up," Lisbeth said, wondering if she looked as ridiculous as she felt, sprawled naked on the floor.

"You were not successful."

Rance sat on the edge of the bed looking at her and smiling. She somehow did not feel the least self-conscious but wished her pose could have been more dignified. She started to get up but struggled like a turtle on its back. Rance was quickly on his feet and reached down. She grasped his hand, and he pulled her to her feet and into his arms.

"You are laughing at me," Lisbeth said.

"Are you hurt?"

"My pride and my butt."

He continued to hold her, and she found the room heating quickly, not entirely because of the fire.

"We broke the agreement," Rance said.

"What are you talking about?"

"We made an agreement that last night would not happen till after we were married."

"Oh, I forgot. Well, there is nothing we can do about it, I guess. You were the lawyer. Couldn't we amend the agreement or something?"

"Well, I guess, since neither of us can claim damages, we could amend it retroactively. In legalese, we would call that an addendum."

"Consider it done. And now that we're not breaching a contract . . ."

Chapter 34

RANCE HAD FOUND Lisbeth an attractive woman from the first time he met her when he and Ben Rice were doing the boundary line fencing. And living in proximity as they had been, few men would have been oblivious to her lithe, womanly figure. But this day as they were pronounced husband and wife, he appreciated that he had not only found a good teammate but been endowed with the bonus of one who was beyond mere attractive.

After they kissed, Reverend Locke, a tall, serious man who had been nothing but kind and accommodating, led the wedding party into the former saloon's curtained-off social room where they were greeted by a small wedding cake, a tray of sandwiches and several side dishes.

Abe Steele, gussied up in a suit and shined boots, said, "This is Martha's doings. She thought it would be time to eat when we finished here and that we should have something special, even if there's just the five of us."

"It's wonderful," Lisbeth said, turning to Martha Bridger and hugging her. "Thank you so much."

Martha, a pretty, white-haired lady with a figure that might be called matronly, said, "It is truly my pleasure. You are a lovely couple. Abe has told me all about you, and I wish you both much happiness. And I hope you will both think of me as a friend you can count on. Now, I must get the coffee from the cookstove." She slipped away, and Rance saw Abe Steele's eyes following her. The old devil had it bad.

Rance and Lisbeth had only met Martha briefly before the ceremony when she appeared through the curtain to the social room, where unbeknownst to the couple, she had been setting out the lunch she had prepared earlier. She seemed a polished lady where social amenities were concerned and very warm and kind. Abe was somewhat on the rough side, but there seemed to be genuine affection between the two. He hoped a romance bloomed.

Rance and Lisbeth did the ceremonial cake slicing together and then the group sat down and enjoyed lunch and conversation. Rance enjoyed chatting with Reverend Locke, a man he estimated to be in his early forties, who had previously been a circuit rider for some fifteen years and whose roots were in Manhattan, Kansas near Fort Riley, where Rance had been stationed briefly for cavalry training.

He learned that the man's father and three siblings, one a sister in Wyoming, were lawyers and that another brother was a veterinarian with a physician's license. An interesting family, he thought. The pastor had not visited since 1866, a year following the war. There were a lot of people like that in the West. Many never saw their families again before they died. Perhaps the growing web of railroad lines would change that. He no longer had an excuse himself for not visiting the graves of those he had left behind in Missouri.

Martha sat on the other side of Lisbeth, and Rance could see they were on the way to becoming fast friends. He was quickly learning that Lisbeth was not as shy and quiet as he first judged her to be. Perhaps it was her justified distrust of males that had made her seem reticent to speak sometimes. She had certainly started to open up with him since his clumsy marriage proposal. He hoped that a time would come when he could truthfully say the words she probably wanted to hear—and hear them back.

The pastor slid his chair back from the table and stood. "I hope you will excuse me," he said. "I must make some home visits this afternoon. It has been a true pleasure for me to be a part of this occasion." He pushed an envelope across the table to Rance. "Your certificate of marriage. I will see that certification is filed with the County Court Clerk. May God bless your union."

Rance had pressed a ten-dollar eagle into the man's palm following the ceremony, and he had started to protest when Rance said, "I insist. We are not a part of your congregation, and you did this with little notice and great dignity." The sum was likely a fortune to the man who would have been glad for a dollar and was likely paid out of the meager offerings found in the collection plate.

After the preacher left, Sheriff Steele spoke. "Party's done, folks. Rance, Lisbeth, I've been holding back some news I got before I came over. I know you hoped to spend a few more days in North Platte, but Hubert at the telegraph office dropped off a telegram from the Cheyenne sheriff. He thought I might want to know a big snowstorm is moving down from the Rockies. You know what that means about two days from now."

Rance knew. The last thing he needed was to get trapped in North Platte by a snowstorm. A bad one would be a threat to his herd. He hated to disappoint Lisbeth.

Lisbeth said, "The mules are rested. We should leave this afternoon. Get on our way even if it's dark before we finish our business here. The supplies from the general store have been ordered. All we have to do is stop by and have them loaded. I need to talk to the livestock agent."

Rance said, "We can go from here to the lawyer's office and see if the paperwork is ready to sign. He said we would get priority, but Asa thought he had another day or two. And you had lumber and building supplies to buy yet."

"No. Nothing urgent. I've been thinking. With a few mules, we could drop that rickety barn at my place, and I can salvage all the lumber I need. There will be plenty left over to make a good start on that house you want to build. There is nothing wrong with the lumber. The craftsmanship was the problem. Besides, we need to lighten our load if we are going to outrun a snowstorm. That lumber would have been two-thirds of our weight."

Something about her response made Rance think of the clasped hands relief on the pedant she wore.

"You sound like you are going to pull out," the sheriff said. "Stop by the office and pick up a badge for your extra deputy. Send word to me when you can. If you need me, I'll see if I can round up a few more men and head up your way."

"Not likely till spring, but I won't hesitate. If there is a confrontation, Print Olive has too many gunfighters to take on alone."

Martha Bridger said, "I will clean up here and package up the leftover cake and sandwiches for you to take with you. You can pick these up at my shop. I have a box of pastries to send with you, too, that you can share with the children."

Lisbeth gave Martha and Abe hugs, and Rance offered Martha a quick embrace and gave Abe a firm handshake. The newlyweds then left to prepare for their departure.

Chapter 35

THE BUCKBOARD CLATTERED up the bumpy road that would eventually take the Coldsmiths and their cargo to a turnoff to a trail that would angle toward the Rising Sun Ranch. Darkness was dropping over them, but the sky was clear and star spangled. North Platte was nearly ten miles behind them. They had pulled out of town late afternoon with a load that rose well above the wagon's sideboards and was covered with canvas tarps and anchored with rope tied with diamond hitches that held the cargo snugly. On top lay the sleeping Australian Shepherd that had joined the family.

Tag had required no coaxing to join the expedition. The dog had stuck fast to his adopted humans as they made their rounds and loaded for departure and had jumped onto the back of the wagon and scrambled to the top of the load as soon as it was anchored. Rance suspected that the dog was not a stranger to a wagon.

It felt like the loaded wagon was moving at a snail's pace, and he knew their return journey would likely take at least a half day longer than the trip to North Platte, and they had been in no rush then. Lisbeth had a buffalo robe tugged about her and had fallen asleep an hour earlier with her head propped against his shoulder. He did not mind a bit. It was a good feeling, and he liked the ease with which they were adapting to the new relationship. After last night's lovemaking, he had looked forward to a few extra nights at the hotel. He had thought it fantasy that they might be such a match beneath the covers. By the hour he was feeling better about the bargain he had made with this woman.

He kept his eyes alert for a place to pull off the trail. The mules needed to rest, and he was feeling the weight of a frantic day himself. A stiff northwest wind had come up the past few hours, and he hoped to find a clearing with tree and brush windbreak along Little Sandy Creek, a spring-fed watercourse that emerged from the Sandhills and eventually emptied into the Platte River. The Sandhills dunes in this vicinity might offer some protection from a ravaging wind, but he worried about drifting at the hollows between dunes where they would be traveling.

An hour later, he saw traces of a wagon trail that turned off into some wooded areas along the creek. He reined the mules to a stop, and Lisbeth lifted her head. She looked at him with confusion. "I guess I dropped off."

"Yep. That's all right. You're entitled to be tired. And I am, too. We are going to stop and rest all of us. The mules need a break, too." He handed her the reins. "Can you hold them steady while I check and see if this trail leads to where I think it does?"

"Of course."

Rance climbed down from the wagon and followed the wagon tracks into the trees. He came to a clearing that at least offered thick north cover and was bordered on the south by the shallow, slow-rolling creek, where most of the timber had been harvested. He could tie the mules where they could reach the creek's edge for water and graze on the dry grass on the upper banks. They had a barrel of corn and could offer the animals a dab of grain as well. The remains of other fires indicated that other travelers had claimed this spot in months past.

Later, after pulling the wagon into the clearing and staking out the mules, they started a fire for coffee and some added warmth. While Lisbeth brewed the coffee to go with Martha's sandwiches and cake, Rance dug out the unused canvas tarp and tied it so it dropped below the wagon bed and formed a wall on one side. He retrieved the two bedrolls and hesitated before rolling them out.

"They should be rolled out together," Lisbeth said. "One on bottom, one on top. Let me put my buffalo robe down first. We can save the other to spread over us if we get too cold. I don't think we'll want to sleep naked, though, or not for long."

He looked at the woman standing next to the fire bundled in her mackinaw, those long legs encased snugly in her new blue jeans. He hoped "not for long" meant what he thought it might. An hour later, under the blankets he got confirmation. Tag whined all the while, though, until he was finally allowed to crawl under the blankets on Rance's side and curl up against his new master's back.

Lisbeth pressed her lips to Rance's with a goodnight kiss that left him wanting more of her. Then she whispered in his ear. "There is not room for both me and the dog in bed when we get home. You will have to choose."

"I have chosen. You win by a dog's hair."

"Not too flattering but good enough." She rolled over and snuggled up against him.

Rance rolled out of the tangled blankets well before sunrise. He started the fire for coffee before he stepped into the woods to relieve himself. When he reentered the campsite, he saw Lisbeth sitting on the bedrolls pulling on her boots. "Me next. Then I'll do coffee if you want to dig out Martha's sweet rolls."

"Temperature has dropped and the wind's not letting up," Rance said. "I don't like this. I'm betting we aren't going to see the sun come up this morning. We have just got to keep moving."

Chapter 36

PRINT OLIVE GLARED at Muskrat Webb, who sat on a bunkhouse bed facing his employer positioned on the opposite bunk. Webb's eyes darted nervously, and he looked like a man who feared his end was coming. He was lucky. Olive was not in the mood for another killing today, but Webb was far from out of the woods on this fiasco. Deacon Scruggs claimed that Webb was the best wrangler on the ranch and could work magic with a horse and rope, and a good scare would either keep him around with his mouth shut or send him packing far enough away that he would not pose a threat. Your men became wary when a man began to execute his own. He had learned that the hard way in Texas many years back when such a killing had triggered near mutiny.

"Muskrat, you claim Coldsmith and some other guy sneaked up on you and Vasquez while you were watching the Coldsmith place. You didn't see the other guy?"

"Well, I didn't get a good look at him. A small feller. Probably the guy that rode with him from the Tufts place before they split, and he took a trail upriver. Guessing he's a neighbor or something. Dark like Ramiro. Injun or Mexican, I'd guess."

Olive said, "Vasquez wasn't backshot. The shooter had to be facing him." Olive knew the man was lying, making the story up as he went. The men had likely been bored by the watch and abandoned their prey for a spell. Not that it mattered much if they had been spotted anyhow. Olive just enjoyed being the cat playing with the mouse.

"Well, maybe that other feller weren't behind us. There was trees all around us, and he could have been in front of us, hiding out someplace. It all happened so damn fast that I can't be sure. I can say this, though. Coldsmith told me to take Vasquez back here and to tell you he was gathering evidence and was going to bring Wollenberg's and Snyder's killers to justice and that he would be seeing you again soon."

Sounded like a threat, Olive thought. Coldsmith was bluffing, trying to draw him out. He had dealt with tougher snakes than the so-called deputy in his time.

Still, the man bore watching, and if he got too close, this snake's head might need to be cut off. The more he thought about it, the more inclined he was to kill the snake.

"Okay, Muskrat, get some rest. It'll be suppertime in a few hours. Be at the chuck house when the bell rings." He stood and walked out of the bunkhouse with Kelly following. Scruggs joined them outside where he had been shooing hands away from the door until Olive was finished.

The three strolled to the stable where Muskrat Webb had left Vasquez tied over the back of his horse. When they stepped inside and escaped the cold wind, Oliver said, "Deacon, after we've talked, I would like you to get two of the hands to bury Vasquez. I showed you where I wanted to put a cemetery. He can have the honor of first occupancy. With the ground frozen and the wind like this, it will be a nasty job. Tell the burial crew they can divide up Vasquez's tack and other belongings betwixt them. I'll throw a hundred dollars in the pot for the horse."

"No trouble getting volunteers for that kind of loot. Of course, the horse is worth twice that," Scruggs observed.

"I'm entitled to that for all the nuisance this guy caused me for a bungled job. Now, we need to talk a bit about Coldsmith."

"What's to talk about? Just stay out of his way."

"I would if he'd stay out of mine. You heard what Muskrat said. The man was letting me know he's coming after me sooner or later. He doesn't seem like the type that doesn't back up his words."

Scruggs said, "Print, you came to Nebraska for a fresh start. You're headed back to doing business Texas style, helping yourself to other folks' cattle, lynch law and such. I ain't bothered so much about using a rope on a man that rustles cattle, but I don't think Snyder and Wollenberg rustled any Olive stock. I'm thinking some of your cows just joined theirs out on public range. I'm hoping you didn't have some of the boys drive a few of your cows in with theirs."

Olive's temper surged. "Are you accusing me of setting those men up?"

"Ain't accusing. Just worrying. We been together a long time, Print. You're my friend, but I was ready to pull out before the move north. You promised things would be different here. So far, I ain't seen it. I'll leave if you give the word. Otherwise, I'll hang on and see how it goes from here."

Olive could not explain why, but he did not want Scruggs to leave. The man spoke his mind to the point of downright aggravation, but he needed him. Both

Scruggs and Kelly had an inexplicable hold on him, a certain competence and blunt honesty in dealing with him that he had never found in other men. Kelly's loyalty so far had been unflinching. Scruggs's backing had always been more conditional, but he could count on Scruggs to tell him outright if he was moving on. He would not run out in the middle of a crisis. Olive said, "I pay you twice what you would get anyplace else."

Scruggs said, "Maybe. It ain't all about money. You wouldn't understand this, Print, but some folks have a conscience. I don't got much of one, but what little I do has been about stretched to bursting."

Olive turned to Jim Kelly. As usual, the black man's face betrayed nothing. "What you got to say, Jim?"

"Nothing. Not now. Except I'm wishing I hadn't watched you hang those young men. We should have taken them to the law and let somebody else sort it out."

"Damn, are you turning rabbit on me too?"

"No plans to go anyplace."

Olive had already decided Rance Coldsmith was a dead man, but he would be patient. He also harbored doubts that Deacon or Jim Kelly would be party to killing a lawman.

Chapter 37

RANCE DROVE THE mule team back onto the wagon trail and headed the critters toward home. The snow had not moved in yet, but the gray sky in the west told him the white stuff was no more than three hours away. The question was how much? He hoped most of the snow had been dumped on the Rocky Mountains and that they were on the end of a storm that was sputtering out.

Rance figured that if a snowstorm did not slow them, they could reach home with one more night on the trail and a long day tomorrow. They would need to find a place for the night where they would not risk being snowed in. He thought of Beaver Creek that snaked through the hills mostly on public lands. The Sandhills encroached into this area and were still cloaked with enough dry grass for the mules, but trees and the firewood they produced were hard to come by. The creek, however, was lined with a fair number of cottonwoods and willows, not the best of fire-building woods but better than nothing. And, of course, the destination offered water for the mules.

He tossed a look at Lisbeth, who already had her gaze fixed on him. Her nose and cheeks were near scarlet from the wind's bite, but she had been silent and uncomplaining about the nasty turn in the weather. It occurred to him that she rarely complained about anything. "Do you want me to get the other buffalo robe out?" he asked.

She had surrendered to Tag the robe she usually kept under the wagon seat. He had crept off the mound formed by the load and moved to the wagon front where the cargo tapered off behind the seat and wedged into a spot that formed a windbreak. An added benefit to man and beast was that Rance could reach back and stroke the dog's head from time to time.

Lisbeth said, "Not now. I will say something if I need it. We should be warming each other some." She scooted over and snuggled up against him. "We are married now," she said. "I hope you have not forgotten."

He smiled. "How could I forget with this memorable honeymoon we're having."

"Don't be sarcastic. I am with you, and you are not my brother anymore. I much prefer you as a husband—so far, anyhow. It resolves a lot of ambiguities for us both."

He was not sure what that meant but replied, "At least we have a road map of sorts now, but you are a woman of surprises, and I've got a hunch we will be redrawing the plan from time to time."

"I hope to never bore you. I have no worry that you will ever bore me. I think we will have a great adventure together."

"You are a good woman, Lisbeth. I consider myself a lucky man."

"Well, Rance, hang onto your luck. It's starting to spit snow."

"Let's hope that's all the snow we get."

At first, Rance thought that, indeed, his luck was holding. The skies were offering no more than a dusting of snow, and until several hours past noon did not slow the wagon's pace. Then the wind turned from nasty to outright vicious. He pulled his stocking cap as far down on his head as he could without blocking his eyesight, and he noticed that Lisbeth's head had disappeared under the hood of her mackinaw like a turtle in its shell. A glance over his shoulder revealed that Tag had dug his way under the thick buffalo robe.

When the dump of heavy snowflakes started and the wind began forming drifts over the hilly landscape, the terrain became less familiar, but so far, the wind was sweeping the trail clean. They had made good time till now, and he figured they should be only two or three hours from Beaver Creek.

An hour later, the wind and snow were not so kind. What had been a white carpet on the trail was now deepening into a twisted feather bed that obscured the roadway and blended into the roadsides, which at some places included dry washes and gullies. If a wagon wheel slipped off the trail's edge the buckboard could at worst tip over and at best be stuck for days.

He reined the mules to a stop and turned to Lisbeth, "Can you handle the mule team?"

She shrugged. "I'm not an expert mule skinner, but I have driven a team on occasion. Usually, it has been a single. Tell me what you want."

"You don't have to guide the mules. Just hold the reins steady. If I yell 'stop,' pull the reins tight."

"And where will you be?"

"I'll be up front. I've got a lead rope in the wagon box. I'll hitch it to the mules and lead them up the trail, test the footing as I walk to be certain we're staying with the ruts."

"How long to the creek?"

"I'm not sure where we're at. Can't see a damn thing with this white curtain in front of us. I'm hoping we can make it in two hours."

Rance no sooner hit the ground than Tag dropped into the snow beside him, staying at his heels as he tied and balanced the rope on the mules' nose bands, hoping the animals would not turn stubborn at the change in routine. He started back up the trail, testing the footing with his feet to confirm they were remaining between the ruts. Then he noticed that Tag had bounced ahead, and when he stepped in the dog's tracks, he was following the center of the hidden trail. Surely the dog did not understand what they were trying to do. Maybe it was a game. Regardless, once he gained confidence in the dog's course, it enabled him to nearly double his speed.

As the snow piled up, the questions were how much longer he would be able to trudge through the drifts and whether the mules could last. He could tell they were wearing down, but what choice did he have? If they stopped here, they would all freeze in place. He signaled a stop to Lisbeth and called to Tag, who reacted to the call and turned. Rance assumed the dog did not yet know his name and likely judged the tone of his new master's voice.

His eyes surveyed the area, looking for a familiar landmark somewhere behind the sheet of white. Then he saw the tree line, snow covered but barely visible winding along what had to be Beaver Creek. The shaky, log bridge should not be far ahead, less than fifty yards, he guessed. They would stop within sight of the bridge, so they could find their abandoned wagon by following the creek.

He walked back to Lisbeth. "The creek is just ahead. There is a gentle slope off the trail to the creek. We're going to try to get closer to the bridge. Then I am going to unhitch the mules. We will leave the wagon on the trail and keep it covered. We need to find the extra canvas tarps and get the buffalo robes and bedrolls together. We still have some sandwiches and cake Martha sent. We will for sure need coffee. It would help if you would think about what might come in handy and try to dig it out. Just stay with the wagon, and I'll take the mules down and find a place to hole up. There is an old campsite on this side of the river if I can find it. And my axe. I will need my axe."

"Let's move," she said, "before we get stuck here."

She was right. They did not need to get the wheels locked in the ice and snow. He returned to his lead rope, and soon the bridge was in sight. After unhitching the mules, he led them down the slope. Tag started to follow, but Rance commanded, "Stay." Darned if the dog did not obey. Somebody had trained him.

He followed the tree line and soon found the old campsite where the creek made a sharp turn west. Around the bend, they would find some shelter from the north wind and a pocket with trees and thick brush on most of three sides with the open side to the south. There was ample room for the mules within the area, and they already appeared to be welcoming the windbreak. He would bring them some shelled corn and clear some of the snow away later, so that the critters could get to the dry grass. With the mules tied, he headed back to the buckboard.

When he reached the wagon, he found that Lisbeth already had the necessities organized. They took what they could and trudged back to the campsite. Lisbeth started a search for firewood, while Rance returned to the buckboard to retrieve the remaining supplies.

Later, with a fire to retreat to for warmth, Rance cut poles for a shelter, and the two fashioned a crude tent by draping one of the canvas tarps over a ridge pole lodged in two forked end posts reaching no more than three feet from the ground. They would not be able to stand or even sit in the structure, but it would offer protection from the wind and snow which most would now call a bona fide blizzard. After brushing as much snow as possible out of the tent site, they stretched the remaining tarp out for a floor and laid the buffalo robes over that before they spread out their bedrolls into a double bed.

After tending to the mules, Rance returned to the fire to find a hot pot of coffee, with Martha's sandwiches and a big slice of wedding cake, sitting on one of the flat stones that formed a fire ring. It occurred to Rance that he was as hungry as he was cold. "You are a mind reader," Rance said, when he sat down next to Lisbeth on the old log he had drug in and rolled next to the fire for a bench. "I'm starving."

"It has nothing to do with mind reading. I was listening to my own stomach."

Rance leaned forward and plucked two sandwiches off a tin plate and placed one on the log beside him, which Tag, sitting on the ground next to his thigh, immediately closed his teeth on. The other he handed to Lisbeth before reaching for another.

Lisbeth said, "I could be jealous, you know."

"What do you mean?"

"The dog was served first."

"Oh, well, you see . . ."

"While you struggle for your explanation, I will pour you a cup of coffee. I already had a cup earlier—hoping I can get rid of it before bedtime. I don't want to crawl out in this to pee in the middle of the night. I swear I would wet my britches first."

"Uh, maybe we should go for separate bedrolls tonight."

"Nope. Remember the clasped hands? We're in this together."

Later, they snuggled together beneath the blankets in the makeshift tent, man, woman and dog. Fully clothed, they were warm enough, and near exhaustion assured that sleep would claim them easily.

When he woke the next morning, Rance smelled smoke, and then the luring aroma of biscuits and bacon wafted through the tent opening. He reached out for Lisbeth. She was gone, and Tag had abandoned him, too. When he crawled out into the deep snow outside, he was blinded for a moment by sunrays peeking over the eastern horizon and sifting through the trees. The tree branches were utterly still.

He turned his head toward Lisbeth who was standing by the fire. "When did you get up?"

"And good morning to you, too. An hour or so ago. It was the coffee's fault. Since I was up, I went back to the wagon and got some bacon and flour and fixings for cinnamon biscuits. We brought the Dutch oven over last night but had nothing to put in it."

"You should have got me up," Rance said. "I don't expect to be waited on like this."

"Don't worry. I won't make a habit of it. You were sleeping so soundly, and I had to get up anyway, so I figured I would start the fire and get breakfast ready. We need to get started. I want to be home by nightfall."

Home. Yeah, it looked like he might be able to make a real home with this woman. "What's the wagon trail look like?"

"Unless it is worse up ahead, it looks passable. The wind must have shifted some, because a lot of it is swept down to an inch or two, and the drifting does not amount to much and doesn't cover the trail, for as far as I can see anyhow."

"Well, let me tend to my business, and then we will eat and start packing up. I would sure like to be home by nightfall, too."

Chapter 38

Late February 1878

S OME DAYS, LISBETH felt she was trying to escape from the middle of a Texas tornado. And she loved it. She loved her life here in the Sandhills, teaching at the school a few days a week, preparing for the eight bred Hampshire gilts that would arrive in North Platte the end of March, and helping Rance with cattle when he needed her. She even loved cooking and baking more than she ever had. She loved those moments during the night after the children were asleep when they could quietly make love while she surrendered to a side of herself that had been a stranger before this cowman entered her life. Most of all, she loved Rance Coldsmith, but, of course, she had not told him so. She dared not risk disturbing this marriage of business and convenience by making him uneasy by such a declaration.

She had learned that Rance was a sensitive man, and she feared he would be troubled by a declaration of love that he could not reciprocate. She had come to terms with that. He was a kind and gentle man and so good with the children. When informed of the pending adoption, Morgan had been ecstatic and took on the Coldsmith name immediately. Marissa was fine with it all but did not seem to grasp all the fuss made by her brother.

She was starting supper, simple fare as usual, a beef and vegetable stew to be poured over fresh biscuits. Leftover cobbler from the last of Tillie's canned apples. She did not expect Rance till later, so she would feed the children and eat with him when he came in.

Rance was riding the range heading north to the public lands and deeper into the Sandhills with Jake Rice, who had been working for Rance with some frequency lately. Tillie thought it wonderful because Ben and Jake fussed and quarreled so much anymore. Besides, fourteen-year-old twins, Matthew and Mark, were capable of doing more of the farm work. Luke was twelve, and John was ten, so Ben had ample labor reserves.

Calving season would start in a few weeks. A few early calves had dropped already. Rance and Jake would be riding out more frequently to check on the cows, hoping to help with calving problems or to bring in an orphan to care for in the barn, if necessary. He had promised Morgan the boy could ride with him on days he was not in school. Lisbeth had added a proviso. The rides would terminate if school projects were not up to snuff or turned in late. Morgan had rolled his eyes at Rance, as if to say, "This is what I have to put up with."

She was anxious to talk to Rance. A representative of a lumberyard out of Plum Creek had stopped by today, trying to sell products and services that were of special interest to folks who lived in sod houses which included most of the rural residents in the vicinity. Rance had planned on a stone house, possibly limestone, but he had learned that the limited limestone available on their land was not good building quality. The cost of shipping stone to their area like Arch Tufts had was just too expensive. The young salesman, Fremont Johnson, had offered lumber bargains and another product that she and Tillie thought might interest their husbands.

Later, after the children were fed, she began her nightly fret. Rance was not returning to the house till after dark lately, and somehow that always made her uneasy. It was not yet eight o'clock, but every fifteen minutes or so she found herself checking the window that allowed a view in the barn's direction to see if he had arrived. Fortunately, tonight he was early, and she got a glimpse of him entering the barn.

She began heating up their supper on the cookstove, buoyed by his appearance. She still had not got accustomed to feeling so happy about the return of her mate. It had never been this way with Carl, only tension and fear that he might be in a foul mood and take it out on her and the children. Morgan and Marissa had learned to hide or keep their distance from their father until they were able to gauge his temperament, which was never joyous.

The door opened, and Rance walked in with a warm smile on his face, Tag at his side. Before he even removed his hat and coat, Marissa leaped into his arms and Morgan was at his side. Marissa kissed him on the cheek, "I'm glad you're home, Daddy," she said.

"Me, too," Morgan said. "Mom said no chess tonight. She wants to talk to you."

"Oh, that sounds ominous."

"Ominous?"

"Sort of like scary. Maybe more threatening, like a mountain lion waiting to pounce on you."

"You might have to write the word down. Missus Rice says we are supposed to bring a new word with us to school tomorrow."

"I'll do that. And maybe we can do a few games of checkers. That won't take so long. And Marissa can help me. She's catching on to that game and should be whipping you in another month or two."

"Huh. More like never."

He put Marissa down and turned to Lisbeth. "Howdy, Missus Coldsmith." He walked over, wrapped his arms about her and gave her a kiss that sent tingles down her spine.

"Howdy back, Mister Coldsmith. That kiss means either that you're wanting more than a kiss or you're softening me up for news that you've got."

"Could be both. But it will have to wait. I'm hungry as a horse, and it sure smells good in here."

"Just think of me as a mountain lion."

"What?"

"Ready to pounce. Never mind. Let's eat and then you can do your checkers. I told Morg 'no chess tonight,' so I guess I wasn't technically overruled. I need to choose my words carefully. I forgot you were a law wrangler once. I've got a bowl of scraps for your partner."

"Delicious," he said, as they ate at the table. "As usual."

"Flattery will get you everywhere," she said. He flushed a bit. She loved to tease him. In many ways he was still a boy around her, not quite knowing how to react to things she said.

"Why don't you tell me about your day? You seem in a good mood."

"Have you ever seen me in a bad mood?"

"Yes. But not too often. You seem to take life in stride. You are an amazing woman."

She was starting to get suspicious now. His behavior was a good step beyond seduction. "Well, Tillie and I were visited today by a Mister Fremont Johnson of the Plum Creek Lumber and Supply."

"And?"

"They are oversupplied with lumber right now, and they are bringing prices down to five per cent above cost with free delivery."

"Sounds interesting. I've pretty much given up on a stone house."

She reached into a pile of papers at the end of the table and plucked out two sheets. "He left me a drawing of what he called a traditional two story." She placed one of the sheets in front of him. "Three bedrooms upstairs, large enough to double up if we had more children."

"You said you didn't think you could conceive."

"Because nothing ever happened after Marissa. But just in case. Either way, I would like for Marissa and

Morgan to have separate rooms if we are going build a house. As you can see, there would be a nice, roomy kitchen and a parlor with a big stone fireplace. I thought the other room off the parlor could be an office and library. There would be room for side-by-side desks and a wall for bookcases or other shelving. It's very simple. The only luxury would be the veranda, which would go along the entire front and then wrap halfway around one side. That's optional, but I thought it would make the house a little different."

"I like that. Of course, my original thought was a single-story house."

"It's cheaper to build up, Mister Johnson pointed out. Half the roof span, less foundation."

"Makes sense. Regardless, this will be a mansion in comparison to where we are living. I want to get you and the kids out of here."

"Rance?"

"Yes."

"I want you to know I have never been happier anyplace in my life than I have during the time I've been with you in this dugout. I would willingly live out my years here if need be." She thought she could have easily added that it is who you are with not where you live that is important. Another time, perhaps.

Ron Schwab

"I'm glad you feel that way. Let me see the materials list."

She handed him the other sheet. "While you study this, I'll put the kids to bed."

When she returned and sat down, she noticed his wrinkled brow. "Something wrong?"

"No, I am just sorting everything out. The materials are about half of what I figured—$2850. Then, you have something for building crew for $2300. That's not much over five thousand dollars. Tell me about this crew."

"Tillie and I figured that it would take you and Ben years to finish two houses trying to pick up what local help you could get after harvests or roundups. And your time is more valuable doing your other work. The building crew is employed by Plum Creek Lumber. They would send four men out to put up both houses. The cost is less because they could set up a wagon camp and complete two jobs without moving. We would have to do all the painting and inside finish work. Ben would build cabinets and the like—we would pay him for ours. I can do bookcases and simple furnishings. Jake is handy, too, so we could hire him for house interior work or painting when you don't need him for the cow herd. Of course, I might try to turn him into a hog man."

"Whoa. Okay, okay. Poor Ben. You women have laid your traps well. I'll bet Tillie's got him hogtied already."

"I'm pushing too much, aren't I? Papa said I need to cut down my bossiness. Carl called me a 'bossy bitch' more than once."

Rance said, "The figures are way under loan approval amount."

"Yes. I thought you would like that."

"Do it."

She could not believe what she was hearing. She had been prepared for an evening's discussion. There would have been no real argument on her part. Rance had brought up the idea of a house. "You mean go ahead with the building?"

"Yes. Do it. But I'm getting into calving season. If you want to get this going while the weather's decent, I'll have to look to you to handle the details. You know where I want the place. That's the only thing that is important to me. I'll do what I need to, but I'm leaving the arrangements up to you, if you are willing to take the project on. I trust you."

"Okay. I'll do it. I will talk to Tillie in the morning and see what Ben said. If they aren't building, I will have to negotiate a new building crew figure, I suspect."

Rance said, "I would bet that Ben has already surrendered. Besides, the wily devil will know this is a great opportunity. Now, I'd better tell you what I'm up to."

She did not feel she had veto rights over anything Rance did. "I am listening."

"Do you know Olaf Iverson? Most call him 'Ole.'"

"I have never met him, but I saw him once in the yard at our place talking to Carl. Doesn't he own some land adjacent to yours on the north?"

"Yes, he owns a half section. He homesteaded a quarter and bought the other quarter for next to nothing from a fellow who starved out."

She could already guess where this was leading. "Would I lose if I bet Mister Iverson is wanting to sell the land?"

"You are always a step ahead of me. You have a knack for beating me to the end of the story. Yeah. Ten dollars an acre for the entire 320 acres. He says he wants to go someplace where the land is meant to be farmed. This is cow country. You can't farm these hills. Ole said he could farm more off forty acres of river bottom someplace than he can out here. Of course, a lot of folks have already discovered that. If I buy, he and his wife will take what they can get in the wagon and head for his brother's place in the eastern part of the state. His brother has located several small parcels with tabletop land that are up for sale."

"You get more land, and you will need more cattle."

"Well, that's true enough, but we can graze the place with our existing herd this year and hold back more heifers for future breeding. Anyway, I can put together some money and borrow a bit more if need be. Ole said I could make up an agreement to bind the deal and that we could take care of the money and paperwork by mail and wire. He just wants to get out of here."

"Will you ever have enough land?"

"I only want what's next to me."

She wondered if there would come a time when they would butt heads on that question. More land meant more debt, more cows, more work. She had already concluded, though, that this man was not one who would die in a rocker on the nice veranda they would soon have. She suspected she was not cut out for that life, either, so perhaps she should just set those worries aside.

Lisbeth said, "There is something else I wanted to tell you about."

"Okay."

"Fremont Johnson was selling something else that you might want to think about." She was already beyond the thinking stage. She was going to press on this one. "He has new self-regulating windmills for sale."

Rance's eyes told her she already had him nibbling at the hook.

"I've heard of such a thing. The blades rotate with the wind, so you don't have to reset to catch it. I would love to have a windmill of any kind, but this would be perfect. Water isn't a problem in our neighborhood. Our water well that the pump is connected to doesn't go very deep."

Lisbeth said, "A single windmill, including installation, costs three hundred dollars. Three would cost $250 each. Tillie says they would take one. I feared I was going spend most of my time carrying water in buckets from the pump outside the soddy to the new house and the hog lots. I would pay for that one. We would need a new well by the house anyway, I assume. This is a godsend, and the timing is perfect."

"Our grasslands have ample springs and creeks, so I'm not worried about the cattle. It might be nice to have a backup, though. I could put one up on the Iverson place and have a tank there. That would make the three for the special price."

"Young Mister Johnson will be dropping back this way in a few days before he heads back to Plum Creek. We need to be ready to place our orders then."

"You know, Lisbeth, you've got my head spinning with all this. Things are happening here. I have a feeling I won't be sleeping tonight."

She reached across the table and placed her hand on his. "Maybe I can help." She winked, and he looked at her and shook his head in disbelief and smiled. "Missus Coldsmith, you can be a naughty lady sometimes."

Chapter 39

July 1878

PRINT OLIVE WAS enraged at the news Deacon Scruggs brought to his home in Plum Creek, which was unofficially dubbed "Olive Town" since he had acquired three-fourths of the properties there and owned the law and others who ran the town. His herds grazed from the South Loup to the Middle Loup rivers. He still maintained line shacks near the Dismal River to the northwest where he pastured smaller herds during spring and summer. He increasingly found himself spending more time in Plum Creek, however, managing the business in more luxurious surroundings.

"You say Coldsmith and that redskin deputy have been snooping about the Wollenberg and Snyder places again?"

"Yep, and Coldsmith visited the log house where the Custer County Clerk keeps the land records. He took down the notary public's name on the Wollenberg deed. That lawyer you hired ain't got a backbone. You can bet he's confessed by now that he didn't see Wollenberg sign the deed. Turns out, too, that Wollenberg was dead on the day he supposedly signed the deed. You wasn't thinking straight when you took the deed to the shyster to notarize. I suppose you signed Wolleberg's name yourself. I'll bet they are looking for papers with Wollenberg's signature on it to compare."

Olive said, "Where's Moon Tilford?"

"He's up at the Dismal outpost."

"Send somebody for him."

"Print, you're crossing a line if you go after the law. No turning back if you do harm to a lawman."

"Who said I was going to do him harm? Just get Tilford down here. I'm leaving you and Jim Kelly out of this."

"I'll send somebody for Moon."

When Deacon Scruggs left, Print Olive began pacing the parlor floor. Enough of Coldsmith, he thought. He would get the word out that the deputy's herd was fair game, and one day soon the nuisance would be eliminated.

Chapter 40

RANCE, MORGAN AND Tag sat by a spring-fed stream that snaked its way through the former Iverson land. From their spot above the farmstead, they could see blades of the new windmill turning at the tower's peak, pumping the water into the stock tank that cattle had already discovered and preferred when grazing in the vicinity. The windmill was also a convenience for the new resident of the soddy there.

Jake Rice had moved from his parents' home several months earlier and asked to rent the house. Rance had made him a better deal. The young man could live there rent-free in exchange for looking after the farmstead and braking the windmill blades when he was on the place and saw water overflowing the tank. Jake was now a full-time employee of the Rising Sun Ranch, splitting his time between Rance's cattle operation and Lisbeth's swine enterprise.

Lisbeth now had seven young sows with fifty-seven pigs that had been weaned for a month or better. She had turned her boar in with the sows with the notion of farrowing second litters before year end. She had told him that gestation time for sows averaged three months, three weeks and three days, a total of 114 in all. They could count on at least two litters a year. She did not like winter farrowing much, but they would be needing the money, she told him one evening after going over the books. She would hold back enough gilts to give her breeding sows of twenty or so by spring and market the remainder. He worried some that hogs were going to take over the place. She had already promised Ben Rice a half dozen gilts that would be ready for spring breeding, given that eight months was the normal first breeding age.

Rance stood reluctantly and dusted off his britches, hating to leave this idyllic spot. Prospects of a nap here had been tempting him, but he wanted to check on the twenty cows he had purchased and turned in with his herd a few weeks back. The new arrivals still stuck together and did not carry his brand yet, so they bore more watching until they accepted his range as home.

With a summer break from school, Morgan, who had turned eleven July 29, accompanied Rance on his ranch duties most days unless his mother drafted him for hog chores, which Rance noted that his recently adopted son did not handle without grumbling some. Morgan had made it clear that he aspired only to be a cowman like his father.

They mounted their horses, Morgan slipping easily into the saddle of the buckskin gelding Rance had given the boy for his birthday. Lisbeth had protested that the three-year-old horse was too spirited for a mere boy. Rance had countered that their son was exceptionally tall for his age at three or four inches over five feet, possibly on track to reach his mother's height in another year. Besides, he was a natural on horseback and had spent hours on the backs of a good number of horses since arriving at the Rising Sun Ranch.

Lisbeth had surrendered easily, and Rance concluded that her remarks were obligatory mother's concerns. Regardless, boy and the buckskin, tagged "Spunk," were a match, and Morgan had assumed total responsibility for care of the critter. He was proud of his son and could not have loved Morgan and Marissa more had they been his own flesh and blood. Sometimes, thoughts of the changes not quite a year's time had brought to his life made his head spin.

As they headed north, they kept their bearing by staying within sight of trees that lined Wildcat Creek which snaked its way to its rendezvous with the South Loup River. Wildcat Creek cut through most of Rance's land, the creek's source deep in the Sandhills to the north. The creek's course could be followed for some distance by a viewer from the second story of the new house that would be substantially completed in another month.

Wildcat Creek passed through a narrow canyon several miles north, and that was where Rance expected to find the herd newcomers. They rode side by side at a slow trot, partially as a concession to Tag. The dog liked to scare up rabbits, and with his ranging, probably covered two miles to make one on their direct route.

Morgan said, "Dad, look at Tag. He sees something in the hills to the east."

Rance slowed his mount and saw that the dog had stopped and tensed, staring at an invisible object in the distance. It could be anything, a coyote, a few deer or even a cow or two. Ranchers had been reporting decreasing cattle numbers in their herds lately and Rance was constantly alert for rustling signs. Abe Steele had told him it was a near hopeless task to nail down the evidence to charge rustlers unless the law officer caught them in the act. There were too many acres to cover and too many reasons that part of another man's herd might be grazing with your own, especially on public lands.

That was why vigilante justice was so frequent in cattle country and why more than one innocent man had died at the end of a rope. Rance was sometimes conflicted, perhaps because of the manner of his father's death. He often found himself more concerned with saving the innocent than catching the guilty.

They came up over a rise, and Rance saw a small cow herd grazing on dune slopes to the northeast. "That could be the bunch," Rance said. "Let's check to be certain, and then we'll head back home."

They reined their mounts in the direction of the grazing animals, riding through the gentle dips at the base of the countless low hillocks. The crack of a rifle echoed, and Rance was almost lifted from his saddle when a slug drove into his left hip. "Morg, head for the creek," he yelled. The treeless sea of grass offered no cover. He slipped his Winchester from its scabbard and swung Rusty around to seek out the shooter. He saw movement in the tall grass on a hilltop some fifty yards back. He got off a wild shot to distract the ambusher, then wheeled his mount and followed Morgan toward the creek, which he figured was a good hundred yards distant.

Two more shots rang out and one hit home, ripping into the back of his left shoulder. There only seemed to be numbness in the wound at first, but then searing pain spread over his upper back and shoulder. The hip wound was barely noticeable in comparison. He could feel the blood soaking his shirt.

As they reached the trees that lined the creek, dizziness was starting to overtake him. When he reined in his horse, he started to dismount, but before a foot hit the stirrup he slid off and dropped on the ground. He blacked out for a moment but came back when Tag began licking his face. To his surprise, Morgan had removed his own shirt and was slicing it into strips with his penknife.

"Morg, you've got to get the hell out of here. Whoever was doing the shooting will be coming after me."

"I won't leave you like this, Dad. I can't."

"Help me with the bleeding, and then I will tell you what you have got to do. We've got a little time. The shooter's horse wasn't in sight, and he will have to get his mount and then track us down."

Rance leaned forward. "Can you see where the slug entered? Cut away my shirt around the wound."

"I see it. Just below the shoulder blade." The boy, seemingly unfazed, began to cut away the bloody shirt. "It's bleeding yet but not pumping out or anything. I don't know what's bad and what's not."

"Give me three of those strips to tie together. You fold one and press it against the wound."

Morgan followed instructions and soon announced, "The bleeding's let up."

"Good. Now I will tie some of your shirt strips together. Then you help me wrap the cloth around my chest, just under my armpits to bind the wound. I can tie the ends snug in front."

In a few minutes, Rance felt they had done all that could be done for the back wound. He reached across his midsection with his right hand and probed the hip wound with his fingers, confirming that the bleeding was minimal. The pain was tolerable.

"I'll get my Winchester, Dad. We can hide in the trees."

"No. We can't risk it. Here's what you must do. Head for home as fast as you can go. Just follow the creek. Take Rusty with you. He will give my hiding place away if he stays here, and I won't be able to ride him anyway. Tag will stay with me. You tell your mom what's happened. Jake should be at the house helping her when you get there. Tell her she needs to have him hightail it over to

Johnny Whitehorse's. Johnny will need a wagon to bring me back."

Morgan was teary-eyed, obviously torn. Rance was proud of the boy, though. He had not crumbled to hysteria like many his age would. "You've got to trust me, Morg. This is the best chance for all of us. Now, clip the lead line on my saddle to Rusty's halter and go. Ride with the wind."

When the boy was mounted, Rance said, "Morg. I love you and Marissa. And do me a favor, will you? Tell your mom that I love her, too."

"I will, Dad." And the boy nudged his buckskin out of the trees and eased his mount into a fast gallop with Rance's big empty-saddled sorrel keeping pace easily.

Chapter 41

RANCE STUDIED HIS surroundings. The trees that lined Wildcat Creek were mostly willows and cottonwoods with a sprinkling of oaks. Much of the undergrowth consisted of prickly gooseberry bushes and young cedars that would someday battle the larger trees for space in the wooded area that consisted of twenty to thirty-foot, irregular strips on each side of the creek. He would like to move closer to the creek, but he would be forced to scoot or crawl. Tag looked at him with sad eyes, obviously confused by the turn of events.

Morgan had left Rance's rifle behind although it was doubtful that his wounded shoulder would allow him to use it. He would have to let the stalker get in close, so he could use his Army Colt revolver. Dragging his rifle by the barrel, he half-crawled, putting most of his weight on his right side, another ten feet nearer the creek before reaching a large cottonwood that he could rest his back against. Raising himself up against the tree and inching into a sitting position, he rested a few minutes to catch his breath. This was where he would make his stand.

He did not have the strength to look for a better nest, and as he looked about, he took comfort from the thick woods and undergrowth surrounding him. His blood-soaked shirt consisted of half-shredded rags now, and the tree bark chafed his bare skin as he leaned back. He was drowsy, fighting to keep his eyes open. He felt Tag sitting beside him and found the dog's presence calming. His thoughts shifted to Morgan. He prayed that the boy had not encountered the shooter, but there had been no choice but to send his son away. If he had stayed, Morgan would have been a witness to the outcome of any confrontation, and the odds favored the ambusher, who would have been unable to leave a live witness behind.

He did love that boy and his sister. Yes, and their mother. He had fallen in love with her quickly after their marriage, although, given their business-like arrangement, he had tried to deny it for a time. He savored the life they were building together and feared making a misstep that might shake the foundation of this magic he had found with Lisbeth. But a few months back, he had decided he owed her the truth about his feelings for her. He had just been waiting for the right time, and now she might never hear the words from his mouth. With that thought, he closed his eyes, and his chin dropped to his chest.

He did not know how long he had slept when he was awakened by Tag's low growling. Instantly, he heard the snapping of twigs and cracking of limbs of something moving through the woods in their direction. They had no bears in the vicinity, so it was easy enough to conclude that the visitor was of the human species, obviously a man who was not terribly concerned about announcing his presence. He had likely found blood to confirm the accuracy of his shooting.

Rance pulled the Colt from its holster, wondering if he could steady his shaky hand enough to get off an accurate shot. He held the weapon in his lap and waited.

"Coldsmith. I'm going to find you soon. I saw your friend ride off. He must have figured you was done for."

Rance offered no response. It occurred to him that the man did not expect to find him alive since his companion had ridden off alone. He was here to confirm death and, perhaps, to find some evidence of it to take to an employer, likely Print Olive. He could think of no one else who would take such steps to see him dead.

He tensed. The man's crunching and crashing through the undergrowth grew nearer. Soon, Rance saw the head and shoulders of a thin man with a black Van Dyke beard slip from behind a cluster of young oaks. He tightened his grip on the Colt, struggling to even lift it.

The man burst into the little clearing with his own pistol raised to fire. "Too late, Coldsmith."

Before the would-be assassin squeezed the trigger, he screamed as a snarling Australian Shepherd sank its teeth into the flesh about his knee. He diverted his gun's aim to the dog, while in panic he tried to pull away from the creature's steel-trap-like hold. Rance raised his Colt with trembling fingers and aimed for the gunman's chest, which had become a moving target. He fired, uncertain whether he had delivered the bullet home before blackness consumed him.

Chapter 42

LISBETH WAS IN a hog pen where the male "shoats," as weaned pigs were called, had been separated from the females. She was bent over a squealing shoat that had its hind legs firmly gripped by Jake's hands, head down and body firmly squeezed between his knees. Lisbeth wielded a small, razor-sharp knife in her right hand. Two quick slices, left hand fingers closing on their quarry, two yanks and two more slices, and she produced two testicles, which she dropped in an awaiting pan on the other side of the fence. So far, she had enough "prairie oysters" to provide several meals for the Coldsmith family and one for the Rice brood.

Jake snatched up the last shoat, and they repeated the process. She was not holding back any boars from the first litters, and these would henceforth be known as "barrows." She had castrated twenty-eight shoats, thus fifty-six oysters. When she established a market for breeding stock in a year or two, she would spare the most promising breeding pigs from the knife to sell to other producers. Any who failed to live up to their promise would meet the same fate when older. She had already decided that her Sandhills breeding stock market would be limited. She would see how this all worked out, since increasing rail access raised countless possibilities outside the local butcher market.

She was climbing over the four-feet high fence of the holding pen when she saw Morgan astride his buckskin coming at a near reckless pace down the slope above the hog pens with an empty-saddled Rusty trailing behind. Immediately, her heart began to race and as soon as her feet hit the ground, she was hurrying out to meet him. She yelled back at Jake, "Keep the shoats in the holding pen, Jake. They get some corn tonight, and I'll turn them out on the range tomorrow."

Morgan reined in beside her. Lisbeth could tell from the frantic look on his face that he brought bad news, but the riderless sorrel had already told her that. "Morg," she said, "where's your dad? What happened?"

"He's been shot, Mom. We were bushwhacked. He's hurt bad, and he wouldn't let me stay with him. He thinks the guy that shot him is coming for him. I didn't want to leave but he said I had to. I'm scared, Mom. We can't lose him. What would we do?"

"Just slow down. What else did he say?" Out of the corners of her eyes, she saw that Jake was coming their way. He would have guessed that something was amiss.

Morgan hesitated and appeared to be searching his memory. "He said if Jake was here, he should go find Johnny Whitehorse and tell him what happened. And Johnny's to take a buckboard. He didn't say much else. I guess he was leaving it to Johnny to help him and bring him back."

Well, she wasn't going to leave it to Johnny. Her mind began running through her options.

"And Mom. Dad said he loves me and Marissa. And I was to tell you that he said he loves you, too."

It was almost more than she could handle. She turned away from her son a moment to wipe away the tears that had suddenly erupted. Damn him. Why hadn't he said something before? And damn herself. Why had she not told him how she felt? If he lived, she swore he would hear "I love you" from her every day they both lived. But now, she needed most to get a grip on herself.

Lisbeth turned to Jake who stood silently with a perplexed look on his face. "You heard the last part, Jake. Rance has been ambushed north along Wildcat Creek. It sounds bad. We'll take our buckboard and the mule team your dad sold us. You need to find Johnny, tell him what happened and get him over here."

"Right away, ma'am." Jake raced away to retrieve his horse from the barn.

She turned back to Morgan. "Morg. Marissa is at the Rice home playing with Missy. I want you to ride over there and tell Tillie what's happened. Ask her if Marissa can stay there until we get back. I know it won't be a problem, but they should know what's happened. When you come back, take care of your horse and saddle one of the others. I'll grab you a shirt. You will have to show us where your dad was at when you last saw him."

She reached out and took the sorrel's lead rope from Morgan. "I'll put Rusty up. I'm proud of you, Morg. You are doing a man's work today."

Morgan muttered, "Thanks, Mom. I just want my dad back." He reined his horse east and headed for the Rice farm, which was no more than a mile distant.

She led the horse toward the barn. If Rance still lived, time meant everything for his survival. She would need to collect all the canteens and fill them with their good well water. She continued with her mental checklist. The kids' feather mattress. A few blankets, although in this heat, cold should not be an issue. She should pack some food for the searchers. Fortunately, she had baked yesterday and should be able to put something together.

She was surprised an hour later when the rescue party members began to arrive. Ben and Tillie Rice both arrived in a buckboard drawn by a mule team.

"My wagon's bigger and got more spring," Ben said. "And you don't need to be driving no mule team this afternoon. I'll unhitch your team and put the critters back in the barn." He did not wait for a response before he climbed down and strode to the waiting mules.

"Tillie," Lisbeth said, "I didn't expect you to come."

"I helped with wounded soldiers during the war, Lisbeth. Did you ever dig a piece of lead out of a man's chest?"

"No," she admitted. "Sick kids are the limit of my medical experience."

"And don't you worry about Marissa. Sue Ellen can handle the herd over at my place just fine. The older kids all have their chores, anyhow."

"I can't thank you enough, Tillie. I've never had a better friend."

"That trail goes both ways, sweets."

"I'm going to saddle my mare. If I don't have to drive a team, I would rather be on horseback, so I can keep up with Johnny." She started for the barn, and then stopped and turned around. "Tillie, Morgan told me that Rance said to tell me he loves me."

Tillie laughed. "You poor thing. I had that figured out way before Rance did. It's about time you both opened your eyes and saw that you've got a marriage that isn't just business anymore, likely never was. That bargain you told me about was just an excuse for both of you."

Chapter 43

A FEW HOURS LATER, Morgan signaled a stop. Lisbeth had lost sight of the wagon carrying Ben and Tillie and the necessities they had rounded up, including a basket of food gathered up by Tillie that dwarfed Lisbeth's offering. "We're close," Morgan said. "Before I left, I did what Dad always tells me. I picked me a landmark. See that burnt-out tree up there, probably lightning-struck? Dad and I were within twenty to thirty feet of it, to the north."

A horse whinnied from the direction of Morgan's landmark.

Whitehorse spoke softly, "Missus Coldsmith, can you and Morgan use them rifles you got in your saddle holsters?"

"Damn right," Lisbeth said.

"Damn right," Morgan said.

"I want the two of you to edge your horses into the cover of the trees and have your rifles ready in case there's trouble. Ain't saying there will be."

"What about me?" Jake asked.

"You follow me. Stay a good twenty feet back."

Lisbeth watched, her heart racing, as Johnny White-horse and Jake tied their mounts to tree branches and Johnny led the way along the edge of the woods toward the blackened tree. Johnny signaled a halt when he reached the area near Morgan's landmark. He disappeared into the trees, and the next five minutes seemed like an hour to Lisbeth. Johnny called for Jake, and the young man followed the voice into the wooded creek sides. Jake soon emerged leading a dapple-gray gelding, a strikingly handsome critter, she thought.

Jake called, as he walked their way, "Johnny found Rance. He's alive, but he said to warn you he's in bad shape and there is a dead man laying not far from him. You can go on in. You will be able to tell where Johnny and I walked through the brush. I'll wait here for my folks and have them take the wagon in as close as they can."

Lisbeth did not have to be told twice. She rushed along the edge of the woods north with Morgan tailing behind till she came to the break in the undergrowth. Then they followed the trail broken by Johnny for more than thirty feet until they came to a small clearing where Johnny knelt beside Rance, whose head and shoulders were propped against a big tree trunk. She dropped to his side, taking quick notice of the corpse half hidden in the brush less than ten feet distant.

"I thought at first the darn dog was going to take me out," Whitehorse said. "He was standing there baring his teeth and growling, but Rance saw me and told him I was okay. Rance was only half awake when I come up to him," Johnny said. "Spoke. Said 'What the hell took you so long?' Then closed his eyes. Paler than a white sheet. Bleeding is just a trickle from the hip. Can't see the back none too good, but I don't see fresh blood or nothing, and I'm guessing he's about bled out."

Morgan said, "You can't see the back wound with him laid out like this. He had me help plug that before I left. That was bleeding most. He didn't seem too concerned about the hip."

"We need to get him out of here," Lisbeth said. "But we should wait for Ben and Tillie and the wagon. I don't think they are that far behind us. He needs water, as much as we can get him to take."

"Water sounds good." It was Rance's voice, weak and raspy.

She pressed her fingers to his cheek, which seemed afire, and bent forward and kissed him softly on the lips. "I love you, Rance Coldsmith, and I'll love you till the end of my days. Do you hear me? I love you."

"Hear you. Did Morg tell you?"

"He told me. Firsthand is better."

"I love you, Lisbeth. I have for a long time. Took me a spell to figure it out."

He flinched, obviously in pain. She took his hand and sat down beside him. He had drifted off again. Somehow, she felt if she held his hand, he could not sneak away to her only competition—death's waiting arms.

Whitehorse said, "Nothing I can do. Best not to move him without more help. Don't want to roll him over or might start bleeding again. I'm going to take a look around. Call if you need me." He slipped away through the trees.

Meaning if Rance died, she assumed.

Morgan remained standing, his fingers absently rubbing Tag's head. "Will he live, Mom?"

"I think so, Morg. But I'm no doctor. Tillie seems to know something about these things. Hopefully, she can give us a better idea of what we are facing."

A half hour later, Ben and Tillie Rice came through the brush and stepped into the clearing. Tillie, upon seeing

Rance, broke away and moved in next to the wounded man opposite Lisbeth. She pressed her ear to Rance's chest and then checked his pulse. "Strong and steady," she said. "I see the hip, but Johnny said there is a back wound."

"Morg said it's close to the shoulder," Lisbeth said.

Tillie said, "We need to get him out of here. He's a lot of man when you stretch him out. We will need Johnny and the canvas tarp I brought. We will put Ben and Jake at his head and shoulders, Johnny at the feet and then Lisbeth you and I will get on separate sides of the middle and try to hold the hip steady. You are stronger than me—you can take the side where he was shot."

With Tillie clearly taking command, they soon had Rance loaded on the feather bed in the wagon. Tillie climbed in and signaled Lisbeth to get in with her. "Let's see what I can do," Tillie said. "I nursed rebel soldiers at the Rice plantation even after emancipation since we didn't have anyplace else to go. I did lots of things a doctor would have done if they'd had one. The old master said I had the touch. It would take us several days to get Rance to a sawbones. That would increase the chances of putrefaction, and that does more killing than the wound itself. I would like to see if he can drink."

Rance had spoken while they carried him to the wagon, but it had been mostly garbled nonsense. Lisbeth took his hand and leaned over. "Rance, can you speak to me?"

"Yep. Been listening to you and Tillie talk just like you thought I was already dead."

His voice was a bit stronger, she thought, and she took it as a good sign that his sense of humor remained. "We want you to drink, Rance, and then Tillie's going to examine your wounds."

"I've seen her dig a locust barb out of a horse's abscess. Hope she's got smaller instruments."

Tillie said, "Sorry, Rance. I brought me the same knife and forceps. Best I could do. But first, I'm getting a canteen. I want Lisbeth to hold your head up and see if you can drink."

He drank more than they had hoped before Lisbeth eased his head down again. She looked at Tillie. "Now what?"

"The hip wound appears to be more in the meat of his butt. I don't think any bone was hit, and the bleeding is pretty well stopped. I want to see his back. You still with us, Rance?"

"Getting sleepy, but I'm here for now."

Tillie spoke to Ben, who stood near the wagon watching with the good sense not to speak unless spoken to.

"We need a fire and then boil some water in those two pots I put under the wagon seat. My instruments are wrapped in the towel in one of the pots. You could bring those to me. Thank you, sweets."

Tillie and Lisbeth, with a bit of help from the patient, rolled Rance over so that he lay face down on the mattress. Tillie ripped the torn shirt fabric away from the wound area and used some of the canteen water to wash around the entry burrow.

"It's what I thought," she said. "I don't think anything vital was hit, or he would be in bad shape by now."

"You make it sound like a little tick bite," Rance whispered. "And if I'm in good shape, I'd hate to see bad."

"No tick bite, but it could be a lot worse." Her fingers traced over the flesh about the entry perforation. "It probably went right through the muscle and got stopped by the wing bone. That's what we called it in Georgia. Out this way, I hear it called shoulder blade, not sure what doctors call it. Main thing is it won't likely kill you. Just got to get it out of there."

"How?" Lisbeth asked.

"I got my forceps and a knife and tweezers. They're for horses, but they'll work. Problem is I don't have enough whiskey to put this man out. I'd like to rinse the wound with what I've got."

"Just do it," Rance said. "Can't hurt much worse."

"You got that water to a boil yet, Ben?"

"Good Lord, woman. I barely got the fire started. Fifteen minutes."

Lisbeth was relieved when Rance passed out at the invasion of the forceps into the depths of the wound. Before he woke up, the slug buried in the side of his buttocks had also been removed.

She ran a cold, wet cloth over his forehead and called his name for several minutes before his eyes opened. "We about done?" he asked.

"Tillie got both the slugs out. You are bandaged. It's time to go home. The rest is up to us."

He was quiet for a time. He seemed to be thinking about something. "Did I tell you I loved you?" he asked.

"You did, but you can tell me again. I won't get tired of it, I promise."

"Love you."

"And I love you back. Now, I will stay here in the buckboard with you, and I'm going to tell Ben to head for home. We can get there not long after sunset. I've got a cow to milk and hog chores waiting. Jake will stay over with his folks tonight and help me out. And I've got another good man in Morgan, so we'll get things done and keep an eye on you in between things."

"Whatever you say. I'm not in a mood to argue with anybody right now."

Lisbeth said, "I almost forgot. Johnny wanted to talk to you when you are able."

"I'm able."

She waved Whitehorse over to the buckboard. The Pawnee came over and leaned against the sideboard and looked down at Rance. "Look like hell," he said.

"Thanks."

"That man you kilt. His dapple gray's shoe has got the break that I seen at the hanging grounds."

"So he was there?"

"Seems likely."

"You good for more riding tonight?"

"On my deputy's tab, I reckon."

"Yep. I haven't been working you that hard anyhow. I want you to take that bushwhacker's corpse over to their ranch headquarters and drop it near the entry before sunup. It's a long ride, but you can stop at Arch Tufts's place on the way back and tell him what happened. He won't let you leave without breakfast and a place to nap."

"How about I take custody of the dapple gray for evidence?"

"You are one wily bastard. Yeah, we do need to hang on to the horse a spell. I suppose nobody else has a claim on the critter, so it can just disappear after we know it's not needed anymore. Don't be trying to wangle any more bonuses for a spell, though."

Chapter 44

PRINT OLIVE SAT at the table in their chuck house meeting place, listening to the bad news Deacon Scruggs was delivering. As usual, Jim Kelly stood with his foot propped on a bench and listened without comment.

"You hadn't been gone for your trip to Plum Creek more than two days when it happened. I guess it was a week ago yesterday morning. It was Muskrat Webb who come and got me. I went and rousted out Jim here, and we went down to the Olive entry sign and found Moon Tilford laying in the middle of the road, dead as a can of corned beef. Single bullet hole dead-centered in his chest."

Olive said, "You should have sent word."

"What good would that have done? By the time we got a message to you, and you got back here, he would have gone from ripe to rotten. It's cold but not freezing water, so we went ahead and buried him up on the hill. I said a few words over him, but they was wasted. Moon Tilford had his seat reserved in hell a long time ago."

Kelly spoke, "It was just a message, Print. I ain't got a doubt about what Moon was up to. And I heard that your deputy friend took a few bullets over near Wildcat Creek not long before Moon came back home. You ain't fooling nobody, least of all, Deputy Coldsmith. He appears to be a patient man, sort of like a cat stalking a bird. You're the bird, Print."

Olive did not like what he was hearing from these two. If they didn't have the *cojones* for this anymore, maybe it was time for a boot in their butts. Their advice was not worth half of what he paid them. They both seemed to be losing a taste for gunplay, especially when a run-in with the law might result. And Coldsmith. Even without a confrontation, his mere presence in Sandhills country had brought the normal Olive operations to a near standstill. The only farmers he had scared out since early spring had sold their land and stock to Coldsmith. He had really coveted the Iverson half section. The other farmer was on leased land and sold his twenty cows to Coldsmith before pulling out. Coldsmith was a small operator, but Olive had a sense that the man had no notion of staying small. There would not be room enough for both.

He decided he would put Scruggs and Kelly on the shelf for now. His younger brother, Bob, had returned from Texas. A year or two short of twenty-five, Bob was long on grit but sometimes short on good sense. Regardless, he would do what big brother asked.

Olive said, "We'll just go about our business, try not to do anything that might encourage Coldsmith to make a move. But I still will not tolerate rustlers. If somebody steals our stock, it's Olive justice they will be facing."

Chapter 45

November 1878

RANCE AND LISBETH sat on the cowhide-covered, stuffed settee in front of the fireplace in the parlor of the new house. They had moved in less than a month earlier, just in time to evade winter in the soddy but too late to savor the wraparound veranda. They loved the house, talked of growing old together there. They sat, mesmerized by the dancing flames, feet propped upon the sturdy coffee table crafted by Ben Rice more for footrest than coffee mugs. Tag slept soundly on the rug nearer the fireplace, having earned house residency, which he had already claimed, by saving Rance's life. No doghouse for this gentle beast.

Lisbeth's head rested against Rance's shoulder, and her fingers interlaced with his. Rance could not have imagined this scene and this life a year earlier. He had recovered from his gunshot wounds for the most part. A stiffness lingered in the shoulder that he had to work out mornings, and an occasional residue of tolerable pain held on to remind him of his close call with death. The hip wound had left a scar on the edge of his buttocks that he only thought of when Lisbeth's fingertips, for some strange reason, toyed with it during lovemaking.

Lisbeth broke the silence. "How long before you are relieved of deputy duties?"

"Abe says Custer County should have its own sheriff by spring. He said he would put a word in for me as deputy if I wanted the job and didn't want to run for sheriff."

"Sheriff? You never said anything about that."

"Because I never considered it. And I will not accept a deputy's job under any circumstance. I'm a cowman, and I want to give my full attention to that—and my wife and family."

"I wouldn't mind some attention when we go upstairs."

He looked at her, and she fluttered her eyelashes. He grinned and kissed her lightly on the lips. "Then you shall have it—my undivided attention."

"You are still troubled about Print Olive, though, aren't you?"

"Yeah, I would like to put him away before I leave the job, but I guess it's not to be. My evidence is just too flimsy. The man will have an army of lawyers if criminal charges are filed against him. What I've got would be torn apart and shredded in a courtroom. At least he is quiet for the moment, and there hasn't been any mischief reported since his man took me down."

"We can make it fine without your deputy money now. I just worry."

"I know, but the end is in sight, and I wouldn't feel right about dropping out when Abe's counting on me."

"I understand that. I just don't think you are finished with Olive, and he likely doesn't consider himself done with you."

"I suppose. Anyway, I'll be turning in my badge in the spring—by the end of March at the latest—replacement or not. And the salary will be welcome till then. The seventy-five yearlings I just sold left us a bit over fifteen hundred dollars after commissions. What's the balance in the Rising Sun account?"

"Nearly twenty-six hundred dollars."

Rance said, "What if I transfer two hundred dollars to the joint account? Abe deposits my salary there, so that should be plenty to live on for the next six months or more. Then I would like to pay five hundred on the Iverson note, and another five hundred on the house loan. That would leave twelve hundred dollars operating money. I probably won't need all that."

"You never ask about the hog money."

"That's your project."

"It is our project with me in charge. I sold forty shoats to different farmers and ranchers to feed for slaughter. Even a cowman enjoys a good ham or some pork chops on occasion, not to mention bacon. I got ten dollars each—almost as much as a full-grown butcher hog, but we couldn't afford to feed them through the winter with so little forage and corn at forty cents a bushel. We can make more money doing this than feeding the critters. And it cuts down chores. The buyers can feed a few out at little cost with slop, a dab of corn and whatever they can come up with. Hogs aren't that picky about what they eat. Anyhow, with the money I had before, I've got over a thousand in the hog account. I'll add five hundred to the house loan. The other we'll have for an emergency. I want to get this paid off. They're holding a mortgage on my old place and your original section as well."

"They've got plenty of security, that's for sure, but I agree. I don't like debt on land we already own."

"You are saying you don't mind if it's for more land?"

He grinned sheepishly, "Well, not so much."

"Let's go to bed. Time to get your mind off the land."

"Could be a challenge."

"Since when?"

Chapter 46

BOB OLIVE HAD just returned from Texas by train. Print Olive was enraged by his little brother's report of what the younger man had stumbled onto in railroad stock pens in Kearney, a growing town in Buffalo County lying southeast of Custer County.

"Slow down and take me through this again now that Deacon is here." They were standing in the wide doorway of the Dismal River stable, and Deacon Scruggs had just returned with several hands from an area north of the river where rustling was suspected. Jim Kelly was scouting possible rustler hideaways.

Print slid the big door nearly shut, leaving a sliver of an opening for sunrays to creep in and provide a bit of light in the structure that had its windows closed because of a merciless wind that was bringing an increasing bitter chill as sundown approached.

Bob Olive said, "I got off the train at Kearney two days back, and I was walking past the cattle pens and noticed a steer with the Olive brand on his hindquarter, so I went over to the pen and saw that the pens were full of Olive cattle. Well, I thought some of our folks must be in town and looked around but didn't find none, so I went to see Dave Anderson, the county sheriff." He looked at Print. "He's one of ours, ain't he, Print?"

"Better be. Go on."

"Well, he didn't know nothing about any of our crew bringing in cattle. So we went and asked some questions of the railroad clerk, and he says a packinghouse buyer staying at the hotel owned the cattle. We found him at the hotel, and he showed us a release for seventy head from Olive Brothers to Ami Ketchum signed by Print Olive. I knew that Print always signed as 'I. P. Olive.' But Ami Ketchum's signature was on the bill of sale to the packing house. Saw it myself."

"Those thieving bastards," Print said. "You hadn't got around to telling me what Anderson's going to do about it."

"He ain't going to do nothing. He said Ketchum has too many gun-toting brothers for him to try to arrest him, especially since Custer County's not in his jurisdiction. Thought I should take it to Coldsmith. I told him we didn't deal with Coldsmith, so he appointed me deputy and said I could deputize as many as I want to bring Ketchum in dead or alive. What do you think about that? The law's after me in Texas, but I'm a Nebraska lawman myself now. He opened his bulky coat. See the badge? Before I give it up, I'm going to get my picture took and send it back to our folks in Texas."

"You done good, little brother. Who are the other deputies?"

"Thought I would ask Barney Armstrong and Pete Beeton. I talked to Barney. He heard that Ketchum is working out of Luther Mitchell's place."

"You sure you don't want my help on this? Nigger Jim could go with you."

"No. I know Ketchum. He's about as dangerous as one of them prairie dogs. I want to do this, Print. On my own. We'll head out in the morning."

After his brother left, Olive turned to Deacon. "What do you think?"

Scruggs shrugged. "I don't know. I guess Bobby's sort of a lawman now. I'm afraid he'll take a notion to stretch some necks if he runs these folks down. Even a deputy can't get by with that without a trial and judge. I like your brother, but good sense ain't never been his strong suit."

"Maybe you could slip word to him tonight that if there's any ropework he needs to get rid of the body."

"Like you did last week on that old feller that got caught poaching a beef."

"Yep. They just got to disappear."

Chapter 47

RANCE REACHED ACROSS the bed, thinking he would snuggle a bit with Lisbeth before they got up to take on another day. But her side of the bed was vacant. He sat up and swung his legs off the bed. Sunrise was beginning to shoot its rays through the curtains, providing enough light for him to dig out his clothes and get dressed. While he sat on the edge of the bed pulling on his boots, he heard voices drifting up from downstairs, Lisbeth's, of course, and the other a male voice.

When Rance went downstairs, he was surprised to find Lisbeth and Archibald Tufts sitting at the off-kitchen dining table drinking coffee. "Good morning, dear." She nodded toward the chair beside her. "Sit down. I've got your cup out, and coffee's still hot. Pour yourself a cup while I get the biscuits. I'm warming up last night's leftovers, but that's the best I can do this early."

Rance sat down across from Tufts, poured a cup of coffee and looked at the older man questioningly. "Good morning, Arch. This is a surprise."

"Good morning, Rance. You've got a beautiful home here, and a gracious, lovely wife, despite our uneasy beginning."

"What do you mean?"

"She apparently heard me ride in before sunrise. I was waiting for the sun to come up before I woke up your household. Well, when I finally came up to the door and knocked, she opened it while my knuckle was still rapping, greeted me with a smile and 'good morning' with a Colt leveled at my gut. I quickly identified myself and explained that it was urgent that I speak with the deputy sheriff. She invited me in, stoked the coals and made a pot of coffee. She heard you moving upstairs, so we had a nice chat while we waited for you to come down."

Lisbeth placed a tin pan of biscuits on the table and gave each of the men a plate and knife. "Butter is in the covered dish. A chunk of comb honey is in the bowl. Rance, you didn't tell me that Arch is an artist. He would like for us to visit him and his wife and select a painting for above the fireplace. I'm really excited about that. Our walls are stark naked. We need to do something about that. It will make a warmer atmosphere to hang some paintings and the like."

Rance found himself slightly annoyed. Arch Tufts came all this way, evidently riding through the night, and they were going to prattle on like this was a social occasion. He buttered a biscuit and covered it with honeycomb, took a bite, savored it a moment and followed with a sip of the hot coffee.

Since Arch seemed preoccupied with decorating his own biscuit, Rance decided it was time to get to business. "Uh, Arch. We're delighted to have you for breakfast. But I don't think you rode the night for Lisbeth's biscuits, however delicious they might be."

Tufts bit into his own biscuit. "If I had known about them, I might have made the ride anyway, but, no, some things are happening that you need to know about. It is about the Olive bunch."

"I am listening."

"Print's youngest brother, Bob, was killed yesterday, and you can be darn sure that all hell is going to break loose."

"Never met him. Did you know him?"

"Oh, yeah. He was a lot younger than Print—I'm thinking not yet twenty-five. Got a wife and a new baby in Plum Creek or Olive Town, whatever folks call it these days. Worshipped Print. Wanted to be just like him, unfortunately. Anyhow, he had been in Texas to visit his folks but had to catch a train out of there because the law's got posters and reward money out on him. I'm not clear on what happened but somehow when he returned, he saw a bunch of Olive cattle in the railroad pens and figured out they had been rustled and sold. He got himself appointed a deputy sheriff out of Buffalo County and got a warrant to arrest Ami Ketchum. Do you know Ketchum?"

"I've run into him a time or two. Seemed a friendly young man, but I was unclear about how he made his living."

"Now you know. I guess, I shouldn't say that. A court hasn't declared him a rustler, maybe never will if I know Print."

Rance said, "So, Bob was killed. Tell me what you know about how it happened."

Tufts finished his first biscuit and reached for another before he spoke. "You are getting this several times removed from the source. I got this from Frank Harrington, a friend of mine who ekes out a living trying to farm on land that should be in grass. He helps out at my ranch and other places when a temporary hand is needed. The only reliable part is the fact that Bob is dead. He died at Frank's homestead."

"Harrington didn't shoot him?"

"No, Frank just sort of got drug into things when Bob, halfway to death was brought to his place. According to what Bob's friends, Pete Beeton and Barney Armstrong, said—they claimed they were all Buffalo County deputies—they heard that Ketchum was at Luther Mitchell's little ranch. I'm not clear on why or if old Mitchell was involved in Ketchum's enterprises or not. Luther would be about my age, late fifties, I'd guess. I don't know him well. Always got stories to tell."

Rance was wanting to move this story faster but decided to let Tufts continue at his own pace. "I don't recall meeting Mitchell. Anyway, I take it they went to Mitchell's."

"Yeah. They stopped at Jim McIndeffer's on Muddy Creek first and talked him into guiding them to Mitchell's place which is back in the hills off the beaten path. McIndeffer was the nearest neighbor that they knew of, and he and Mitchell had homesteaded about the same time. Anyhow, McIndeffer led them to the place and then found himself a safe spot on a hill overlooking the ranch yard, so he's the one that saw how it all played out and told Frank Harrington about it. He saw Missus Mitchell on a wagon, steadying a mule team while Ketchum was trying to tie a bull to the back of the wagon."

"But not Luther Mitchell?"

"That's right. Next thing, Beeton was riding into the ranch yard. McIndeffer learned later, they were trying to get a fix on where Mitchell was and that Beeton asked Ketchum about shoeing a horse. Ketchum said they were returning a bull to a neighbor, and he didn't have time— Ketchum does blacksmithing, you know, and could likely make a good living at it."

"I have never used him but heard he did good work if a man could track him down," Rance said.

"Yeah, a man's got to be available and tend to business if he wants to make it. Anyway, as Beeton was returning to report to Bob Olive, the woman went into the house. That's when Bob and his boys moved in to make an arrest. They had their guns set to fire but Ketchum, like a fool, pulled his own revolver. He got off a shot, but then took one in his arm or shoulder, it appeared. Barney Armstrong had a nasty foot wound when Frank met up with him later. All hell broke loose, I guess, and Luther Mitchell comes charging out of the house with a rifle. He served in the Union Army and knew how to use the weapon. He sent the deputies looking for cover and fired a slug into Bob's side. Bob held fast to his horse, and Beeton took the reins and led the critter away with Ketchum and Mitchell still raining gunfire. That's when McIndeffer left the hill and met up with Bob and his boys. McIndeffer could tell Bob wouldn't make it back to Olive headquarters and suggested they go to Frank Harrington's soddy, which was less than a mile down the creek. That's how Frank got involved."

"So what did they do about Bob?" Rance asked.

"Not much. He was bleeding from gut and mouth by this time. Frank offered a bed and McIndeffer stayed on to do what he could for Bob. Barney headed for Plum Creek to tell Bob's wife—her name's 'Mint,' I guess—and Pete rode to the South Loup headquarters ranch to notify Print.

"So did Print Olive get there before Bob died?" Rance asked.

"Yeah, he got there late that afternoon, and the wife arrived before sundown the next day."

"So what did Print Olive say?"

"Frank didn't know much about what went on after Print got there. He pretty much got booted out of his own house until it was all over. But he said Print was in a rage. Vowed that Ketchum and Mitchell would hang. Frank took him seriously. That's why I'm here. This is Custer

County jurisdiction, and I didn't want you to get blind-sided."

Rance sighed. "I appreciate that, Arch. I really do. Looks to me like I need to take Ketchum and Mitchell into custody. That's if Olive hasn't already caught up with them."

Chapter 48

PRINT OLIVE SAT in an old rocking chair pulled up to his brother's bedside. He had no illusions that he was engaged in anything but a deathwatch. He had taken over the chair upon his arrival the previous afternoon, even slept in it last night, refusing to leave Bob's bedside except to tend to natural urgencies.

He was grateful that his brother slept and did not seem to be suffering intolerable pain. He was reasonably lucid during brief waking moments. But this was a hell of a place to die, a mud shack for God's sake. Before riding away from headquarters and following Pete Beeton to this pigpen, Print had ordered prompt assembling of a temporary casket and had instructed Pete to leave directions to Frank Harrington's farm. Pete had given him no reason for a scintilla of hope for Bob's survival. Deacon would bring the wagon bearing the wood box for the remains, and Jim Kelly would likely accompany him astride a horse, joined by several of the Olive hired guns.

He pulled his timepiece from his vest pocket and saw that it was a few minutes past three o'clock. The bright sun kept the temperature outside above freezing, and an early snow had largely melted, so there should be no weather delay for the wagon. He reminded himself, however, that a wagon trail allowed for few shortcuts. Some delay should be expected. He wondered about Bob's wife, Mint. She would likely remain in Plum Creek and await word.

Bob stirred on the bed. Print noticed the blankets were blood-soaked again. They had probably used up Harrington's blankets by now. Pete snoozed on a church pew-like bench next to the door outside. He would see what the hired gun could rustle up in the way of saddle blankets and the like. Maybe Harrington still had something usable stashed away.

"Print?" Bob Olive croaked.

"I'm here, little brother."

"Don't leave me, Print. I don't want to be alone when it happens. I'm not afraid. Ma's probably got word by telegraph and is praying for me by now."

"I'm not going anywhere, Bobby." He took his brother's hand in his. It was cold as ice.

"Print, I only wanted to be like you. That's all I ever wanted."

Tears rolled down Print's cheeks. He could not recall the last time that had happened. Bob relaxed, and at first Print thought his brother had died, and it sent his own heart racing. He was relieved when he found that Bob had dropped off to sleep, and the inevitable had been delayed.

There was a soft rapping at the door. "Come on in."

Deacon Scruggs and Jim Kelly stepped in. Deacon said, "Hated to interrupt, Boss. Just wanted to let you know we were here."

"And you've got the box?"

"We do. Any orders?"

"Just wait out at the barn for now. Check with me every hour or so. I need some blankets. These are soaked with blood. Tell Pete and see what you can come up with. I don't think he will make it till dark. We're going to take him to Kearney when he's gone. There will be some night travel, if I'm right."

"I'm damn sorry, Print," Scruggs said. "We'll be ready to do what has to be done."

"Sorry, Print," Jim Kelly added.

A few hours later, a young woman burst through the door. Petite, dark-haired and wearing a man's riding garb, she was a pretty thing even in her grief, Print thought.

Mint Olive said, "Is he . . ."

"He's alive." Print got to his feet and surrendered the rocking chair to his sister-in-law.

"I would like some time alone with him," she said.

Print shrugged, tossed a few more logs in the fireplace, pulled his coat on and went outside. He found that Deacon Scruggs had replaced Pete Beeton on the bench, and he sat down beside him and began to roll a cigarette. "It won't be long," Olive said. "She didn't want me in there."

Scruggs said, "It's natural she'd want some time with her husband."

"She doesn't like me much."

"Now that's a surprise."

Print gave Mint Olive a half hour, and then he reentered the house. He walked over to the bed where Mint was holding her husband's limp hand. The pallid, drooping face and the standstill of Bob's abdomen told him that his brother was dead.

"I'm sorry," he said. "The men who did this will pay."

She looked up at him and glared. "And more people will die. You killed Bob, Print. You just the same as pulled the trigger on that man's gun. Whether you asked him to go after those men or not, he did it to please you. Everything he did was to get your attention."

Print said, "Bob should be buried in Texas. In the family plot. You will return to Olive Town and gather up your things and your baby. I will send Jim Kelly with you, and he will escort you on to Kearney. We will take Bob to a funeral parlor in Kearney to be embalmed and buy a nice casket. I will wire my parents, and you will accompany the casket home on the train. I will arrange for one of the other hands to go with you since Jim might not be welcome at your destination. After you have departed, I will tend to the remaining business."

Chapter 49

December 1878

ARCHIBALD TUFTS SLEPT most of the morning at the Coldsmith house, catching up from his night ride to report to Rance. The deputy in the meantime rode to Johnny Whitehorse's cabin and asked him get his gear together and meet at the Rising Sun headquarters at noon, suggesting he might alert the rarely present Primrose that he might be gone a few days.

Johnny replied, "She's not here. She took her pony and rode away two days ago. Going back to the reservation, she said. Doesn't like Pawnee ways, whatever the hell that means. Might be with child. Don't know. I'll go get her when I'm done with this deputy business. You said by spring."

"Yep. But I think we are about to earn a year's pay. Anyhow, bring a spare mount and come over early and we'll feed you before we ride out. Arch Tufts will ride with us as far as his place."

"Okay if I bring that dapple gray I've got in custody? That guy's a sweetheart."

"It looks like custody is permanent. I don't see why not."

Later, after the horses were saddled, he led Rusty and his spare bay gelding over to Lisbeth, who had seemed rather subdued all morning. Morgan and Marissa stood on opposite sides of their mother, neither offering a smile. "You are a cheerful bunch to behold," he said.

Lisbeth stepped over to him, wrapped her arms about his neck and gave him a lingering kiss. "You are a loved man," she said. "Take that with you and remember it before you do anything reckless. We need you here, Rance. After that man shot you, I worry every time you ride out. That badge can't disappear soon enough for me."

"I love you, Lis, and Marissa and Morg, too. I have every incentive to come back. I intend to be careful." He stepped over to Tag where he sat about ten feet back from the others with sad eyes focused on Rance. He knelt and stroked the dog's head and scratched his ears. "Sorry, boy. We're going to be covering a lot of ground on this trip, and your mom needs you here to keep a lookout and help Morg and Jake with the cows." The dog just gave Rance a mournful look that would send him off with a good dose of guilt.

He mounted Rusty, and the three men rode off leaving a trail of dust behind them. He tossed a look over his shoulder before he disappeared over the rise and saw that Lisbeth and Morg were heading toward the hog pens. Marissa had likely already made it to the warmth of the house. Lisbeth was working too hard. Jake would help her with hog chores twice daily and keep an eye on the herd as best he could, but they could really use another man if they expanded the operation, as he knew they would.

They were almost to Arch's house late afternoon before it occurred to Rance that it was the first day of December, the start of a new month that would close out another year.

"Where's the Mitchell place from here, Arch?" Rance asked.

He pointed to the row of hillocks that ran endlessly northwest of his house and provided a scenic backdrop for the residence. "Just behind the hills, you will find Muddy Creek. About a half hour ride downstream will take you within sight of the Mitchell farm. I doubt if you will find anybody there by now, but it's a start. Swing back here for supper, if you like. We'll have rooms if you want to stay the night out of the chill. I love this country but come winter I sometimes think of south Texas."

"Don't wait for supper, but we'll come by if it's not too late."

"Don't concern yourself about the time. The wife will set some supper back."

Rance and Whitehorse moved on, following the creek as Tufts had suggested. They came to a farmstead set down in a lowland bowl surrounded by the rolling hills. A barn had been burned down to its foundation, and the roof of the small sod house had been torched. A wagon attached to a mule team stood outside the house, indicated someone, not likely a resident, of the roofless house was inside. They rode in at a walk.

"Let's split," Rance said.

Whitehorse nodded agreement, and they veered off in opposite directions. It would make it more difficult for someone with a scattergun to take them both with a single blast, and any other gunmen would be forced to choices as well. As they neared the wagon, an older man with a white beard and bib overalls looped over the shoulders of a wool sweater emerged from the house with an armload of rifles. He froze when he saw the visitors.

Rance called, "Come on out. I am Deputy Sheriff Coldsmith and my partner is Deputy Whitehorse."

The man walked slowly toward the wagon, obviously no threat to the law officers with the burden of weapons he could not get into firing position. Rance dismounted as the old man dumped the arsenal in the wagon.

"I'm George Mitchell," the man said. "I'm Luther's older brother. Luther dropped by my place and asked me to get his guns to a safe place. I stayed away for several days because I didn't know what might happen over here. My place is a mile due east. Then I was going to come over, and I saw the smoke from my place and waited another day."

"A lot of guns."

"Hell, I got three, maybe four, more armloads, not counting sidearms scattered about. I'll miss some that are better hidden, but I ain't hanging around here any longer than I got to. When it comes to guns, Luther's plumb weak north of the ears. He's sure as hell got more guns than money or cows."

"We're looking for Luther and Ami Ketchum. Do you know where they are at?"

"No secret that I know of and I sure ain't looking for trouble with the law. They was headed for Loup City when I seen them. They was going to talk to Judge Aaron Wall there. He's Sherman County Judge and sort of a family friend and handles legal work for most of us. They felt they was in more danger from Print Olive than the law. I don't know if they made it or not. They're dead if Olive got them."

Perhaps the judge had already arranged for one of the other county sheriffs to take custody of Mitchell and Ketchum. Regardless, Rance decided he was not letting go of this one until he had confirmation. They would return to Arch Tufts's place, grab a good meal and three or four hours' shuteye and then move on to Loup City in the middle of the night.

Chapter 50

LISBETH STEADIED HERSELF on the handrail as she stepped slowly down the four stairs that led off the veranda. She had struggled with dizziness and nausea since rising and had been grateful for the railings that ran the full length of the staircase to the second floor.

Morgan and Marissa were in the barn already, Morgan tending to the milking while his sister grained and tossed hay to the few horses held in stalls overnight. Morgan would carry water from the nearby well to the animals when he finished milking. The kids were busy with their chores and schoolwork, but she was proud of the way they had taken on responsibilities at the ranch. They were thriving as young Coldsmiths, and beyond the unpredictable physical disasters that always lurked, she was confident in the futures they were building at Rising Sun Ranch.

During Rance's absence, Jake Rice was riding the range into the encroaching Sandhills, identifying locations of grazing herds. The canyons, and sometimes near mountainous dunes, often made it difficult to keep track of the cattle which tended to break up into multiple groupings as they foraged for lusher grass now that the food source was dormant. That left the hog chores to her. Fortunately, she had marketed all the shoats and all she had to care for was the breeding stock. On the other hand, there was little forage now, which required the feeding of more corn and thus, more labor and cost.

Lisbeth and Jake had installed large barrels intermittently along the outside of a wooden fence nearest the barn, where bins of corn were installed. Feeding troughs that would serve four or five sows each were spaced along the fence interior, so the feeder could dip buckets of corn from the barrels and dump them over the short fence and into the troughs. Lisbeth thought the buckets were much heavier than usual today and found herself pausing to catch her breath before she moved on to the next barrel. Tag joined her while she was pouring corn into the troughs and seemed to be looking at her with concern.

Finished feeding the sows and followed by Tag, she walked tentatively to tend to the boar who was kept in a separate pen with his own A-frame house outside of breeding season. She did not want him breeding young gilts, all of which were his own progeny. She had talked to several small farmers who would rent Big Guy for breeding in the spring, and she would find another boar to service the first-timers. Exchange or rental of boars and bulls was not uncommon to avoid adverse consequences of inbreeding.

Big Guy was a 750-pound giant, a good hundred pounds heavier than the average Hampshire boar. He had an aggressive disposition, and she took special care when she was around him. She and Jake had trimmed back the boar's tusks a few months earlier, so he could not damage the sows during his romantic interludes, but his dagger-like teeth could still do damage. When she arrived at the boar pen, she saw this was not to be her lucky day. The boar had rooted the trough over, as he was inclined to do when not timely fed, and he was grunting loudly in complaint.

She picked up a solid stick in case she needed to give the boar a sharp whack on the snout to back him off while she turned the trough back over. She was climbing over the fence when her head started spinning, and her knees crumpled, and she fell on her butt. Big Guy started grunting and charging toward her. Her eyesight was blurry as she searched for the stick she had dropped. She heard Tag barking frantically and saw the dog flying over the fence, landing between her and the charging boar. She was aware of a melee of squealing, growling, grunting and barking as the combatants collided. She tried to struggle to her feet before blackness overtook her, and she collapsed back into the pen corner chosen by the boar for emptying his bowels and bladder.

When she awakened, she found herself naked in the clawfoot tub in the downstairs water closet that drained into a nearby gulley, but was still filled by buckets and pots of water. She was greeted by Tillie Rice's kind doe eyes.

"Just relax, sweets," Tillie said. "That's the rinse water going out the tub. As soon as that's done, Sue Ellen will bring more water, and you can soap away the pig shit smell."

"How did I get here? I know I passed out, and Tag was having a tussle with Big Guy. Is Tag okay?"

"Tag is fine. A few wounds, but they don't need stitches. I'll doctor him a bit before I leave. It seems that Morgan heard a ruckus over by the boar pen, and when he got there, he saw you lying in the mess and thought you were dead. He opened the gate to the pen, and Tag chased that big boar out. Morgan saw you were breathing, so he got Marissa up there to stay with you and Tag, got his horse and headed to our place for help."

"I guess we needed it."

"You sure did. I couldn't bring you back by shaking you a bit, but I couldn't see any injuries. Ben carried you to the house and set you in the tub. I took over from there. Figured the water would bring you back."

Sue Ellen was pouring warm water in the tub, and Lisbeth savored it, feeling drowsy and invigorated at the same time. "Thank you, Sue Ellen. I'm feeling much better."

Tillie said, "Sue Ellen's going to fix something for you and the kids to eat. She'll stay the day. Longer if needed. I'll check on you this evening if she doesn't send Morgan for me before." She handed Lisbeth a washcloth and a bar of lye soap. "Can you wash yourself, or do you need help?"

"I think I can do it."

Tillie said, "Now, tell me what happened."

Lisbeth told her about the nausea and dizziness she had experienced that morning.

"Was this the first time this ever happened to you?"

"It's the worst I've felt, but I've had a little of the same thing for several weeks when I first get up in the morning. And I've lost all my energy. I drag all day long."

Tillie shook her head knowingly. "When did you have your last monthly?"

"I don't know. Missed the last few, but that's what happens to me. I've never been regular since Marissa was born. I thought it was likely something was wrong, and I wouldn't be having any more babies—which didn't distress me any when I was married to Carl."

Tillie said, "Well, I'd bet our farm, sweets, that you are with child. That being the case, maybe you could slow down a mite. Now let me help you out of the tub. We'll get you into the parlor in front of the fire, where you can sit the rest of the day."

Lisbeth accepted her friend's help stepping from the tub. "A baby. That can't be."

"Don't know why not, sweets—unless you and that man of yours are still playing the brother-sister game. And I wouldn't believe you if you said you were."

"I wonder what Rance will say?"

"I'm guessing he will bust his buttons and strut around like a stud horse. He'll be thrilled, of course. Why wouldn't he be? But let's keep this between you and me till you have had a chance to tell him. He should be the next to know."

Lisbeth dried herself off and slipped into clean underthings and a robe Sue Ellen had fetched from the upstairs bedroom. She walked into the parlor with Tillie at her side, but the dizziness had abated, and she felt energized. Obediently, however, she sat down in the stuffed chair and was quickly entranced by the flames dancing in the fireplace, savoring their warmth. She did not even notice when Tillie slipped out of the room. She prayed Rance would be home soon. She wanted nothing more than the man she loved back again, by her side and hand in hand.

Chapter 51

PRINT OLIVE HAD sent word back to ranch head-quarters for a posse to be organized to search for the fugitives and burn down the Mitchell place even before his brother was embalmed. In Kearney, he arranged to publish notices of a seven-hundred- dollar reward for the capture of Mitchell and Ketchum. He also sent telegrams to sheriffs of nearby counties with whom he had established "financial relationships." Several were on their ways with deputies to join the search.

On December 3, Olive received notice that the sheriffs of Merrick and Howard counties had captured the wanted men at a farm northeast of Kearney and that they were incarcerated in St. Paul, the county seat of Howard County. Print, now at his Plum Creek home, had no desire to travel a day or two to Saint Paul. Beyond his relationship with the sheriff there, he felt he had no control of the arrangements there. To further aggravate him, the sheriffs of both Merrick and Howard counties, as the arresting officers, were claiming the reward money. B.J. Gillan, the sheriff of Keith County held the arrest warrant, so he was claiming the reward as well.

Ogallala, the Keith County seat, was many miles west of Plum Creek, but Gillan, a fellow Texan and longtime friend of Olive, had returned by rail to help with the search and, unbeknownst to the other lawmen, was staying at Olive's Plum Creek residence. Olive declared that the reward money would be paid to Gillan and that he would share with the others contingent on their continued cooperation. It was agreed that the prisoners would be delivered to the more substantial Kearney jail for temporary holding. Print Olive insisted, however, that the reward money would not be paid until the prisoners were delivered to Custer County where the crime had been committed.

Print sat down with Gillan at the Plum Creek residence. Gillan had worked for Print for several years in Texas before moving north to Nebraska and leaving his questionable reputation behind. He was a thin, weathered man with a scarecrow build, a year or two over forty but looked mid-fifties.

"Do you think the law will hang them, B. J.?" Print asked.

"Not a chance. They already got a couple lawyers. They would hang here in cow country, but they will get a change of venue. Mitchell might get some prison time. Ketchum didn't pull the trigger, so he might even get off, hands slapped for the rustling—a fine maybe."

Print sighed. "That's what I figured. This is what I want you to do. You can split the reward with the other sheriffs or not. I don't give a damn. You get another five-hundred-dollars for doing what I tell you."

"Not much I wouldn't do for that kind of money."

"The courthouse for Custer County is at a placed called Custer. It consists of a two or three-room log cabin. There is no real jail there. No town, for that matter. Just a place. They would have to lock the prisoners up in a room. There is no elected county sheriff at the present. There is a deputy working under the supervision of the county sheriff out of North Platte. He's too smart for his own good. If he gets word of what's taking place, he will be waiting at Custer in the shack they call a courthouse to receive the prisoners. They will end up in North Platte, and then my plans are dead."

"I understand."

"I want you to appoint one of my men as your deputy, but you are going to call him the Custer County deputy."

Gillan said, "Sounds shaky."

"It won't be questioned. Everybody wants to be rid of this problem. Your job is to go with your new deputy to Kearney and take custody. Bring them on the train here. We will arrange for horses and wagon to haul the prisoners. Then you head north toward Custer. I will have a map sketched with landmarks for you and give you a good head start. I will meet you up the trail and relieve you of your prisoners. You will get your money at that time. I recommend splitting some of the reward money with the other sheriffs just to keep their mouths shut."

"I'll do that. I'm getting nervous as hell about this. I ain't going any deeper after I turn over the prisoners to you. I'll be heading back to Kearney to arrange the reward cut and then I'm taking a train back west to my county."

"Just do your part. Then it's my concern."

Chapter 52

RANCE AND WHITEHORSE reached Loup City early afternoon and found it easy enough to locate the home of Judge Aaron Wall, which had been the apparent destination for Mitchell and Ketchum. The judge was a pleasant, middle-aged man, who served as county circuit judge for at least three counties in the area. He was a member of the lawyers' bar, a rarity among rural county judges, most of whom were farmers or businessmen who handled judging as a sideline. Wall also practiced law to the extent it did not interfere with his judicial responsibilities.

Rance and Whitehorse sat in front of the judge's desk in a small study that had book-lined shelves on two walls that ran floor to ceiling. Rance had never enjoyed much of a library during his lawyering years and found himself a bit envious.

Wall leaned back in his chair on the other side of the desk, scratching his bearded chin thoughtfully. "They were here, but I obviously had some ethical problems assisting them. They were not official fugitives at that meeting, but, of course, I knew they would be soon enough. They were more fearful of Print Olive than the law, probably with good cause. I sent them with a letter to my brother who lives ten miles east of here, asking that he provide refuge until I arranged for their surrender to authorities."

Rance thought the judge could have just taken them into voluntary custody at his house and notified Abe Steele in North Platte or the Kearney sheriff. Olive would not have dared taken the men from a judge's house. "Tell us how to find your brother's place, and we will take them into custody."

"Too late. I received a telegram late morning. Posses from all the counties around here have been looking for Ketchum and Mitchell. They were found and have been taken to the St. Paul jail."

Rance knew he should feel relieved. He did not. He wanted to talk to the men and satisfy himself they were safe from Olive's clutches. "Where is the telegraph office? I should contact Sheriff Steele in North Platte for instructions."

"General store across the street. It's also our postal relay. With less than thirty residents, we can't support any competition."

Rance said, "I guess that's my next stop. Thank you for your help, Judge." He started to rise when the judge raised his hand, signaling for him to wait.

"Deputy Coldsmith. I am not on Print Olive's payroll. I was approached by a man named Scruggs about arranging a meeting with Olive. I declined the invitation. Olive's reputation preceded him, and I wanted nothing to do with the man. That said, I am aware of his power and ruthlessness. I prefer not to face him in mortal combat if I can avoid it, but I do draw lines. But I hope you know that a fair number of lawmen are in his camp, either on his payroll or subject to blackmail by him. He seems to make it his business to know everything about anyone whose assistance he might need. I cannot tell you whom to trust. That being the case, I suggest you trust no one until you satisfy yourself otherwise."

Rance already knew this, but he appreciated the man's concern. "Johnny and I will watch our backs."

The telegrapher at the dirty, cluttered general store, turned out to be a fuzzy cheeked young man not many years out of boyhood. He was adept with the telegraph keys, however, and Rance suspected he would depart this isolated outpost for greener pastures one day. His skills were in demand around the country. His name was Albert.

Rance and Whitehorse sat at a small table nursing sarsaparillas and stale ginger cookies, while they waited for a response to the telegram Rance had sent to Sheriff Steele. It had been nearly two hours since the message was sent. Rance had asked if Abe had heard about the Bob Olive killing. If the sheriff had not heard of the incident, more explanation would be sent. Between rail and telegraph, Rance assumed Abe had been alerted. There were likely newspapers reporting the killing by now, perhaps even the arrests had come to the public's attention.

The clickity-clack of the telegraph told him that a reply might be coming in. How many messages would this little cluster of houses receive in a day? Albert appeared to be working earnestly taking down the message, and he soon got up from his desk and carried the message to Rance, who took it and began to read aloud. "DEPUTY RANCE COLDSMITH. STOP. WORLD KNOWS. STOP. TAKE CUSTODY OF PRISONERS. STOP. DELIVER TO NORTH PLATTE. STOP. ABE STEELE ACTING SHERIFF CUSTER COUNTY."

Rance took it that Abe had designated his and Rance's titles on the message so Rance could show it to others to evidence his authority. "Well, Johnny, I guess our next stop is St. Paul."

"As long as Jake sees to the horses at my place, I got nobody waiting for me at home. We can be gone all winter if need be."

"I'm sure as hell not going to be gone all winter. I'm going to pick up the prisoners and get them to North Platte the fastest way possible."

Chapter 53

RANCE'S MOOD TURNED sour after they spoke with the Howard County deputy sheriff at St. Paul. Ketchum and Mitchell had been taken to Kearney to be held by the sheriff there until the legal niceties could be worked out. Custer County was not yet served by a county prosecutor, and Judge Wall, as a county judge, would not have jurisdiction over a murder case. He supposed a district judge serving multiple counties could set up a temporary courtroom at the log cabin courthouse in Custer but finding an impartial jury would be next to impossible in ranch country. Somebody else could figure that out. He had to get to the prisoners.

A day and a half wasted. They had been out almost five days now, pushing the horses more than he liked. They would have to slow the pace some and hope for the best, but it would take a good two days, resting the animals, to get to Kearney. This was assuming a snowstorm did not blow in.

They stopped at the general store for food supplies. Rance found a used pup tent there and purchased it, thinking that it would be easier to set up and warmer than the canvas tarp tossed over low-lying tree branches. Life in the new ranch house had sure as hell spoiled him.

It was midafternoon when they rode out of St. Paul at an easy canter. Rance sidled his mount close to Johnny Whitehorse. "I don't like the gray skies in the west. Is it going to snow?"

"Don't think so but forget about warm sun on your back for the next few days."

"I can't figure why they moved the prisoners so quickly. Nobody's got authority to be making these decisions. We come as close as anybody. I don't like it."

"You think Print Olive's involved, don't you?"

"Smells like it. Once we get hold of Ketchum and Mitchell at Kearney, we're checking our horses in at a livery and grabbing a train to North Platte. Then this becomes Abe Steele's problem, and we're heading home."

"No bonus for this, I'm guessing."

"No bonus. That dappled gray you are riding is your bonus."

Midmorning two days later, they arrived in Kearney, a thriving railroad town pushing two thousand population. As they led their horses down Main Street, Rance caught sight of several tempting restaurants. Maybe he and Johnny could grab a decent meal before they departed with Ketchum and Mitchell.

They went directly to the Buffalo County sheriff's office adjacent to the courthouse. When they walked in, they encountered a craggy-faced man with a brushy, salt and pepper mustache, dozing with his Stetson pulled forward on his forehead and feet propped on his desk. They waited a few moments for the man to wake up. The badge pinned to his sheepskin-lined vest said this was the county's duly elected sheriff.

Without opening his eyes, the man finally spoke. "What do you want?"

"I'm Rance Coldsmith, acting Custer County Deputy Sheriff. This is Johnny Whitehorse. He's also a deputy."

The sheriff swung his legs off the desk and sat up, dark eyes almost canopied by thick, shaggy eyebrows, eyeing the newcomers suspiciously. "How do I know you're who you say you are?"

Rance pulled back his coat to reveal the badge pinned to his own vest and plucked Sheriff Steele's telegram from his trousers' pocket and dropped it on the desk. As the sheriff perused the paper, Rance said, "Sheriff Abe Steele by virtue of being Lincoln County Sheriff is acting Custer County Sheriff. You must be aware of that."

"Uh, yeah." He stood up. "My name's Dave Anderson. I was holding the prisoners, but they ain't here. They left on the train a few hours ago."

"What do you mean?" Rance asked. "You just turned them loose?"

Anderson's face reddened. "Hell, no. The Keith County Sheriff, B. J. Gillan, and a young deputy from Custer County took custody."

"There is no other Custer County deputy," Rance said. "And what in the hell is the Keith County Sheriff doing here?"

"Just helping out. Sheriffs from half dozen counties have been involved in the search."

"The crime was committed in Custer County. Have you been in touch with Abe Steele about this?"

"I ain't. I don't know if anybody else has. I just stumbled into this, trying to help out."

Rance wondered who he was helping. Print Olive, maybe? "I heard you were the man who deputized Bob Olive in the first place."

"Well, yeah. I didn't know Steele had a deputy assigned to Custer County."

Rance sighed. This was not finding Ketchum and Mitchell. "Where was Gillan taking the prisoners?"

"To Custer. Sheriffs involved all agreed that's where they should be. They was going to take them to the courthouse there. Let somebody there decide what to do. County Clerk would probably get hold of Judge Boblits to handle things. There ain't no telegraph service to Custer, so we couldn't get instructions anytime soon."

"You could have sent a rider. Less than two days there and back. There's a telegraph office in Loup City, so you could have contacted Judge Wall. He would have sent someone for Boblits." E. J. Boblits was Custer County's part-time Judge. As a county judge, his jurisdiction was limited, but he could issue warrants for search or arrest. Olive dared not cross the man, and Rance was confident Olive did not own the rancher-judge.

"But I think you will need to explain why Abe Steele wasn't notified. Frankly, Sheriff, this whole thing stinks. I'm wondering if Print Olive is leading this parade."

"I don't like your insinuations, Coldsmith."

Rance chose to ignore the man. "You say they were going to Custer. Railroad doesn't go there."

"They was going to Plum Creek first. They was going to pick up a wagon and team for the prisoners and then head north to Custer."

Plum Creek, also known as Olive Town. No chance that the stopover was a coincidence. "Where's the telegraph office? I'm going to notify Sheriff Steele about what has happened and have him send a message to Sheriff Gillan to hold the prisoners there for us."

"Won't do no good."

"Why not?"

"Telegraph service is out at Plum Creek. That's what Gillan told me before he boarded the train this afternoon. Said I wouldn't be able to reach him. Our telegraph office is at the Union Pacific depot. You can check and see if it's still out."

It would be until Gillan left Plum Creek for Custer or wherever he was headed, Rance figured.

Chapter 54

PRINT OLIVE AND Jim Kelly waited at the Plum Creek railroad depot for arrival of Gillan and the prisoners. Kelly had driven a mule team with a double-seated wagon to the station. Water, food supplies and blankets had been packed in the wagon bed. Print figured the wagon could make Custer by tomorrow evening but, of course, it would never arrive there.

Kelly had ridden in with four gun-hands from the ranch headquarters the previous night. Olive did not anticipate a need for near that many men, but he was taking no chances. Barney Armstrong and Pete Beeton, who had been with Bob Olive the day he was shot, were already in town.

Olive and Kelly stood by the wagon in silence until Olive spoke. "I expected Deacon to be here."

Kelly said, "He's gone."

"What do you mean 'gone?'"

"He packed up his things and rode off yesterday morning. Took his spare mount. Said he was done with Print Olive."

Olive could not restrain a surge of anger. "That's a hell of a way to show his gratitude. Not even a handshake and goodbye."

"Didn't want no fuss about it, I'm thinking."

"You fixing to run, too."

"Maybe."

"What's that mean?"

"If you got a necktie party in mind, I ain't wanting an invitation."

"You've hung a few rustlers in your time."

"Lost my appetite. And times is changing."

"When we ride out from here, you can go back to headquarters. Take Barney with you. He's gotten jumpy as frog legs in a skillet."

Kelly nodded.

When the train pulled into the station, Olive strolled over to the two passenger cars and waited for Gillan and Harry Barrows, the gun-hand deputy, to appear with their prisoners. Gillan exited first, stepping down on the planked platform, raising his hand in greeting to Olive. He was followed by Ketchum, whose left arm was in a sling, his right wrist handcuffed to the older man who trailed him. Gillan steadied Ketchum, a big, bearlike man who stumbled onto the platform, dragging his companion behind him. Deputy Barrows, a young, gangly man, came last.

Mitchell appeared weaker than his wounded comrade and averted Olive's glare. Ketchum, younger than Olive had expected, probably not far into his twenties, glared back and spat on the platform as if offering a challenge. Beeton and Armstrong both had agreed that Mitchell had been the man who pulled the trigger on the rifle that took Bob's life.

Olive stepped over to Mitchell, grasping the man's hairy cheeks with both hands and squeezing like a vice, jerking his head upward and forcing the man's dull eyes to meet his. "Are you the man who killed my brother?" he asked.

Mitchell just stared ahead, his face expressionless like he did not even see the rancher. Olive released him and turned to Ketchum.

The smirk on the man's face made Olive want to shoot him on the spot. "What have you got to say for yourself, Ketchum?"

Ketchum did not reply and did not flinch at Olive's glare. The silence angered Olive more than a verbal assault. He hungered to see fear in these men. He wanted them to plead for their lives.

Gillan said, "Harry, you keep an eye on these two. I want to talk to Print in private."

The freshly minted deputy nodded and moved nearer to the prisoners.

Gillan waved Olive to follow him, and they were ten paces distant before Gillan spoke softly. "They got lawyers, Print. They was told to say nothing. I'm thinking it would be best to just take them to Custer or find that deputy you mentioned—Coldsmith—and let him have them."

"Do you want your reward and bonus money?"

"Just saying."

"Load these sons-of-bitches in the wagon and head up the road to Custer. You can stay the night at Dick James's ranch. He's the Dawson County sheriff. Harry knows the place. We'll intercept you before you reach Devil's Gap tomorrow." He handed Gillan the map sketch. "I'll give you your money. You turn the prisoners and wagon over to me. We'll have two saddled horses for you and Harry and you go back to Plum Creek. You can return to Kearney by train and arrange any reward split with your friends. After that, get the hell back to Keith County. We don't even know each other. Understand?"

"That suits me fine."

After Gillan pulled the wagon out of town, Olive waited a few hours before departing with his gunmen on a horse trail that wound through the hills roughly parallel to the wagon road. With the wagon's slower pace, they would easily arrive at the meeting place before the wagon. He was not especially happy that two local businessmen tagged along. Bill Green, a local tavern owner, and Jack Baldwin, a hotel manager and alcoholic, had heard about a possible lynching and insisted they wanted to be a part of it. The gallon of whiskey Baldwin brought with him especially perturbed Olive. Still, the support and participation of two local businessmen could be a positive thing.

A few miles out of town, Jim Kelly and Barney Armstrong split off from the other riders and headed in the direction of the ranch headquarters. As dusk approached, Olive and his outfit set up camp along Muddy Creek, a short distance into Custer County. As the icy wind swept down from the north, he began having second thoughts about his quest. Later, though, he began to blame Ketchum and Mitchell for the unpleasantness he was being forced to endure. Wrapped in his bedroll near the fire, he struggled to snatch a few hours' sleep. At least tomorrow it would be over.

Chapter 55

RANCE LEARNED THAT another train would not pick up passengers to Plum Creek until the next morning. He was not certain what, if anything, was happening there, but if it were nefarious, he was certain the plans would be well on the way to execution before their arrival. Regardless, they would have to go on to Custer by horseback. They needed to re-supply and pull out.

Rance sent a telegram to Abe Steele updating him on developments. While waiting for a reply, Rance and Johnny indulged in big steaks, fried potatoes and apple pie at a place called the The Rancher's Oven. It was a dumpy, dirty place, but they were not attired for hotel dining. Fortunately, as he had often found, the fare was far better than the atmosphere. The food could not come close to that he had become accustomed to since Lisbeth's arrival at the Rising Sun, however. Lord, how he missed her and the kids and the life they had there. It had been over a week now. He could not be out of the deputy business soon enough.

After eating, they stopped at the telegraph office and picked up Abe Steele's message. Rance read it and told Johnny, "Abe's taking the first train he can catch to Plum Creek. He probably won't be there till day after tomorrow. We are to meet him there with the prisoners. He will have at least two deputies with him. They will take custody, and we can go home."

Whitehorse nodded approval. "Do you think there will be prisoners?"

"I don't know. I'm baffled by all this. We don't even know who the good guys are. I'm glad Abe's coming to take this over. In the meantime, we've got to try to find the prisoners. We start at Custer, I guess. You know this country better than I do. Any shortcuts?"

"Not many. Land gets rougher when we go back north and west. You know that. I can find trails that pass between hills, but none are straight enough to let us go at a gallop or even a trot for long distances. Changing horses will help, but allowing for us to grab four hours shuteye and rests for the horses, I guess we could be at Custer by noon tomorrow, if we get some luck."

"Not soon enough. But I guess I'll have time to think about what we do when we get to Custer and don't find any prisoners."

Chapter 56

PRINT OLIVE HEARD the wagon bouncing along the main wagon road before he saw it. He and his "posse" were dismounted and waiting on the trail that intersected with the road, hidden by a hog-backed ridge that ran for some distance along the trail before dropping off to allow the natural passageway for the road.

"Pete, you come with me," he said. "The rest of you wait here."

Olive nudged his horse forward and onto the road, raising his hand and signaling the wagon to stop. He reached into his saddlebags and plucked out a bulging envelope. He dismounted, waiting for the wagon to reach him. When the mules were reined to a stop, Gillan turned the reins over to his deputy and climbed out of the wagon and walked over to Olive. Both prisoners sat in the wagon's second seat, watching them warily.

Gillan said, "I've been thinking, Print. I would be fine with the seven hundred dollars reward money, and we could just call off the exchange. I can take the prisoners on over to Custer and have them in somebody else's custody by noon."

Olive handed him the envelope. "Twenty-four fifty-dollar bills in there. Twelve hundred dollars. I've met my part of the bargain. Now, Pete will take over the reins. You and Harry go get the extra horses we brought and get your asses back to Plum Creek. Like we talked, you and I don't know each other."

Gillan tucked the envelope in his coat pocket. "A stop in Kearney and then I'm on the train to Ogallala. I'll be turning in my badge there and moving on west someplace."

"Good luck to you, B. J." Olive extended his hand, and the men shook.

After B. J. Gillan and Harry Barrows departed, Pete Beeton took the wagon reins. Following Olive, the party went another mile north on the main road to a fork where a rarely used wagon trail veered northeasterly through Devil's Gap, a canyon route that was occasionally used by the few farmers and ranchers who lived beyond the short canyon's exit.

The posse trailed the wagon, and when Olive tossed a look over his shoulder, he noted that Green and Baldwin lagged even further behind and were so drunk they could barely sit on their horses. He had been a fool to let them trail along. Still, now that they were with the posse, it was better that they remain so that they were a part of the event and not inclined to come forth in case of unpleasant repercussions.

As they rode through the canyon, Olive saw the tree he had remembered, a sturdy oak with a low-hanging limb. "Pull the wagon under the tree, Pete."

When the wagon was positioned, Olive instructed two of his hired guns to take their lariats and make loops and slip them over the prisoners' heads. Ketchum and Mitchell were roughly pulled to their feet and held in place until the loops were tight around their necks and the other rope ends were tossed over the branch and tied.

Olive nudged his mount up next to the wagon and addressed the two men. "Now you got anything to say for yourselves?"

Silence.

He looked at Mitchell, who seemed not to understand what was happening, and Olive seethed with anger. He pulled out his Winchester rifle and levered a cartridge into the chamber. "I want to know why you killed my brother."

Mitchell looked at Olive as if he did not know what the man was talking about. Olive squeezed the trigger and the crack echoed through the canyon as a slug dug into Mitchell's side. The force threw him over the side of the wagon, almost dragging Ketchum with him because their arms were still cuffed together. Olive's men pulled Mitchell back upon the wagon and left him sagging from the rope. Olive could not tell if Mitchell was still alive or not and did not give a whit one way or the other. He wanted this over. "Swing 'em."

The wagon lurched forward, and Beeton drove the wagon out from under the two men. Their feet barely cleared the frozen ground. Mitchell's body was still, but Ketchum's legs and feet kicked in an eerie dance, and he swung his injured arm wildly as the rope dug into the flesh of his thick neck and eventually strangled him.

"Let's go have an early supper, boys," Olive said. "We're just two hours from ranch headquarters."

Green and Baldwin sat on the ground with a jug between them, swilling whiskey and cheering and clapping at the show they had just witnessed. Olive figured they could find their ways back to Plum Creek. He paused once and looked back before they left the canyon. The two men were standing next to the suspended bodies with the whiskey jug like they were trying to share a drink with the deceased. Not much later he saw smoke rising from the canyon. His first instinct was to turn back and check it out, but then he thought better of it.

Chapter 57

I T WAS CLOSING in on two o'clock when Rance and Whitehorse left the house which constituted the courthouse and unofficial town of Custer. Judge Boblits, whose ranch home was located within five miles of the courthouse, had been alerted about delivery of the prisoners and was sitting in the makeshift office that was shared with whatever public official needed one at the time.

Boblits had been relieved at Rance's appearance with instructions from the acting sheriff and had signed an order directing delivery of the prisoners to Rance. He agreed to remain at the courthouse until late afternoon in case someone should arrive with the prisoners or should Rance require further court approvals or support.

They decided to remain with the public wagon road that took users south of Custer and would have been the sensible route to and from Plum Creek by wagon. According to the Buffalo County sheriff, Ketchum had a serious arm wound that included a possible broken bone that had not been splinted or otherwise treated, and the men were shackled together. It seemed highly unlikely they would be traveling by horseback. They were in the road for little more than an hour when the rancid odor struck Rance's nostrils.

He asked Whitehorse, "Do you smell that?"

"Over the hills to the east. Smoke."

Rance could not sight it in at first, but his eyes finally focused on a narrow spiral of smoke rising over the hills and feathering out into the wind east of where they rode. "We need to check that out. The last time I smelled anything like this was when I was riding with General Mackenzie in Texas and we came upon the remains of a Comanche raid. It was burning flesh."

Whitehorse nodded, "Not good. Devil's Gap, I think. Follow me."

When they rode into the canyon, they were greeted by the smoldering forms of two men hanging from a thick tree limb, the charred, nearly naked figures still joined by the handcuffs. As they dismounted, one of the ropes that had been nearly burned through snapped and the body of the smaller man, probably Mitchell, Rance guessed, dropped to the frozen earth. The corpse's arm remained raised in the air because it was still shackled to the other body which was now tipped at a strange angle.

Rance retrieved the skinning knife he kept sheathed in his saddle bags, sickened by the putrid odor that he felt that, like a skunk's discharge, could never be washed from his clothing. He cut the half-burned rope that had dug several inches into the bigger man's neck, and the body fell onto the other corpse, the two crossed figures forming a near perfect "X."

He gestured toward the empty whiskey jug lying on the ground near the tree trunk. "Think that would fuel a fire like the one that ate these two?"

"Yep. Soak their clothes and hair. Looks like one might have had a beard where the face is near gone. What do we do with them?"

"I want you to go back and tell Judge Boblits what we found. See if he can get a wagon to come out and pick up the bodies. Tell him I said I would like for him to see the scene. I don't want these men left out here overnight, but they likely won't get them back to Custer before dark. At least in this cold weather, the bodies aren't going to decompose. They just need to get them inside a barn or something so wild critters don't show up for dinner."

"What are you going to do?"

"I'll get the bodies wrapped in a tarp as best I can. Then I am going to arrest Print Olive. I'll ride up to his place, take him into custody and follow the wagon trail back to Plum Creek. I'm hoping Abe Steele will be there. I'll turn Olive over to Steele along with my badge. I failed to save these men. I'm firing myself. After I do that, I'm going home. I suggest you do the same."

"Do you know where to find Olive?"

"His ranch headquarters is a lot closer than Plum Creek. He would want to let things cool down some before he showed his face in town. I thought I would see if Arch Tufts would take me in for the night. I'll pick up Olive in the morning and see if we can make Plum Creek in a long day."

"You sure you want to do this alone?"

"Yeah. Olive's not a total fool. He's probably having some second thoughts already. I'll tell him that Judge Boblits knows what I am doing. He won't risk adding murder of a lawman to the charges."

Chapter 58

ARCH TUFTS HAD insisted upon riding with Rance to Olive Ranch headquarters. "Just in case you need a witness," Tufts had said. "Leave your extra horse here at the ranch. Snowbird and Coyote Man will pack food and anything else we might need for the trip to Plum Creek. We'll swing by and pick up the horse after we have Print Olive in custody."

"You don't have to do all this, Arch," Rance had said.

"I've been waiting too many years to see Print Olive get his comeuppance. No way I'd miss being a part of this."

It was midmorning when they rode up the entry road to the Olive headquarters. There were at least five men scattered around the site who obviously were not engaged for ranch chores. One who stood at the corner of the house, a rangy full-bearded man Rance guessed to be in his mid-forties, strode toward the newcomers as they approached the house. His thin lips and narrow eyes were set in a frown.

"What's your business?" He asked.

"I want to speak to Print Olive. Tell him Deputy Sheriff Coldsmith is here."

The man started to say something but then apparently thought better of it and hurried to the front door of the house. He knocked, and the door opened a crack. He spoke to someone that Rance could not see and then returned to his post at the corner of the house. A few minutes later Print Olive strode out, tugging a thick quilted coat about him as he walked toward the two visitors.

"To what do I owe the pleasure of the visit?" Olive asked sarcastically.

Rance said, "I am here to arrest you for the murders of Ami Ketchum and Luther Mitchell. Please arrange to have a horse saddled. We will be delivering you to the acting county sheriff of Custer County who is waiting in Plum Creek to welcome you."

"You know that this is a waste of time, don't you, Coldsmith? But, okay, I won't make a fuss. I need to get to a telegraph office, and my home is in Plum Creek. My lawyers will take care of everything after that. This is all just a misunderstanding."

"Get your horse."

Chapter 59

HUGE SNOWFLAKES FLOATED from the sky and started frosting the rolling hills surrounding the ranch when Rance rode into the yard on Rusty, leading the bay gelding behind him. Both horses whinnied. Rance figured the critters must know that they were home. Later, he would see that they were treated like royalty. Cozy stalls, brushings, grain and fresh well water. They had served him well for nearly two weeks.

Tag appeared from beneath the house veranda and commenced barking, bounding across the yard toward him. Rance knelt and wrapped his arms around the dog, submitting to a good face licking.

Morgan was coming out of the barn carrying a pail of milk and looked in the direction of the barking dog. He saw Rance. "Dad," he yelled. "Dad's home." He set the bucket down and raced toward his father. Rance got back to his feet but Morgan almost knocked him over when he crashed into him with open arms that wrapped around his father's waist.

Rance looked down and saw tears running down the boy's cheeks, dripping over a smile that brought tears to his own eyes. How he loved this boy who had come to him in a half-grown package. Then arms wrapped about his leg, and he released the reins of his mount and reached down to pick up a giggling Marissa and lifted her up over her brother, pulling the girl against his shoulder.

"I had a hunch you would be home for supper."

Rance looked up and saw Lisbeth walking his way.

He put Marissa down, and Morgan stepped aside as Lisbeth claimed her husband, kissed him warmly on the lips and held him tightly. "Do you know how much I love you?" she asked.

"Yep. Almost as much as I love you."

"It has been over ten days," Lisbeth said. "Christmas is just two weeks away."

"And we are turning into snow people," Rance said, suddenly aware of the snow accumulating on their hats and coats.

Lisbeth said, "The cow is milked. The hogs are fed. I'll go up to the house and finish supper. You can put your horses up and then hurry up to the house."

"I'll take care of the horses, Dad," Morgan said.

"Good," Lisbeth said. "Then your father will have time for a bath before we eat."

"I could take offense at that," Rance said. He unbuttoned his coat and opened it. "Notice anything?"

Lisbeth frowned. "I'm sorry, no."

"Keep looking."

"Your deputy's badge is gone."

"I'm not a lawman anymore. From now on, I'm a full-time cowman."

She smiled. "Okay, cowman. That is something to celebrate. Now let's get to the house, and you can get that bath taken. I'll scrub your back while you tell me what you have been up to. But first I have something to tell you."

Chapter 60

THE BLINDING SUN'S glare off a foot of snow that shrouded the surrounding hills turned the rider approaching from the west into a moving blur. The wind had moved on a few days earlier, and the quiet spread over the land was almost eerie. Sundown would arrive in an hour or less, and Rance thought it strange that someone would be visiting this late in the day. His hand instinctively caressed the grip of his holstered Colt.

He moved back into the shadow provided by the veranda roof, his eyes remaining fixed on the rider. He could make out a pack horse trailing behind the rider now, and as the man drew nearer, he recognized the sturdy visitor who sat erect in the saddle. He relaxed and hurried down the porch steps and gentle slope that took him to the ranch yard where he waited.

"Abe, for God's sake, what are you doing out here?" Rance asked.

Abe Steele dismounted from the big black horse that carried him. "Could have said, 'Abe, how good to see you,' or something of the sort."

Rance extended his hand and received a firm grip from his old friend. "It is good to see you, but you are not an expected guest."

"And just how would I make myself expected? Send a rider ahead to tell you I'm coming?"

"You win. Let's put those horses up in the barn. You've got supper and a room for the night."

"I was sort of counting on that. Hope Lisbeth won't be upset by the surprise visitor."

"She will be excited to see you, especially if you offer news from the outside world."

Later, when Sheriff Steele accompanied Rance to the house, Lisbeth greeted him with a happy squeal, a hug and kiss on the cheek that should have assured him of his welcome to the Coldsmith household. He still had said nothing about the reason for his visit, but Rance knew Steele well enough to let the ornery cuss pick his own time. He only knew that a casual social call would not have brought him all this distance in the cold.

Fortunately, Lisbeth was already frying up two chickens for supper, looking to salvage enough for the next day's noon dinner. She sliced a few more potatoes, and with her canned green beans put together a feast topped by apple cake, half of it frosted for the kids and Abe, who was partial to sweets. Rance supposed Abe's relationship with Martha had done nothing but feed that habit.

After supper, the Sheriff surrendered to a chess challenge from Morgan, who humiliated Abe twice before the lawman pled that he had business to tend to. Finally, with kids in bed and fresh coffee on the table, he sat down with Rance and Lisbeth.

"This young woman has taken you a long way, Rance. Beautiful home, kids, meals fit for a king. I hope you know what a prize you caught."

"I do know, but somehow I don't think you rode all this way in the middle of winter to tell me that."

"Well, where do I start? First, I guess I should tell you I'm done with being Custer County sheriff as of the first of the year. Somebody else has been appointed to serve till election. Name is Rupert Syms, a small farmer who just moved to the county. Know him?"

"Nope."

"Younger fella with a family. Probably temporary, but the salary will help him for a while, and I don't look for serious trouble in the foreseeable future."

Rance said, "I'll try to look him up and get acquainted."

"Thought you should know that trial for Print Olive is going to be set for early April. A district judge by the name of William H. Gaslin, Jr. from the Hastings area has stepped in and taken charge of the whole works, although some say he doesn't have authority. Word is he sees the publicity as a step to being governor. He plans to conduct the trial in Hastings, his home bailiwick."

Rance said, "I hope he works out venue issues to satisfy the lawyers. Try the case in the wrong jurisdiction, and there could be serious problems with a verdict."

"I don't understand all that stuff. I came here mostly to tell you when the trial's taking place. You will have to testify. I will, too. But you found the bodies of Ketchum and Mitchell. You know the background of all this better than anybody."

"I thought this could be coming. I am grateful to know the date. Not happy it's in the middle of calving season. I'll have to arrange for help. I suppose Johnny Whitehorse will get drawn into this, too."

"I'm guessing not. He didn't see anything you didn't. Would the prosecution want to call an Indian to testify if they don't have to?"

Rance thought about the question. He supposed there would be risk of some biases among jurors who had connections to the Indian wars. "You might be right. Well, I assume somebody will give me a subpoena or notice of some kind. They will want me to meet with the prosecutor before I testify. But I wasn't a direct witness to the hanging. I worry that nobody will actually place Olive there."

"One of his hands and a Plum Creek businessman, Bill Green, are going to testify to save their own hides. They expect a few others to make a deal. Olive also bragged to some of his hands about what he done. One of them, Muskrat Webb, come to me on his own and volunteered. Man fears for his life, and I'm holding him in the jail under protective custody for now."

Rance said, "I met up with him once. I think he's a decent man who got in with the wrong bunch."

"Have you seen any newspapers lately?"

"Nope. We collect all we can once a month if we're lucky, when either somebody from the Rice place or ours gets to North Platte or Plum Creek."

"I got a few in my saddlebags I forgot to bring in. I'll leave them with you in the morning when I leave. This is all big news around the state. I arranged to ship the bodies of Ketchum and Mitchell to an undertaker in Kearney. While the mutilated bodies was laid out on planks behind the business, a photographer slipped in and got pictures. They made the Lincoln and Omaha newspapers, and the feller that took the pictures is advertising copies for sale. Heard he's got orders for thousands."

Rance said, "A public circus like this can be nothing but trouble."

"You know, a lot of cowmen have talked to me. I think Olive would walk away free as a bird if the trial was held in Custer or Lincoln or one of the other cow counties."

Rance sighed, "I fear you are right."

"Well, I'll leave the papers, so you can get a feel for what's going on. I got one other thing to talk to both of you about."

"I'm listening."

"Martha and me is getting hitched."

"I knew it. I knew it," Lisbeth said, smiling and beaming. "I'm so happy for you both."

"Congratulations, Abe. She's a wonderful lady, and you aren't such a bad guy yourself."

"There's more."

"Go ahead," Lisbeth said.

"We would like the two of you to stand up with us. Small wedding, June 1st."

"We'd love to," Lisbeth said. "I can't wait." She paused, "Oh, I guess I shouldn't speak for Rance."

"You can speak for me on this. I'm in."

"And I'm resigning as Lincoln County sheriff effective the day before the wedding. Martha wasn't sure she could handle the worries of being married to a lawman. Rance, you know I said I wasn't going to run for reelection anyhow."

Rance asked, "So, what are you going to do? Just play cards, gossip and drink coffee at the tavern like some of the other geezers do?"

"Nope, I'm starting a new career as a businessman."

"What kind of business?"

Steele's face flushed near scarlet. "I'm going to be partners with Martha in Grandma's Delights. She's teaching me baking, and she needs help at the counter. She's doing a lot of baking for the eateries now. I ain't all that bad a cook, and I'm excited about it, to be honest."

"I think it's wonderful," Lisbeth said. "I love being in business with my husband. You will just carve out your own niche."

Rance agreed, but he still had trouble visualizing his old friend in the baking business. It sounded like a horrible end for a man like Abe.

Chapter 61

April 1879

The Olive Trial had been in progress for nearly a week when Rance arrived in Hastings to testify. He had met with C.J. Dilworth, the Nebraska Attorney General, who was said to be an astute politician, the previous evening about his testimony. Slim with a perfectly coifed head of black hair and neatly trimmed handlebar mustache, he looked the role of a distinguished lawyer. It was unheard of for the attorney general to become a direct participant in a local trial. Usually, any involvement by that office was via an assistant attorney general or other lower ranking employee of the office. Judge Gaslin had also appointed another lawyer as district attorney *pro tem* to prosecute, pushing the regular district attorney, whom Rance considered very competent, into a nominal role. Aspiring Republican officeholders were drawn to the trial like bees to honey.

The attorney general had tried to refresh Rance's memory to a version of the hangings that made Rance almost, but not quite, a direct witness to the hangings. Rance did not tell the man of his own experience in the law, knowing that a man of the attorney general's ego would have looked upon a country lawyer as a mere bumpkin. Rance wanted Print Olive convicted, but he would not stray from the truth to accomplish his own wishes. He had reached the point where he just wanted to make his appearance and head home to look after his calving cows and their new babies.

Wearing a suit for the first time since his wedding, Rance now sat in a row of chairs reserved for witnesses behind the lawyers' tables in the hall that had been designated a special courtroom for the occasion. The location was Liberal Hall, a structure originally built and used by Unitarians. Over 400 people had been attending the trial daily, and Rance noted the hall was packed today. He estimated at least a dozen lawyers surrounded the prosecutor's table at the front of the auditorium and at least that many gathered at the defense table. Every prominent Republican lawyer in the state had lobbied for a spot on the prosecution team, according to newspaper columnists.

Print Olive also was defended by an army of lawyers, the best that money could buy, and among some ranchers and many others they would be deemed warrior heroes and, regardless, would welcome the public attention.

The bailiff used a cone-shaped amplifying device to call the court to order and announce the judge's appearance. It took some time to quiet spectators, but the noise subsided when the judge threatened to thin noisemakers from the crowd. Rance was troubled by the fact that soldiers were spaced every twenty feet or so along the walls to enforce his order and to assist the bailiff with maintenance of peace in the bizarre courtroom.

Judge Gaslin, a bulky man with a clean-shaven face and gray hair struggling to survive on a balding pate, fit the role of a judge. His face was set in a sober expression, and he had been endowed with a booming, commanding voice. A desk had been set on a stage at the room's front, elevating him a good three feet above the lawyers, defendants, witnesses and court staff. Jurors' chairs were lined up in two rows to the judge's left on the stage. Rance suspected this was by the judge's design to assure that his importance was not overlooked by the horde of newspaper representatives and photographers recording the event. The press enjoyed designated seating off to one side below the stage where the members received a clear view of the proceedings and could hear most of what transpired.

This was the fifth day of the prosecution's case, and it was anticipated the trial would continue for weeks. Rance's testimony this morning would follow that of Charles "Muskrat" Webb, who had just been called as a witness and been sworn in, taking his seat in a lonely chair below the stage with judge and jury looking down.

Even with the advantage of preferential seating, Rance could hear only bits of the examination and cross-examination by the lawyers. Muskrat Webb, whose eyes were darting back and forth, looked like he feared for his life, and his responses to questions were so soft, Rance did not pick up a word. Still, he could not help but admire this young man for his courage in coming forward. It occurred to Rance that most of the observers would not be hearing a word of what was going on. Why in blazes were they here? Curiosity? First-hand gossip rights? He could not imagine. He would be gone the instant after he was excused.

When Rance was called, he strolled to the witness chair, paused in front of the judge's desk, raised his right hand and took the traditional oath to tell the truth. He sat down and was approached for questioning by Dilworth, the attorney general. The examination was brief, focusing mostly upon Rance's discovery of the hanging corpses of Ketchum and Mitchell. Dilworth was attempting to paint a grisly portrait of the scene, and the former lawyer in Rance knew how to help him.

Rance was surprised when the defense declined to cross-examine. Yet, it was possibly good strategy. There would be the risk of Rance's investigations of the other murders coming to the attention of the jury. There would have been objections to his responses, but juries did not erase memories all that well.

Rance was excused, and at the first recess, got up and walked out of the hall. Outside, he saw Muskrat Webb unhitching his horse and strolled over to him. "Mister Webb, may I speak with you a moment?"

Webb turned to Rance with the look of a man ready to run. "Mister Coldsmith," he said, nodding his head.

Rance came up and extended his hand, and the wrangler fumbled nervously with his horse's reins before freeing his right hand and accepting Rance's.

Rance said, "I just wanted to thank you for coming forth to testify in this case. There has been a lot of evidence submitted in the trial, but most of it is irrelevant. Your testimony was important because you had nothing personal to gain. They now have testimony of several who were present at the hangings, but it is somewhat tainted by the fact they are talking to save their own skins. You showed some courage. I admire that."

"Thank you, sir."

"Do you have a job?"

Webb laughed. "No rancher around here will have me after this. I guess I'll be moving west, maybe Montana."

"I'd hire you. I need a good hand. I can't promise my wife wouldn't have you tending a hog now and then."

"You're serious?"

"I am. Think on it. If you are interested, come by the ranch and we can talk terms."

"I will think about it. I sort of got hooked by this country, and I don't got money to move on."

Rance plucked a ten-dollar gold eagle from his pocket. "This is a loan. Use it to move on if you want or to live on till you make up your mind."

"I don't know what to say. But I won't turn it down. Thanks. I just may be up your way this next week to talk about a job."

Chapter 62

December 1879

ARCH TUFTS SAT across the table, sipping a cup of coffee while Rance read the story in the *Nebraska State Journal*. Tufts had made a business trip to Plum Creek a few days earlier and while there had picked up an extra copy of the newspaper to take to his friend. This issue was half-filled with stories about Print Olive, who, having been found guilty of murder in the second degree, had been sentenced eight months earlier to life in prison at hard labor in the Nebraska State Penitentiary in Lincoln. His lawyers had appealed the verdict to the Nebraska State Supreme Court on the basis that Judge Gaslin's court had lacked jurisdiction in the case.

Rance folded the paper and laid it on the table. "I'll read the rest later, Arch. I appreciate your making the trip to bring this to me. You went through a lot of trouble."

"Well, I've been wanting to bring the Sandhills landscape painting for Lisbeth for months. I promised her a year or more ago. I wanted her to come and pick one, but it didn't work out, so I chose my favorite and brought it along."

"She will love it. It's a beautiful piece. I like the deer grazing in hills above the Dismal River. It is the Dismal, isn't it?"

"It is. Tell me what you think."

"I just did."

"Don't play games. About Print Olive."

"Well, he served eight months, and now he's free. I told you I was worried about jurisdiction. The Supreme Court has remanded the case back to Custer County."

"So they have a new trial and go through this all over again. Do you think a jury here would find him guilty?"

"I doubt it. And it will be a challenge for prosecutors to put a case together again. Half of the witnesses have left the country. Of course, Muskrat Webb is working for me now, and I'm still here, but I doubt if the men who testified against Print during the first trial can be found.

If any are turned up, they might not live to trial date. I would bet the new trial will not happen."

Tufts stood to leave. "Well, I'm sorry I missed Lisbeth and baby Cassandra, but if she won't be back till evening, I'd best be on my way."

"You will hear from her about the painting. I'm just sorry you won't be here to see her face. I can't thank you enough, Arch, for everything. I'm a lucky man to have a friend like you." Rance got up to walk with Arch to get his horse.

"That boy of yours is growing up," Arch said, as they strolled to the barn. "It was good of him to see to my horse. How old is he?"

"Twelve, last summer."

"He's a big cuss for his age. You going to make a cow-man out of him?"

"He likes the cattle work well enough, but horses are his real love. He's breaking the darn things already but only when his mom isn't around. He's got a rare touch with horses."

"I forgot to mention," Tufts said, "and it was one of the reasons I came over. Rumor is that Print Olive is going to be pulling up stakes here if he doesn't end up back in the penitentiary. If so, that means land and cattle will be coming up for sale. I don't suppose you will be looking to expand again."

Rance looked at him with disbelief. "What do you think?"

Tufts laughed.

A few weeks later, Rance was not surprised to hear that Judge Boblits had conducted a semi-official court session in the log courthouse at Custer. Ranchers swarmed the building to praise Print Olive's efforts in ending cattle rustling in the area. The judge ordered the case dismissed, and Olive walked away a free man.

The evening following receipt of news that the Olive case would not be retried, Rance stood at the top of the hill that overlooked the ranch house. He loved to watch the sun disappear behind the higher hills to the west from this spot, and tonight the sky provided a kaleidoscope of colors as a backdrop to the rolling dunes. A biting northwest wind stung his face, but the sky was clear. That could change suddenly if snow followed the rumors of nasty weather in the Rockies.

Last spring, Rance and Lisbeth had made a habit in the evenings of walking hand in hand up the wide, sandy trail that led to this spot, but after Cassie's birth, their joint visits had tapered off to his going alone. A new year and the beginning of a decade would be upon them in several days, and tonight he vowed he would spit out the bitter taste Print Olive's release had left in his mouth. He enjoyed a happy, healthy family now. He was paired with a woman he loved more than life. He knew from experience that such times could be fleeting, and that fate could intervene to alter the course of life's journey in an instant. To hell with Print Olive and his ilk. He would not allow them to sour the life he was building here. It was time to turn the page to the next chapter.

Rance was not startled when he felt the touch of Lisbeth's fingers on his hand as she took it in hers. He had not heard her coming up the trail, but he had sensed her nearness.

"Morg and Marissa will look after Cassie for a spell. Tag will supervise from his spot in front of the fireplace. If you don't mind company, I think we should get back to the ritual of doing this together," Lisbeth said.

"I like that idea." Rance turned toward her and kissed her lips softly.

Author's Note

Print Olive maintained his Nebraska ranching operations for almost two years after his release from prison. In 1881 he purchased a ranch in the Dodge City, Kansas area. He commenced liquidating his Nebraska properties, a portion of which he sold to his brother, Ira, who had already acquired separate property along the Platte River valley south of Plum Creek.

Olive ranched near Dodge City, thereafter, also maintaining a small cattle ranch along the Colorado and Kansas border. On August 16, 1886, he confronted Joe Sparrow in a saloon in Trail City, Colorado over ten dollars that the man owed Olive. Although Olive was unarmed, Sparrow drew his pistol and shot the rancher, who died of his wounds at the age of forty-five.

Jim Kelly remained in the Nebraska Sandhills area and worked in Ansley, Nebraska until his death. A stone donated by the community and a local monument company was placed in the cemetery in 1959 to honor his memory. The stone reads: "James Kelly, 'Nigger Jim.' Died February 7, 1912. Legendary Figure of Custer County."

Much has been written about Print Olive and his days in Texas and Nebraska. Separation of fact from fiction is a challenge when it comes to this historic figure, since many stories are contradictory. Olive's involvement in this novel was incidental to the story of the fictional Coldsmith family, and a novelist's literary license has been exercised when necessary to advance the plot.

A valuable resource in writing this novel was *The Ladder of Rivers, The Story of I. P. (Print) Olive* by Harry E. Chrisman, published by the Dawson County, Nebraska Historical Society.

About the Author

Ron Schwab is the author of the popular Western series, *The Law Wranglers*, *The Coyote Saga*, and *The Lockes*, as well as several standalone novels, including *Grit*, a winner of the Western Fictioneers Peacemaker Award for Best Western Novel, and *Cut Nose*, a finalist for the Western Writers of America Best Western Historical Novel.

Ron and his wife, Bev, divide their time between their home in Fairbury, Nebraska and their cabin in the Kansas Flint Hills.

Made in United States
Orlando, FL
17 January 2023

28782236R00268